Book Three of the Family Shadows Series

City Shadows

Jeanne Moon Farmer

Word Light Press

City Shadows
Jeanne Moon Farmer
Book Three of the Family Shadows Series
Copyright © 2013 by Jeanne Moon Farmer
ISBN: 978-1-938643-06-4

Word Light Press
P O Box 94-8636
Maitland, Florida 32794-8636
theshadowbooks@gmail.com

AUTHOR'S NOTE: *City Shadows* is a work of fiction. Names, characters, events and incidents are either the products of the author's imagination or used in a fictitious manner. Any resemblance to actual persons, living or dead, or actual events is purely coincidental.

City Shadows is a fictional story set against the background of Miami and I have tried to include the flavor, sounds and sights of that city as the story flowed through the three books from the 1950s to the 1980s. But, these were years of change, growth, problems, and issues that could not be ignored if the story was to authentically represent Miami.

My story is fiction but I have borrowed from Miami's history and included the turbulent years of drug trafficking and violence. My characters are fictitious; any resemblance to people, living or dead, is coincidental.

Cover Design: Rik Feeney (www.RickFeeney.com)

Photographs: © Pixattitude|Dreamstime.com
© Tom Dowd| Dreamstime.com

Acknowledgments

When a book is completed it means saying good-bye to old friends. There is a moment of melancholy as I close the files on the McDeal and Anderson families. Most especially, I will miss Carter and Jocelyn, Lawrence Fitz, Margo and Michael, Sam and Lara, Sunni, and Lulu Sarsyn. For three years, all of the characters that filled the pages of the *Family Shadows* series have been a real part of my daily routine. But, their story is told and it is time to move on to the new stories and characters that are saying loudly, "it's our turn."

My heartfelt thanks go to Beverly Haskins and Diane Mullen. This dynamic duo continues to make me a better writer. They have read, reread, edited, suggested, and kept me focused on the relevancy of every word and every page. Their red pens are the first to correct my grammar and word usage, and often it is their questions that prompt me to rethink and rewrite in order to make the story more interesting or more cohesive. I can't imagine putting words on paper without their advice and counsel. I am blessed by their friendship.

The best Book Club "sisters" in the world are my Beta readers and my cheerleaders. For fourteen years we have read, laughed, shared, and eaten at some really great restaurants. They continue to encourage me to "write us a good book."

Family is a big part of the team that makes my writing possible. They have already been introduced to the characters and storyline for my next books and I can't wait to see which characters grab their attention. I know they will begin debating with me and advocating for their favorites very soon. My sons, brother, and sister-in-law, enrich my writing and life!

A special thank you to my brother, Buddy, for helping me with the research for this story. We combed the archives of the *Miami Herald* and other periodicals, and discussed the documentary, *Cocaine Cowboys*, until our families grew weary of the "Miami talk."

Although neither of us lives in the city today, our Miami roots run deep.

My story editor, Nancy Quatrano, continues to amaze me. Our partnership gives me the freedom I need to bring my writing to life. Her insights and suggestions tighten my stories and keep the momentum of the plot moving forward. She puts her heart and soul into understanding who my characters are and how they should go about telling their stories, and, even better, she understands who I am as an author. It is a privilege to work with her.

Rik Feeney, my publishing coach, continues to help me understand the ever-changing publishing business. His knowledge—and ability to communicate what he knows—always goes beyond remarkable. Most important, he helps me laugh at myself when I begin to take it all too seriously. He steers me in the "write" direction.

Special thanks and hugs to my husband. His love, understanding, and encouragement are my anchor.

In the middle of writing **City Shadows** I lost the other anchor in my life, my mother, and it took me a few months to get back into this story. Even in my sadness, I could still hear her voice asking the familiar question, "When will that new book be finished?" She always knew I would be a writer—there is no way I am going to disappoint her. Thanks, Mom.

Dedicated with love to Gary and Ian -
you complete my family

Jeanne Moon Farmer

Prologue

Miami 1983

Postcard perfect - blue sky, fluffy white clouds, hot, balmy, and sandy beaches. It was the kind of day the Chamber of Commerce could use to lure thousands of tourists to Miami. Except the tourists were leery of coming near a city where drug wars and violence blocked out the beauty this kind of day offered.

Miami was no longer safe and the national media had begun referring to it as "Paradise Lost." Fear-filled publicity was destroying the tourist industry and overshadowing the beaches, the sunshine, the allure of the tropical Eden. Paradise had sold out to the devil called cocaine and lost its soul to the drug traffickers who were creating a city that was out of control. Drug money was building a concrete and glass skyline to rival any city in the world, but people lived in fear, and corruption was the norm rather than the exception. Yet, the sky was still blue, the breeze continued to whirl across the sand, and the sun warmed the skin of the innocent and the lawless without discrimination.

Jocelyn McDeal leaned over the balcony and wondered at the paradox of Miami, the place she had called home since her birth twenty-seven years ago. Good and evil; beauty and ugliness; tranquility and travesty. It was all there and it was unnerving. She heard the traffic flow past on Biscayne Boulevard and watched in the distance as a speed boat pulled a skier across the bay. Could the beauty she looked at this morning really mask the horrors she had been told existed? The horrors she read about every day in the news?

She closed her eyes and struggled to change her thoughts. She needed a diversion this morning. Her eyes were tired from working long hours on the latest manuscript written by her boss, Lawrence Fitz, and her nerves were jangled by the anticipation of a chiming doorbell. She took a breath of the salty air and tried to relax.

The trap had been set and she had agreed to be the decoy. It had seemed like a good idea at the time, but as reality hit, her bravado was fading. Any minute now the doorbell would ring and she would be face-to-face with the evil, the ugliness, the terror. She would no longer be able to pretend it didn't exist.

She knew the FBI, the DEA, and the Miami Dade police had her covered. She wasn't alone and she wasn't the one responsible for capturing the person who rang the bell. All she had to do was answer the door and invite a major player for one of the biggest drug cartels in this hemisphere to come inside. How hard could that be?

The ugly side of the paradox had to be stopped. Drugs were being openly shipped through the port, corrupt customs agents and police were turning a blind eye, and the rival cartels were staging unbridled warfare on the streets. Miami was a nightmare and she might be able to play a small role in stopping it. All she had to do was open the door.

Her boss, a former FBI agent, had helped orchestrate the plans that she was part of and she believed with all her heart that he had made her safety a priority. If she knew who was going to be on the other side of the door, it would make it so much easier.

The sudden unwelcome chime of the doorbell broke the quiet and, startled in spite of her thoughts, she walked over and opened the door.

"What a surprise," she gasped. "I wasn't expecting to see you."

PART ONE

a poem is a city filled with streets and sewers,
filled with saints, heroes, beggars, madmen,
filled with banality and booze,
filled with rain and thunder and periods of
drought, a poem is a city at war....

— Charles Bukowski

Jeanne Moon Farmer

Chapter One

Jocelyn McDeal
Miami, October 1982

"Lawrence, the new book is really good. You hooked me with the characters, and the story-line leaves me wanting to know more." She hesitated. "But, do you think you can get away with a Miami crime exposé that hits so hard at what's going on right now? All your other books have been about things that took place years ago." A frown crossed Jocelyn's face as she looked across the desk at her boss and mentor.

"This story can be told without getting me in hot-water, Jocelyn. If TV shows can get away with bringing Miami's crime story to the living rooms of America, surely my book won't tip the apple-cart too much. I'm not naming names and you know I wouldn't betray any of my contacts. It'll be all right. So, please, my dear, stop worrying." Lawrence gave her his best smile and turned back to the papers on his desk.

"If you say so. But talk to Elena Martinez about protecting yourself before you put any more effort into this one. Okay?"

It was hard for her to imagine that the distinguished, white-haired man sitting across from her had spent fifty of his eighty years working for the FBI. She would have an easier time believing that he had been a history professor at Harvard. But, Special Agent Lawrence Fitz, now retired, had been one of the best and he was a genius at criminal investigation. He liked to tell her that all he did was *solve the puzzle*. But, she had been around him long enough to know that he saw pieces of the puzzle that no one else could see.

"I don't think I need an attorney, but I'll pass my ideas by Elena and see what she says. You worry too much, Jocelyn." He shifted in the chair and turned to look out the window. "You are going with me to Maddie Sonnet's celebration tonight, aren't you? It's not every day that someone we know passes the bar."

"I wouldn't miss it. Do you know if she took the job with Elena and Eric's law firm?"

"She received very good offers from three of the largest defense firms in town and I doubt if Randall, Martinez and Cannon can come close to matching those offers." He closed his eyes and folded his hands in front of him. "You know, Jocelyn, I wouldn't be at all surprised if she chose to go with the prosecutor's office. She's always told me her reason for going to law school was to get people like the men who killed her husband off the streets. But you never know what motivates people." He sighed. "I don't think she's made up her mind." He pushed his glasses higher on his nose. "It would be just like her to make a big announcement at the party."

"Her husband was a policeman, killed in action, right?" Jocelyn was trying to remember what she knew about Maddie's past and realized she didn't know much about her at all. "Goodness, look at the time! I've got to run or I'll be late. The Miami Herald goes to press with or without me, but I don't want to miss my deadline." She gathered her things and almost ran out of the office.

"Pick me up at seven o'clock, Jocelyn. I don't want to miss one minute of this party." Lawrence called after her as she headed out the door.

"Ben and I will be here on time. See you later." She smiled when she thought about her boss's obsession with time. He hated to be late and expected others to feel the same way. Over the years, he had instilled that sense of punctuality in her. She could hear him laughing at her now, knowing there was no way she was going to miss a deadline.

Working two jobs was beginning to be hectic, but Jocelyn McDeal loved both worlds and wasn't ready to give either of them up. She had done editing and research for Lawrence Fitz since she was a freshman in college and had just been promoted from copy editing to feature writing at the *Herald*. Some day she would have to choose, but not today. *I love Lawrence and he needs me. There's no way I could just walk away. And, if I left the newspaper, I'd miss out on all the excitement. Hectic or not, it's what I love doing.*

*****

At twenty-seven years old, Jocelyn McDeal understood that she was one of the fortunate ones. She was living her dream even if it meant she was a workaholic. Two full time jobs gave her all the excitement, glamour, and professional satisfaction she could handle. And, dating Ben Jordan gave her a sense of relationship. Even on hectic days like today when she felt overwhelmed, she knew she wasn't ready to change the career parts of her life.

Working as a feature writer for the *Miami Herald*, one of the largest daily newspapers in the nation, gave her a sense of accomplishment and kept her current with the world. The paper's energy and vitality permeated every corner of the *Herald's* building and she walked a little taller every time she stepped inside. It started with the smell of ink and paper and it flowed through all the people who worked to make sure the news was in the hands of Miami's residents every day. She worked long hours during the week to fill the column inches allotted to her "City Speaks" feature that ran in the Tuesday and Saturday papers.

While the newspaper gave her an adrenalin rush and kept her pulse racing, it was her job with Lawrence Fitz that kept her grounded. He was a grandfather figure to her - a mentor and muse. He had rescued her from an impossible situation when she was eighteen years old, had been there to guide her through her college and career choices, and had encouraged her to forgive her family and repair her relationship with her dad. Most of all, he had been there to help her through the hurt caused by the break-up of her relationship with Mark Sanders.

Not a day passed that she didn't think of Mark, and sometimes those thoughts made her feel guilty about the life she had made for herself with Ben Jordan. But, no matter what her heart told her, a relationship with Mark was beyond impossible. He was her first

13

cousin and there was no way the family or the Catholic Church would ever bless their marriage. Lawrence had been there to support her when she finally made the decision to walk away from Mark and only Lawrence understood how much she still loved him.

Over the years, Lawrence had folded her into the crevices of his life, and last year, when his beloved wife had died of cancer, Jocelyn had been able to repay him somewhat by being there for him. As she tried to comfort him, she witnessed the dignity of his grieving and saw that the deepest love might be about letting go.

Lawrence was one of the most multi-faceted people she had ever met. His ability to observe, research, and bring all the pieces of an investigation puzzle together had made him an ace crime-solver and the FBI had rewarded him with promotion after promotion. When age forced him to retire, he used his years of experience and talent to produce brilliant mystery/thriller novels that attracted a huge following. She admired all of those aspects of the man, but her greatest respect and love for him came from his kindness, his honesty, and his gentle spirit.

Lately she had begun to notice how much he relied on her. His step wasn't as spry, his eyesight wasn't as sharp, and his memory wasn't as quick. Little things, nothing catastrophic, were becoming more frequent and she instinctively knew she wouldn't leave him. He had more books to write, more stories to tell, and many more things to teach her. Even as she watched him slowing down, she realized there were so many more life lessons she had to learn and she wanted to share them all with him.

*****

Walking into the newsroom at the *Herald,* Jocelyn knew immediately that something big had happened. The large room where her cubicle was located seemed charged with the excitement and spontaneous conversations that always accompanied a breaking story. As she approached her desk she called out to a fellow reporter, "Hey, Denny, what's going on?"

"They just found the body of a two-year old boy on the steps of the downtown mosque! It was gruesome. The poor little thing had two bullet holes in his head."

"That's horrible! Do we know anything else?"

"He was wrapped in a white cloth and, get this, he was holding three red roses. I've seen the pictures and they made me sick. I can't imagine how the photographer feels."

"Who was the little boy? Do they know?"

"One more victim of the drug wars. The baby's passport was next to him and looks like he's the son of one of the Emperitza's henchmen."

She looked puzzled. "What are you talking about?"

"The dad's one of the guys the FBI has identified as a hired gun for the cartel. Apparently, it was a drive-by shooting and the kid took the bullets that were intended for his dad. They don't know who put the baby's body on the steps, but they're guessing it was the parents. Bad enough to have your kid shot to death, but then not to give him a proper burial is really rough. "

"That's heartbreaking." A knot formed in Jocelyn's stomach as she listened to her colleague. "When's it going to end, Denny? I feel like we live in a war zone with all of this senseless killing. It's destroying our town. Ever since that *Time* magazine article dubbed us "Paradise Lost," the tourists have stopped coming and the murders keep happening." She sat down at her desk and dialed a familiar phone number.

"Have you heard the latest?" She lamented. "A two-year old got caught in the cross-fire and was killed. It's insane, Lawrence, and makes me more nervous about this new book of yours."

Even with his reassurances, when she hung up the phone she couldn't get rid of her feelings of dread and foreboding.

*****

What does one wear to an "I passed the bar" party? Jocelyn groaned as she stood inside her closet and tried to choose an appropriate outfit. Ben would be knocking on the door in ten minutes and all she had on was underwear. She knew that wouldn't bother Ben, but she didn't want to give him an excuse for them to run late. Out of desperation, she grabbed a coral silk shirt and black slacks that she could dress up with a few accessories. Sometimes she wished she had the whimsy of her good friend, Ruthie, or the fashion sense of her step-mother, Sharon. *That woman can make a paper bag look chic.* But this was the best she could do with her limited imagination and budget. Besides, tonight was Maddie Sonnet's big night and everybody would be looking at her.

Maddie was beautiful, confident, and personable, but Jocelyn knew the woman's life hadn't been easy. Right out of college she had joined the Miami Dade police force, but left when her policeman-husband had been killed in action. For years, she had worked as a private investigator to put herself through law school and tonight her friends and family would be celebrating her new career. Jocelyn felt comfortable around Maddie and knew she would have liked her even if she hadn't been the daughter of Lawrence's FBI partner.

Pulling her shoulder-length brown hair up with a coral ribbon put the finishing touch on her hasty attempt to look presentable and as she twirled in front of the mirror she decided for a short, slightly slender young woman, she looked pretty good. The deep brown of her eyes and hair was highlighted by the coral blouse and she wondered why she didn't wear the color more often. When the doorbell rang, she dropped her apartment key in her pocket and headed for the door. She forgot about being rushed and tired and started looking forward to having some fun.

*****

It was a lively party. The music was loud and the champagne flowed. Jocelyn guessed there were fifty or sixty people crammed into Maddie's small house and back yard. She was trying to keep her eye on Lawrence, but he was having too much fun to stay in one spot for long.

"Ben, I've lost Lawrence. Have you seen him in the last half hour?"

"Jocelyn, the man is having fun. Leave him alone and let him enjoy the party." Ben's voice showed his irritation at the attention she was giving the elderly gentleman. "In fact, why don't you enjoy the party a little bit more? All you've done this evening is fret over him."

"Are you jealous of Lawrence?" Jocelyn teased.

Ben threw both arms around her and nuzzled her neck. "No, sweetheart. I know who's taking you home."

"I wish Maddie would make her announcement so we could get out of here. Come to think of it, I haven't seen her in a while either. I bet she and Lawrence are in some corner solving the problems of the world." She looked around the room but didn't see them. "Ben, would you fix me a drink. I'll look around and be right back."

Ben left with her glass and she wandered through the living room. She was about to head outside when she thought she heard voices down the hall. Turning toward the bedrooms, she decided that was a good place to look. Two of the doors were opened and a quick look told her no one was in those rooms. Just as she was about to turn around, the door of the third room opened and a very disheveled Eric Randall walked out of the room followed by an equally disheveled Maddie. It was apparent they had had too much to drink when Eric tripped and Maddie began to giggle like a school-girl.

When Eric recovered his footing, he turned and pressed Maddie against the wall. Jocelyn stood in shock as she watched Eric move one hand under Maddie's blouse and the other under her skirt. "I haven't had enough. Go back in the bedroom, Maddie. I never get enough of you." Eric wasn't whispering, so Jocelyn heard every word and could see the pulsing movements of his hands against Maddie's body.

"Eric, I have to see about my guests. I'll come back in a few minutes." Maddie whispered. "Besides, your wife is probably wondering where you are."

"Just a few more minutes, Maddie. I want you again and I can't wait. And, I've got some more good stuff." Eric's voice was smooth, even though he was breathing hard, and there was a demanding edge to his words. Jocelyn watched spellbound as Maddie melted against him and began to respond to his touch.

They were climbing all over each other as they stumbled back in the bedroom and closed the door. Within a few seconds, Jocelyn heard the bed begin to creak and she blushed. *Oh, dear God. Maddie and Eric Randall. They were so in to each other they didn't even see me standing here. Damn, I wish I hadn't seen this! Poor Elena.*

"Did you find Lawrence?" Ben's voice startled her and she turned to face him. "You look like you've seen a ghost. What's the matter?"

"You won't believe what I just saw. I need that drink!" Jocelyn took the drink he offered and walked back down the hall.

"What's going on?" Ben questioned as he followed her out to the front porch.

It was quieter on the porch and the breeze felt good on her reddened, warm face. "Ben, I just saw Maddie and Eric Randall together."

"So what? They've worked together and I assume they're friends."

"No, Ben. I mean they were *together*. Literally. They walked out of her bedroom as I was standing in the hall and I watched them jump on each other. I wasn't three feet away and they never saw me!" Her voice was rising and she was getting more animated as she talked. "They must have been having sex and continued out in the hall. Then they went back in the bedroom and I heard the bed creaking!"

"Slow down! You're getting yourself all worked up." Ben said as he placed his arm around her shoulder and drew her close.

"I'm not *getting* worked up! I *am* worked up!" She exclaimed. "Do you know what this means for Elena?" Jocelyn's voice sounded quieter and sadder as she looked into Ben's eyes. "The worse part was I heard him tell her he had 'some more good stuff.' That can only mean one thing, Ben. He was talking about drugs."

"You don't know what he meant, Jocelyn." Ben laughed. "That may have been his ego talking." He drew her closer and held her in his arms. "Let's go find Lawrence and see if he's ready to go home. I doubt if Maddie is going to make any big announcements tonight."

As they turned to go inside, the screen door opened and Lawrence walked out on the porch. "There you are. I was wondering if you're ready to leave."

Jeanne Moon Farmer

Chapter Two

Carter McDeal

"Boss, have you got a minute?" The young man called to Carter McDeal as he crossed the parking lot behind the Miami Transit Company office. "I need to tell you something."

"What's up, Joey? Your girlfriend giving you a hard time?" Carter joked with the young man who had been his assistant for the last year.

"Yeah, but that's not a problem." He chuckled, then his face got serious. "Last night, one of the cleaners found a package under a seat on one of the buses that runs the route to Liberty City."

"That's not unusual. Did he turn it in or what?" Carter wondered why Joey was bothering to tell him about the package. People left things on buses all the time.

"Carter, it was an ordinary-looking package - wrapped in brown paper, tied with a string - but when he picked it up it came unraveled and there were about twenty small packs of white powder inside. Scared the guy 'cause he's on probation, so he took it to dispatch. They called the cops and I guess we'll be hearing from them this morning. Just wanted to give you a heads up"

"It's probably some nice old lady's talcum powder."

"That's not what the cleaner thought. We'll see what the cops say." Joey laughed. "I'd like to be a fly on the wall when the owner comes to Lost and Found looking for that package." He turned serious. "You know, if that package turns out to be coke, it's probably worth thousands. I'd hate to be the guy who has to explain that to his boss."

"You think the cops are going to come to talk to me?"

"Guess that depends on whether the cops that came last night are on the take or not. We'll know soon enough." They entered the building and started down the hall. "I've got the charts ready for your meeting this afternoon. Do you want to go over them before the morning gets too hectic?"

"Give me about thirty minutes to get my day organized and then bring 'em on. I need to be really prepared if we're going to save that run to Opa Locka." Carter turned into his office and didn't give the package or the police another thought.

*****

"Sharon, why don't you call Jocelyn and see if she wants to meet us for dinner? Hopefully, this meeting won't last too long and we can meet her around seven o'clock somewhere in Coral Gables? Pick a spot and let me know. I'll call you later." Carter hung up the phone and tried to concentrate on the charts that Joey had prepared. He knew he had an uphill battle ahead of him at today's meeting, but he was going to try his best to save that route. Working people depended on it.

Some days he longed to be back in the driver's seat of a bus rather than in his office trying to manage routes, fight unions, make decisions, and be a boss. All his life, he had worked for the company, but he knew he had been less stressed when he was driving the Route Six bus.

*****

Later that evening, he watched as his daughter entered the restaurant and was shown to their table. She was a pretty, young woman, and he was proud of the way she carried herself as she walked toward them. He stood up as she approached the table and gave her a kiss on the cheek.

"Hi, sweetheart. I'm glad you could join us on such short notice."

"It's always nice to have my dad buy me dinner. How could I pass up the offer?" Jocelyn leaned down and hugged Sharon, then

22

took her seat at the table. "What are you guys up to? We haven't had a chance to talk in a couple of weeks."

"Working and working." Sharon offered. "We did go to the boat show at Dinner Key on Saturday. Other than that, we are getting old and boring. You know how your dad is. He'd rather sit at home and watch the clouds go by." She reached over and patted her husband's shoulder.

Carter gave his wife an indulgent smile. "We've been thinking about taking a cruise next month. Wanna take some time off from work and go with us? We're looking at the western Caribbean and Cancun."

"Sounds great, but no thanks. There's too much going on right now. You know Lawrence is finishing up a new book and I'm struggling to keep up with him."

"I like his character, Joe Fielding, the FBI agent that always gets his man." Sharon said. "I'm sure that anyone who knows Lawrence can see him in every book he writes. Either that man has lived one dangerous and exciting life or he has a very vivid imagination. What's this one about?"

"I think most of what he writes, he's lived. Or at least someone he knows has lived it. He's used to being on the edge and that's what concerns me about this new book. He's taking on the Miami drug trafficking operation and I think it's risky. My boss doesn't like to remember how old he is and that he's out of practice dealing with the bad guys."

"You're right. But, Lawrence isn't going to take any chances." Carter looked across the table at his daughter and spoke directly to her. "He wouldn't put you in danger. I know him better than to think he'd take a risk with you." He had known the man since before Jocelyn was born and trusted him to make good decisions.

"I'm not worried about me, Dad. I just think it's the wrong time for this book." She turned to Sharon. "Did you hear about the two-year old that took a bullet for his dad? If the Emperitza, or whatever she's called, is behind what happened to that kid, she is one ruthless, cruel woman."

"I heard it on the news and it makes me concerned for all of us. Why do you think that woman is behind this?"

"The little boy was the son of an alleged henchman for the cartel and the police know he used to work for her. It adds up that she might be trying to get even with him about something."

"I've lived in Miami all my life and this is the first time I've ever felt uncomfortable traveling around this city." Sharon shook her head and looked down at her menu. "But, let's change the subject. This one creeps me out. How are things with you and Ben?"

"We're fine. We went to Maddie Sonnet's party the other night. You know she just passed the Bar?"

"Tell me again how you know her." Carter knew Jocelyn had talked about the woman before but he couldn't remember in what context.

"Her dad and Lawrence were partners in the FBI. You know, she and her late husband used to be on the police force. She quit when he was killed, and then put herself through law school working as a private investigator. I met her when she was working on the Alli Anderson case."

"Right. I remember now. Beautiful woman, if she's who I think she is. Tall, kind of exotic-looking redhead." Carter cut his eyes at Sharon to see her reaction.

"I'll agree that you have wonderful taste in women." Sharon's eyes twinkled when she looked at Carter. "Just look at the company you're keeping tonight."

"You have a good memory, Dad." Jocelyn paused before she went on. "Have you seen Elena lately?"

"No, why?"

"Just wondering. Do you know her husband, Eric, very well?"

"Honey, I don't really keep up with my attorney's private life. Years ago, when she was defending me, she and Eric weren't married. I don't know him well at all. Why do you ask?"

"You know I like Elena. First, because of how she helped you, and then Lawrence and I worked with her on the Alli Anderson thing. I think she's great, but I'm not sure I like her husband."

"Hopefully, you don't have to deal with him often, then, if that's the way you feel." The look on Jocelyn's face told him there was more to the story than she was telling. But he wasn't about to ask.

"I'm starving. What are the two of you going to order?"

*****

Later, as Carter and Sharon were getting ready for bed, he looked over at his wife and asked, "Are you really afraid to live in Miami?"

"I don't know if I'm *afraid*. Let's just say I'm more cautious than I used to be. There are areas, especially on the beach, that I try to avoid. And, it worries me that half my clients must be drug dealers or worse."

"What are you talking about?"

"Carter, where is all this money coming from? I'm a good interior designer and I've always made a good living at what I do. But in the last two years, I've made more money than either of us could have imagined. And, I'm trying not to judge when I say this, but most of the people I've worked for lately don't seem the type to live in million dollar houses." Sharon rubbed cream on her face and turned to look at Carter. "I've had to decide to either go out of business or take on clients that I know must be earning their money from drugs. It's everywhere."

"You're right about that. They found several thousand dollars worth of coke on one of the buses this week and I had cops all over asking questions. They ask questions, but it doesn't seem like they're *doing* anything about it." He walked over and took her in his arms. "I had fun with Jocelyn tonight. She's bright and interesting and seems to be making some good choices for herself. I just wish she would find someone to love. I don't think Ben is the love of her life."

"Honey, it's going to take her a long time to get over Mark. Give her time."

"Look how long it took me to get over you!"

They both laughed.

*****

Carter couldn't remember not loving Sharon. He had loved her since the first day he saw her when they were in the tenth grade. In those days he had been too shy to even talk to her and had watched her from a distance for all of that school year. When he finally got up the nerve to ask her to a school dance, it had shocked him that she said yes. That dance changed his life.

Sharon took a shy teenager who lived alone with his mother and made him think he could accomplish anything. She taught him to laugh, to not take life so seriously, and to dream. And, his dream was a life with her. They were inseparable and planned to marry as soon as they finished high school, but the Korean Conflict interfered with their plans. While he was in Korea, she met someone new and made a different life for herself. He went back to his old life - no more laughs, no more dreams.

It took the worst day of his life to bring them back together again. When Jocelyn was seventeen years old, he was charged with kidnapping her. His mother, Gracie, who knew the story of Jocelyn's birth was dead and there was no one to help him clear his name. Sharon had read about it in the newspaper and called him. She was divorced by then and wanted him to know she believed in his innocence. She and his attorney, Elena Martinez, were the ones who fought for him, supported him, and encouraged him through the ordeal. Although the day he told Elena the truth, she thought he was crazy.

"Jocelyn was left on our doorstep."

"Oh, Carter, you can do better than that," Elena's face showed her disbelief.

"You wanted truth, and that's it. Jocelyn was in a box that someone left on our doorstep on June 16, 1956. She looked to be about a week old. I thought I caught a glimpse of her mother as she was walking away from our house, but I'm not sure. The box the baby was in had a couple of bottles, some formula, and a note. I wanted to call the authorities but my mother kept putting it off until it didn't

seem important any more. That's the truth. Now who is going to believe that?"

Nobody would have believed him if Jocelyn's mother, Roseanne, hadn't stood before the judge and affirmed that the story was true.

He knew he had never stopped loving Sharon and over time, she remembered that she loved him. She was the one who encouraged him to reach out to a very angry Jocelyn, and slowly he had reestablished a relationship with his daughter. Jocelyn had been slow to forgive him for all the lies that had been told about her birth and he was afraid he had lost her. Eventually, she let go of her anger and he formally adopted her. Thank God, Sharon had never let him forget that love is patient and worth fighting for. Because of it, today, he had Sharon and Jocelyn in his life.

From the day the charges against him were dropped, Sharon had been there helping him move forward. Because she believed in him, he began to dream again. Now they were married, he had gone to college and received a degree, and he had moved from driving a bus to a management position in the transit company's downtown office.

But he worried about Jocelyn. She had fallen in love with Mark Sanders and when the truth of her birth was told, Mark turned out to be her first cousin. For years, she and Mark had tried to forge a relationship in opposition to the church and the family, until Jocelyn realized that she wanted children and that was very risky when first cousins married. His daughter had walked away from the relationship, but he saw the truth in her eyes every time he tried to talk to her about her new boyfriend, Ben Jordan. Unfortunately, she was still in love with Mark. Carter's story had a happy ending, but for the life of him he couldn't see any kind of ending for Jocelyn and Mark that wasn't heart-breaking.

He rolled over in the bed and snuggled up against his sleeping wife - the love of his life - and prayed that someday his daughter would find a man who could push Mark Sanders out of her heart.

Jeanne Moon Farmer

Chapter Three

Sharon McDeal

"Yes, Mrs. Moreno, I have ordered the fabrics and production will begin as soon as they're delivered. Please understand, because of the quality and quantity of the fabrics you've chosen, orders like yours often take time. Once the fabric is here, it will take approximately two weeks for the draperies to be completed." Sharon listened to the angry voice on the other end of the phone and wished she didn't have to deal with Mrs. Moreno. This client had been demanding and manipulative from the very start and flaunted her money as though she was wearing million dollar bills pasted all over her body.

"As we discussed yesterday, the furniture has been shipped, the carpets and wallpaper will be installed as soon as the painters are finished with their work. We're right on schedule, Mrs. Moreno, and your beautiful new house will be ready for the holidays. I promise." She sighed.

"Yes, I'll come by this afternoon to make sure the workers are doing their job." Hanging up the phone, she sank back in the chair and vented her frustration with a string of words she rarely said aloud. *That woman wants miracles. The renovation design was just completed last week!* Deciding it wasn't worth raising her blood pressure, she continued the work she was doing on another client's project.

*****

Later that afternoon, as she stood in front of the palatial home of the Moreno's, she asked herself again why she had taken the project. The Moreno's puzzled her and she wondered how the couple could afford this place. Every time she visited the house, Jose Moreno was sitting by the pool in his swim trunks talking on the phone and smoking a cigar. She guessed he was probably in his late forties, but he must have worked-out every day to keep his body as well-toned as it was. His South American heritage was obvious in his dark hair and olive skin and heavily accented English. He had never acknowledged her presence, which Sharon thought was odd. *As long as he pays the bills, who cares?*

Ava Moreno was his opposite. She was very young, maybe twenty-two, tall, blond and voluptuous. When Sharon first met her, the young woman had been dressed from head to toe in silk - pants, shirt, and scarf - and her long, curly hair had been twisted around her head and held in place with beautiful ruby-studded combs. Her make-up was flawless, her other jewelry impressive, and her conversation laced with expletives. After that first meeting, Sharon never saw her in anything but a bikini and magnificent jewelry. Long legs and the way she carried herself, made Sharon wonder if she had once been a dancer.

Other than the stream of inappropriate language, the first meeting had gone well. But once the contract was signed, Sharon regretted every minute she had to spend with the woman. From daily phone calls, tears, and threats to find another interior designer, the woman gave her a headache. Putting her personal feelings aside was the only way she would get the job finished.

Once Sharon had been buzzed inside the gate, she knew she couldn't get back in the car and just drive away, so she lingered longer on the driveway than she should. In all her years in the business, it was the first time she could remember not wanting to go inside and deal with her client. Stalling for a few more minutes, she let her eyes enjoy the beauty of the house and its surroundings. It sat on a triple lot among lush vegetation and a velvet lawn that ended at the seawall.

The wide-swept vista of the bay behind the house completed a picture of peace and serenity. To one side of the house was a five-car garage and she knew from previous visits that five expensive cars were housed there. She had seen three Mercedes, one Ferrari, and another exotic car she couldn't identify. On the other side of the house was a pool, an enclosed tennis court and a small guesthouse. She watched two men working in the flower-beds, two others cleaning the Olympic-sized pool that took up more than half of the side lawn, and another sweeping the tennis court. *Keeping up with a place like this would be a chore and probably requires an army to maintain. I think I'll keep my little house in the Grove.*

The quiet was broken by the voice of a maid calling her to come inside. "Senora McDeal, por favor. Senora Moreno está esperando."

Sharon smiled and walked into a house that was in seeming chaos. Painters, electricians, and plumbers were everywhere, working frantically as Mrs. Moreno shouted orders and paced from one room to the next.

"There you are! Who hired these morons? I've tried all morning to get them to change the color in the dining room and all I get are grunts!"

"Good morning. Why do you want to change the color? We've ordered everything to go with the rose beige and if you change the color we'll have to start from the beginning. Let's sit down and talk about it." Sharon tried to keep her voice as calm as possible, but she knew her facial expressions showed her exasperation. "The color you chose for that room is a good blend for what you've chosen for the rest of the house. What's the problem?"

"I don't like it! That's the problem. And, I want it changed today! Do you understand me?"

"Please sit down and talk to me. What is it that you don't like?"

"The room's a rosy beige and I want it changed to a sea foam green. I saw that in a magazine this morning and I like it better. So, change it." Today, Mrs. Moreno had matched her electric blue bikini with two sapphire and diamond bracelets and sapphire earrings and as she talked, she tossed her jeweled arm back and forth in front of Sharon's face.

"Sea foam green is lovely, but I don't think you'll like the effect of that color in the dining room. To show off all the dark wood in that room, there needs to be a warmer color on the walls and floors.

Remember, that's why you chose the rose beige. It maintains the room's charm." She pressed her point.

"A sea foam green deserves a room where there's an abundance of light." Then she smiled. "I've got an idea. Why don't we use the sea foam green for that guest bedroom we were discussing yesterday? That room is on the corner of the house where there are windows on two sides of the room, plus it has French doors. We haven't ordered the furniture or rugs for that room yet, and the green would give the room a cool, inviting appeal."

Mrs. Moreno sat quietly, her lips pushed out in a pout. "I wanted green in the dining room."

"All right. I'll go stop the work. But you have to understand that doing this will mean the house won't be ready for the holidays." Sharon stood up and began to leave the room.

"No way! You can put on extra people. I want the color changed and I expect the house to be ready before Thanksgiving."

"Certainly, Mrs. Moreno. I'll stop the workmen and then we can begin looking at color swatches, wall paper and new rugs. Every order will have to be put on rush, but I'll do my best to get it done." She sighed as she walked out of the room.

*****

"Third time Garcia can't deliver. La Emperitza de Cocaina won't like that. You take care of him anyway you have to." He listened for a few seconds, then shouted in the phone. "Don't give me that BS. I ain't asking what you think. Don't call me 'til it's done." He lowered his voice. "I better be reading about it in the morning paper." Jose Moreno slammed down the phone and turned in surprise to see an attractive middle-aged woman standing behind him.

"Quién eres?" He growled. "What are you doing? What you hear?"

"I'm sorry, Mr. Moreno, I didn't mean to startle you and I wasn't listening to your conversation. My name is Sharon McDeal and I'm the interior designer working with your wife on the renovation of your home. I was on my way to the dining room to stop the workmen."

"Why the hell you stopping work?" He threw his hands up over his head as he walked in the room. "Work gives me a headache. Finish and get these people out of my house!"

"Of course. Perhaps you could discuss your headache with your wife. She wants to make a change that will delay the work."

"Ava! Get in here! What's the matter with you?" His face was getting redder as he turned and started shouting at his wife. "I told you I want these people out of here and now this lady is telling me they will have to be here longer because you want to make a change!"

"Aw, sweetheart, I just didn't think you would like rose beige in the dining room." Ava purred like a kitten as she walked closer to her husband. "I know you like green," she said as she rubbed up against him, "and all I want to do is make you happy." She ran her fingers through his hair as her smile turned into a pout. "You know I'll do anything to make you happy." Her voice lowered to a sultry whisper as she moved her lips against the side of his head.

"Okay, okay! Make the damn room green but do it in a hurry! I want these people out of my hair!" His voice softened. "Red, green, whatever you want."

As Sharon watched in embarrassment, he grabbed Ava and his hands began to roughly knead her bottom. When Sharon cleared her throat, he suddenly jerked his hands away and abruptly pushed his wife to the side, winked at her, and stomped out of the room.

*****

"How was your day?" Carter hugged Sharon and gave her a quick kiss.

"It was a headache kind of day. The Moreno's are impossible." She saw a puzzled look come over his face. "Oh, sorry. They're the people I've been telling you about who bought that huge place on Key Biscayne. You know, the bimbo that has given me so much trouble?"

"If you're calling someone a bimbo, maybe I need to meet her." Carter teased. "I might appreciate her charms more than you do."

"Not on your life. Although I will admit, her charms are out there for everyone to appreciate. Carter, this woman is bizarre. All she ever wears is a bikini and a jewelry store! And, every day, her demands get more impossible to deal with. I've never had so many change orders."

"Sounds like you need a nice glass of wine. Give me a minute to change and I'll meet you in the garden with some bubbly."

"I like the sound of that. I'll see you on the patio." Then she hesitated. "Carter, I know you're going to think I'm crazy, but I think I over heard Mr. Moreno give an order for someone to be killed."

"Honey, you've been reading too many newspaper headlines. Don't let your imagination get the best of you." He hugged her again. "Let me get you a drink and we'll talk."

Chapter Four

Jocelyn

"Ben, there's a sidewalk festival in the Grove on Saturday and I told Dad and Sharon I'd meet them there for lunch. Why don't you go with us?" Jocelyn was curled up on the couch in her apartment watching television with her boyfriend. Exhausted from a busy day at work, she was enjoying some mindless time of doing nothing and not thinking of anything consequential.

"I'll have to pass. I'm playing golf with Dad in the morning and I think he said Mom was going to meet us for lunch."

"That sounds like a fun day. You haven't played golf in several months."

"Yeah, when you're the lawyer in the firm with the least seniority, you work most weekends." He shrugged his shoulders and continued to watch the program.

"Can we be serious for a few minutes?" Jocelyn sat forward on the couch and turned to look at Ben.

Without taking his eyes off the TV screen, he answered. "If you'll let me finish this show, I'll give you my undivided attention."

She walked to the kitchen and made herself a cup of tea. She was bored, bored, bored. Lately, she and Ben had less and less to say to each other. When he wasn't working, he was glued to the television. She couldn't remember when he hadn't worked on Saturday and it surprised her that he was taking time to play golf with his dad. How long has it been like this?

They began dating when he was working part time at the newspaper to put himself through law school. Yes, he was usually serious, but they used to have some good times. She thought of the fun things they used to do together - concerts, sailing, walking on the beach, parties - certainly he had times when he had to study, but he made time for her. Not like now when all they did was sit in her apartment and watch TV for a few hours each week. They weren't even married but it felt like they'd been following this routine for fifty years. *For crying out loud, Daddy and Sharon have more fun than I do!* And, not for the first time, she wondered if her unhappiness was really about Ben?

"Is that show over?" She asked as she plopped back down on the sofa.

Ben reached for the remote and muted the sound on the TV. "What needs my serious attention?"

"What do you know about the drug activity in this town?"

"Why? You thinking of taking up snorting or something?"

"You're not funny, Ben."

*****

"The last chapter of the new book is great," she called to Lawrence. "It scares me to think that I'm so out-of-touch with what's happening in Miami. Is all this stuff you're including in the book really going on? How did Miami get to be the center of the cocaine trade?"

"Jocelyn, my dear, you know," she could hear the indulgent smile in his voice, "I always base my fiction on reliable information and fact. My character, Agent Joe Fielding, is living the combined stories of real agents in the Bureau. I may take some literary license to make the plot move along, but you know I'm drawing from actual events." Lawrence sighed. "Unfortunately, location, corruption and greed made Miami ripe for the picking."

"If there's so much corruption, how do you know who to trust? You've made law enforcement, the port authority, and the customs agency look as rotten as the bad guys. What if you're touching on things that will make these people mad? Won't they come after you?"

"Why? I haven't given away any trade secrets. My story uses the cocaine trafficking as a backdrop. Besides, it's documented in every newspaper in the country. Those people don't have time for me. What threat would I be?"

"Lawrence, I'm worried that the female character you've created may too closely resemble that woman they call the Emperitza." Jocelyn wrinkled her brow. "Do you think she's actually as ruthless as your character? And, why did you call your character the Scorpion?"

"I don't want you to have nightmares, but the real Emperitza is every bit as evil and probably more so." Lawrence shook his head. "From everything I've heard she would just as soon kill you as look at you. She's someone to be reckoned with and the people in the drug business know it."

"You make it sound like she rules Miami."

"She does rule her part of Miami and I wouldn't be surprised if she isn't one hundred percent behind the murders and drug wars that your newspaper writes about every week." He reached over and patted Jocelyn's hand. "Honestly though, she has no reason to even look my way, so stop worrying. Now, you've got a book to finish editing, so go back to work and remember that what you're reading is fiction."

"If you say so." She wasn't convinced and knew the worry lines on her forehead emphasized her concern.

*****

"Alli Anderson has a concert at the Orange Bowl next week and I just happen to have two tickets up front. Would you like to go?" Ben asked.

They were sitting in the garden at her dad's house enjoying the gentle ocean breeze and the last few sips of the frozen daiquiris that Sharon had served after dinner. Jocelyn had been lost in her concerns about Lawrence's new book and barely heard Ben's question.

"What did you say? I'm sorry. I was thinking about something and didn't hear you."

"I have tickets for Alli's concert next week and wanted to know if you'd like to go. A guy in the office bought them months ago and can't use them."

"Yeah, that might be fun. I've never seen her in concert and from everything I've been told she puts on a dynamite show."

"Your ex-boyfriend doesn't play with her band any more, does he?" She sensed an edge in Ben's voice as he asked the question.

"No, it's been a couple of years since he left the band. Mark told his mom that Alli is a wild child and he couldn't handle it."

"No matter, I love her music." Ben put his glass down on the table and stood to leave. "I've got to be in court early tomorrow, so I need to go. I'll say good-bye to your dad and Sharon and let myself out." He leaned over and kissed the top of her head. "Dinner was great."

"Will it ever slow down, Ben?" she asked with a heavy sigh, not bothering to get up.

"We've had this conversation before, Jocelyn."

She could feel the impatience in his voice, but tonight she wasn't going to let it bother her. "I know we have. But that doesn't make it any easier on our relationship." Turning her head, she looked in his eyes with a sense of resignation. "Thanks for stopping by. I'll talk to you later in the week."

When the French doors leading into the living room closed, she realized she didn't know when the concert was or what the plans where. *Oh well, what does it matter? I've learned the hard way that making plans isn't Ben's thing.* When she had drained the last drop of rum and lime juice from her glass, she stood and walked across the garden to the guesthouse where she lived.

As she climbed the stairs to her bedroom the disappointments and emptiness of her relationship with Ben felt like a heavy weight on her shoulders and somewhere in the vicinity of her heart there was emptiness. There was nothing to hold on to any more. Ben didn't have time for her and he had no intention of changing.

She had two choices—stay or leave. But venturing into the dating world depressed her. She had never been in that world before and she didn't think she had the skills to be successful. The only guys she had ever gone out with had been her friends long before they had started dating. She had met Mark when she was a kid volunteering at the little theater and Ben when he was doing a summer internship at the newspaper. Both relationships had grown out of friendship and she didn't have any other male friends.

Turning around on the stairs, she decided to see what her dad and Sharon were doing before she let her mood descend into feeling sorry for herself. She was almost running by the time she crossed the patio and went in the main house. "Dad, Sharon, where are you guys?"

"In the kitchen scraping the crumbs off the cake plate. Come join us before they're all gone." Sharon's voice was playful and inviting. "We'd love some company."

"Ben left early. Does he have a big case or something?" Carter frowned as he glanced at his daughter. "I thought he'd stick around for awhile."

"He never sticks around, Daddy. You know that." She tried to keep her tone casual.

"That young man doesn't know how to enjoy himself," said Carter.

Both women laughed. "Honey, who does that remind you of?" Sharon teased. "There was a time when you didn't know that, either."

"Lucky for me I had the two of you to come to my rescue." Carter grabbed his daughter and gave her a big hug. "Spending time with the old folks might not be so bad this evening." His expression changed as he let go of Jocelyn. "We were talking about the murder of that baby and some of Sharon's more interesting clients. Maybe you can answer some of our questions since you have a front row seat at the newspaper."

"Right. Like I know more than what you read in the paper!"

"Your dad had some strange things happen on a couple of the buses a few weeks ago. Did you know they found packages of drugs taped under seats on several of them? One route was to Hialeah, the other to Liberty City. The police think somebody is using the bus system to courier drugs."

"That's creepy. I've been worried about Lawrence, but I never thought I'd have to worry about you, too." Concern filled her eyes when she looked at her father.

"There's no reason to worry about me. But, why are you concerned for Lawrence?"

"His new book will be published next month and it's a story about the drug cartel." She took a seat at the table and scraped some icing off the remaining piece of cake. Licking her fingers, she looked at Sharon. "What's interesting about your clients?"

"Not so fast. Tell us more about the new book." Sharon leaned toward her. "And, please don't tell me Lawrence is writing some kind of exposé."

"Have you heard anything about this supposed woman called the Emperitza? It's alleged that she runs the whole show and Lawrence says she is meaner than a snake."

"What does she have to do with Lawrence's new book?"

"His story is about a woman they call the Scorpion who runs a cocaine cartel and the more I'm learning about the underworld in Miami, the closer his story seems to match what's happening all around us. What if the mob or cartel or whatever these people call themselves, decide they don't like what he's written?"

"Lawrence knows what he can print and what he can't. His publisher won't let him cross any lines." Carter tried to sound convincing. "Have you told him how you feel?"

"Of course, but what good does that do? If he wants to tell an exciting story, he's not going to concern himself with personal safety." Jocelyn shrugged her shoulders and continued to scrape the icing off the cake. "Sometimes I think he believes he's his own main character, Agent Joe Fielding!"

"That's probably closer to true than we realize. After all, Lawrence Fitz was a top-notch FBI agent in his day." Carter playfully slapped her hand when she reached for the cake plate again. "Save me some." He hesitated then spoke more commandingly. "Jocelyn, two bits of advice. First, stop worrying about Fitz. Second, be careful. Just keep your eyes and ears open."

"You want to stay and watch some TV?" Sharon changed the mood with her light-hearted invitation. "That new show, Miami Vice, is on tonight. Maybe those tough guys will give us a clue about our city's dangers." She winked at her step-daughter. "And, they're so good looking!"

Jeanne Moon Farmer

Chapter Five

Alli Anderson

The concert circuit was a grind, but she loved the adrenaline high of performing in front of hundreds of adoring fans. The pace she'd been working for the past three years would have been physically and emotionally exhausting if she didn't have a few energy boosters she could rely on to keep her going. All of the years she had hated her mother for depending on drugs and alcohol were forgotten now that she needed them. She reclined in the lounge chair in her dressing room and tried to chase thoughts of her mother from her mind. But today, Margo kept intruding.

Alli Anderson, daughter of one of the best loved Diva's ever to grace world stages, had been a whirlwind success from the moment she stepped on stage three years earlier. It had started when cancer stole Margo's voice and cut short her career. Alli had jumped at the chance to take her mother's place on the concert tour and show the world that her star could outshine Margo's. Her concerts sold out in minutes, her albums were consistent best sellers, and she had three hit songs that had gone platinum. *Not bad for a twenty-two year old!*

Her version of her mother's songs had launched her career, but now she was performing her own music, designing her own costumes, and working with the choreographer to arrange her own backup dancing. "Vibrant, stunning, refreshing, crazy," were just a few of the critics' descriptions of their newest darling, the wild child whose amazing talent was selling out performances wherever she appeared. She and her mother, Margo, had changed places - Alli was the star and Margo was her shadow. It always thrilled her when she thought about it that way.

The frenzied pace of her life would be daunting to most people, but for Alli it was the elixir that fed her. The hunger was always there, demanding that she turn the wheels faster and faster. Everyone said she was out of control, but she knew that wasn't true.

"Alli, ten minutes 'til show time!" the stage manager shouted through the closed dressing room door. "It's time to rock and roll, Sweetheart."

That was her cue. There was only one thing left to do before she appeared on stage to thrill another audience with her voice, her seductive moves, and her high energy. Sitting up, she reached in the drawer of the table by her chair for the small, white packet of cocaine. As she prepared to snort the line of white power that she laid out on the table, her body and mind anxiously awaited the sensation that was only a few seconds away-the rush of adrenalin, the euphoria, the power, the feeling of majesty that intensified her love affair with herself.

Within a few seconds the powerful drug hit her brain and she was ready to give the audience what they had come to hear—and more— so much more.

*****

"The lady has a big order for ya." Toro Mendoza, the band's drummer, spoke quickly into the phone. "Hey, she's willing to pay and you know it." He continued to listen to the voice on the other end of the line. "Man, we're leaving for Chicago in the morning and she has to have the stuff before we get on that bus. You have somebody deliver to me at the hotel in two hours or we find a new place to shop."

Toro hung up the phone and turned to Alli, "Don't cut it so close next time. I may not be able to get you what you need on an hour's notice."

"You always come through for me, Toro. I'm not worried." It was intermission and she could feel the earlier euphoria evaporating. With another hit she would be able to give the audience what they wanted in the second half of the show.

"Alli, you've got to slow down. You're using way too much of this stuff." The drummer looked at his boss with concern. "I'm not preaching, Alli. Don't get me wrong. But, I'm just saying to go easy on the powder. It can really mess with your head if you use too much, especially when you're mixing it with booze."

"I know what I'm doing, Toro." She laughed. "You stopped preaching and now you're meddling. Isn't that how it goes?"

"Whatever you say, Sweetheart." He walked to the door, then stopped. Clearing his throat, he took a good look at the beautiful young woman who thrilled millions every night with her vibrant performances. "Just remember how messed up I was last year. You don't want to go there."

Alli turned from her dressing room mirror and looked at the concern on the man's face. "Hey, stop worrying about me. I'm fine."

"I know this tour is strenuous, but it will be over in two weeks and we can all get some rest. It scares me that this is the second big order I've made for you this week. I'm just saying, slow down a little."

"You're right. My energy's been dragging the last few days. That's all." She smiled. "Thanks for caring. I'll be all right." She watched as he opened the door to leave. "Let me know as soon as the delivery gets here and, Toro, this is between us. Right?"

"Yeah, boss. Just between you and me." He walked out the door and closed it behind him.

Alli turned back to the bright lights of the make-up mirror and tried to ignore the dark circles under her eyes. Since the opening of the tour, she hadn't stopped partying and it was catching up with her. She promised herself that after tonight's show she'd go back to the hotel and rest. But, she was having the time of her life—she was the center of the universe—and she loved it. Ignoring the slight tremor in her hands, she reached into the tote bag next to her chair. She fumbled around until she grasped a small bottle of vodka. Her hand caressed the smooth, cool glass and a sigh of relief escaped her lips as she opened the bottle and brought it to her mouth. The fire of the first sip burned awareness throughout her body and within seconds she felt herself coming alive again.

She opened her eyes and shouted at the face in the mirror. "I am Alli Anderson and I rule rock and roll! Nothing can stop me! Do you hear that, Margo? Nothing can stop me!"

*****

Todd Madison, Alli's bodyguard, watched from the wings as she worked her magic on the audience. Her voice boomed, her gyrations rocked the stage, and her seductive dance had people screaming for more. Every night for three years he had watched her sell herself to millions of fans who never seemed to get enough of what she offered. Night after night her performance ended in demands for more. —Just the night before, she had responded to five curtain calls and had done three encores before he and her manager had stopped her. Once she left the stage, it wasn't over. After a quick change of clothes, she had partied with a group at one of the downtown clubs until the club closed at two o'clock, and then she had invited some hanger-on to her room. From his room across the hall from hers, he had heard the man leave around six this morning.

Alcohol, drugs, sex—the pattern was the same, but the intensity had been steadily increasing. Her manager was upset about missed rehearsals and her accountant had talked with him briefly about her spending sprees and the number of large checks she was writing to Toro Mendoza. As a former police officer, he was finding it more and more difficult to turn his back on his suspicions that Toro was supplying Alli with drugs—most likely cocaine.

Todd paced back and forth, wrestling with his concerns, his questions, and the voice in the back of his head that kept nagging at him to call her father. For days he had been struggling with his conscience. Was it his role or responsibility to police her actions, or was his one and only job to make sure she was safe. His long history with the family wasn't helping to ease his mind. Alli's mother, the great singer, Margo, had struggled with addictions that had eventually impacted her career and health long-term, and he knew how hard Alli's father, Michael, had worked to keep Margo from destroying herself.

Alli was his boss, but she was twenty-two and could do what she wanted. His job was to protect her. Millions of people wanted a piece of her—some adored her and just wanted to see or touch her, others were pure evil and wanted to do her harm. For three years, he had successfully kept her safe in the outside world, but he was losing the war to protect her from herself.

His steps quickened, his mind raced. Abruptly, he stopped pacing and felt his body relax somewhat. The person he needed to talk to was Margo's former bodyguard, Sam Baxter. The man had lived through the same struggles he was having and he would know what to tell him. The final stop on the tour was a sold-out performance at the Orange Bowl in Miami and he and Alli would be home for the summer. He could wait two weeks, but as soon as they landed in Miami he was going to call Sam and ask his advice. Either that or he was going to have to quit this job before his worries over Alli got the best of him.

Jeanne Moon Farmer

Chapter Six

Lawrence Fitz

Satisfied. That's how he felt about the new novel that was to be released in the coming weeks. His research was sound, his contacts had provided the facts he needed to make the story as realistic as possible, and his attention to detail was bound to keep the readers interested.

He knew Jocelyn was concerned, even though he had tried to allay her fears. She thought the story was too close to the truth. But he was determined to let the world know what was happening in South Florida and this book was a fictional account of the ugliness that was overshadowing the beauty of Miami. Every time he thought about his beloved adopted city, he got angry again. He had been in law enforcement all his life and was appalled at the corruption and lawlessness cocaine was imposing on most of South Florida. With the amount of money that was pouring into Miami, how was it possible that nobody was investigating where it came from?

He flipped through the manuscript. Joe Fielding, the protagonist in all his novels, is an FBI agent who knows the ropes. In this new book, Joe uses his cunning and resources to uncover the heart of the cocaine operation in Miami. As the story unfolds, Joe finds himself the target of a small time drug dealer who eventually leads him to the woman who is the master-mind with strong connections to the Columbian cocaine cartel. Joe knows she is dangerous and out-smarting her will be virtually impossible. So, in the make-believe world of the novel, Joe makes it his goal to dismantle the operation, not to capture the woman. By the last chapter, the operation has fallen apart and the woman has been forced to take refuge in South America. Throughout the book, the FBI agent reveals the myriad ways that the cartel can be destroyed.

If a make-believe agent can find answers, then why in the world can't the real men and women of law enforcement see what's right in front of them? He was disgusted with the customs agents, Coast Guard, police force, and county government that were allowing mayhem and murder to consume the city. And, how much more had to happen before the FBI and federal drug enforcement agents got seriously involved?

That kind of thinking only raised his blood pressure, so he let it go and turned his thoughts back to the release of his book. His editor liked the story, but the publishers had been hesitant to run with the new book. Over and over they had asked him to tone down the story, but he had refused.

"It's fiction!" he had almost shouted at Mason Garret, the vice president of the publishing house. "Yes, I've used some incidents that have actually happened, but they're all documented in the *Miami Herald*. So, there shouldn't be any legal issues for you or for me." He had defended his right to write the book and his publisher's right to print it, but in his heart he knew it was going to ruffle some feathers once it hit the book stores. After weeks of negotiation and haggling, he had taken out a chapter the publisher felt was inflammatory and they had finally agreed to go to press.

The advanced reader copies of the book had been sent to the reviewers and the reviews looked promising. The book would be released in a few months and it looked like he had another bestseller. Lawrence smiled. He had never imagined that his years as an FBI agent would reap such financial rewards. His last chat with his accountant had astounded him. Between the books and the movie deals, he was a very wealthy man——a rich man with no heir. It was unfortunate that he and his wife had no children, but he had made generous provisions in his will for each of their nieces and nephews, several charities, and the church. But, the smile on his face was because of the provisions he had made for Carter and Jocelyn and Maddie. The two young women he loved like a granddaughters, and the man he wished had been his son, would inherit the bulk of his estate. Yes, thinking about them made him very happy.

*****

A woman's screams startled and alarmed him and he rushed to the door to see if he could help her. But, before he could get to the door, it opened and Jocelyn stumbled into the foyer.

"What in the world is going on, Jocelyn? Was that you who screamed? My dear, you look like you've seen a ghost."

"Lawrence, thank God you're safe!" she gasped, then threw her arms around him. "I thought something terrible had happened to you." Drawing in a shaky breath, she dropped her arms and looked at him. "Have you been outside this morning?"

"What on earth are you talking about? No, I haven't been outside, but what has that got to do with the screaming I just heard?"

"Open the door and take a look." She motioned to him and followed him back to the front door.

He winced when he saw the door and then shook his head. "Jocelyn, call Tom West down at Miami Dade Police headquarters and tell him what has happened. I'd like for him to send a crime unit, but I doubt seriously if they'll find any fingerprints." He closed the door, blocking out the sight and smell of the dead chicken impaled by a large knife to the outside of the door and the death threat smeared underneath with dried blood.

Jocelyn hung up the phone and sat down on the sofa. "What do you think this means, Lawrence? I can't stop shaking." She crossed her arms in front of her and leaned forward in the chair. "Whoever did this must have tortured that poor chicken. It's sickening." She looked across at Lawrence who was sitting nonchalantly in his chair. "Doesn't this upset you? It has me freaked out and you're just sitting there like nothing has happened!"

"Nothing has happened, my dear. It's probably a teenager playing a prank on me."

"You're not taking this seriously." She stumbled over the words. "Why did you want the police involved?"

"Why? Because prank or not, I certainly don't want this to happen to any of my neighbors in this building." He took a breath and chuckled almost to himself. "Can you imagine if Mrs. Harriman or Mrs. Steenburg had opened their doors to that sight?"

He watched as Jocelyn continued to fidget. "Don't worry. This is nothing for us to be alarmed about."

"It's about the book! I knew something bad was going to happen because of that book. You're in danger. Can't you see that?" With this realization, her anxiety level began to increase.

"You're letting your imagination run away with you, Jocelyn. Let's wait to see what the police have to say before we start making wild judgments about my safety." He walked into the kitchen on the pretense of pouring himself a cup of coffee. When he was certain that Jocelyn couldn't see him, he closed his eyes and took a deep breath. As much as he hated to admit it, he knew the implications of the chicken on his door. But nothing would be gained by allowing Jocelyn to witness his concern. He sat down at the table and made mental notes, searching for the right words to say when Tom West arrived. Although he and West had a law enforcement connection through a case they worked together years ago, he didn't want their conversation to further alarm Jocelyn.

He was deep in thought when the ringing doorbell made him aware that time had passed. As he stood up to return to the living room, he prayed that the conversation he was about to have would not be unhealthy for Jocelyn. He needed to make sure her fears were put to rest.

"Hello, Tom. Thanks for responding so quickly."

"Holy cow, Agent Fitz. You've got yourself a messy door!" The officer shook his head as he surveyed the scene. "It won't be too long before that chicken will stink up this whole building. I'll call for a team to get here ASAP. We've got to get this mess cleaned up. Any ideas on what might have caused this?"

"It's probably just a prank, but nevertheless, I wanted you to take a look."

Jocelyn looked at the police officer and said, "I think it's way more than a prank. He's trying to downplay this, but I think it's a serious threat. Look at those words. "IT'S YOUR TURN. They're significant."

Tom frowned, "What do you think that means?" He looked at Lawrence and waited several minutes before he got a response.

"I'm not sure, but it could have something to do with my latest book," Lawrence responded reluctantly. "I use those words as a death threat in one of the chapters."

"Sorry, I didn't know you had a new book out. I'm a big fan, Lawrence." Tom smiled. "What's this new book about?"

"The publisher has sent it out for review and it will be in the book stores in a month or two. It's a fictionalized story of the drug trafficking problem in Miami," Lawrence offered.

"Jeez, Lawrence, you sure do like to play with fire. Do you mind if I sit down?"

"Have a seat, Tom" Turning around, he realized he hadn't introduced Jocelyn. "Sorry, I've really forgotten my manners. This is my assistant, Jocelyn McDeal."

Smiling at the belated introduction, Jocelyn extended her hand to the officer and asked, "Would you like a cup of coffee?"

"Thanks, Miss McDeal, but I just finished a cup." He pulled out a note pad and started writing. "Let me ask a few questions. Do you have any idea when this could have happened?"

"I'm not sure. Jocelyn discovered it when she arrived this morning." Lawrence laughed. "First, I didn't hear any strange sounds during the night. Second, I don't have a clue, and third, if this is related to the book, then it could have been done by anybody who wanted to earn five dollars."

"You're right. As soon as my guys have checked it out, I'll get back to you." Tom stood and turned to leave. "Lawrence, I know you aren't going to like hearing me say this, but maybe you should think about hiring somebody private for a few weeks. I know you're ex-FBI, but remember, you're retired and don't have the authority you used to have."

"Thanks, Tom. I'll take your advice under consideration."

"I've asked that the patrol car make extra passes around this building during the evening hours, but that's about the best I can do."

After the police had completed their investigation, Jocelyn began. "I agree with Tom West. You need to have somebody looking out for you and I know the perfect person. I'm calling Sam Baxter right now."

"No thank you, Jocelyn. I know you're concerned, but I don't need Sam." Lawrence tried not to sound irritated. But, the situation was about to get on his nerves.

"Please, let me call him. At least talk to him."

"Has everyone forgotten that I have been the protector just about all my life? I'm retired, not debilitated, and I don't need protection."

"Lawrence, for the first time since I met you, you're not being sensible or rational. If you're not worried about yourself, then please be worried for my safety. Remember, I'm part of your team and I spend a lot of my time here. Think about hiring Sam to protect me!"

He walked over to the sofa and looked down at Jocelyn with tenderness. "You're right, my dear. I would never forgive myself if something happened to you. All right, call Sam and ask him to come over for a chat."

*****

"Sam, I really don't think it's necessary for me to have a twenty-four hour guard. But, Jocelyn is very uneasy right now and I thought you could help me figure out a way to allay her fears." Lawrence spoke matter-of-factly with the man who had once been the bodyguard of the pop singer Margo. "Her anxiety about this novel began long before it was sent to the publisher and it has accelerated because of the unfortunate incident with the chicken."

"Mr. Fitz, Jocelyn is right to be concerned and I hope you're taking this threat seriously. I think you're lucky they gave you this warning. From everything I know, these people usually shoot first."

54

"I'm convinced this is some kind of prank. I don't think I'm in danger. I've talked with several of my contacts and they haven't heard anything on the street that would indicate I've been targeted."

Sam seemed to be assessing the elderly gentleman before he spoke. "I know you just finished writing your latest book, Mr. Fitz, but if you touched a nerve with the Emperitza, she's not going to take it lightly."

"Please, call me Lawrence." He laughed. "If we're going to be working together, the mister thing is a bit formal, don't you think?"

"All right, but changing from mister to Lawrence doesn't change our reality. I think you've been warned. Now, it's up to you to decide whether you want protection or not. And, I agree that you need to take Jocelyn's safety into consideration." Sam looked around the apartment. "Does anyone else live here with you?"

"No, no Sam, I live alone. My wife died a year ago and now it's just me. We never had children, so I don't even have family that comes to visit. Of course, Carter and Sharon McDeal and Maddie Sonnett stop by every now and then, and Jocelyn is in and out all the time. In fact, she has her own key. But, no," his voice softened, "I live a fairly solitary life. That's why I can get so much writing done."

"What about friends? Isn't Maddie's father your former FBI partner? Don't the two of you see each other often?"

Lawrence laughed. "Maddie's father is old and decrepit. He never leaves his house except to ride around the golf course in that cart of his. He doesn't even play the game anymore." He looked at Sam with a twinkle in his eye. "James and I are the same age, but I hope I never get as old as he is."

"I know you're not going to like what I'm going to suggest. However, I think you need to change residence for the time being." He added before Lawrence could protest. "Just for a few weeks. Until we can see what kind of surveillance you're under."

"There you go again, thinking the drug traffickers are after me! This is all so unnecessary, Sam."

"Your choice, Lawrence. But, you're wrong, and I think you know it. If you were to hire me this is what I would suggest. First, you need to move out of this apartment for a while. Second, we need to keep the car you and Jocelyn use under scrutiny. I wouldn't want someone to place a bomb under the hood. Third, we need round the clock on you and Jocelyn. And, fourth, we need your contacts to do more than listen to the talk on the street. We need someone inside who can keep us updated on what the plans are for you."

"I love this, Sam. It's just like old times. Except I was always the one sitting where you are today." He leaned forward in his chair and took an earnest look at the man in the chair across from him. "This is much ado about nothing, but I will go along with it for a limited amount of time."

"I think that's wise. Now let's get to work. Is there a place you can move to for a week or two?"

Lawrence looked thoughtful. "Jocelyn moved out of the guesthouse at the McDeal's a few weeks ago. I'm sure Carter and Sharon wouldn't mind if I moved in there for a short time. I'll call them later and discuss it."

"That's perfect. I have several people I've worked with in the past and I'll start making some calls. If Claire McGuire is available, she's my first choice for Jocelyn. Claire was part of the team who protected Margo. She's good and I trust her. She'll work well with Jocelyn. And, Lawrence, I'm assigning myself to you. If you're agreeable?"

"I'm not going to put up any more arguments. But, this is short-term, Sam. As long as you realize there's a time limit, then we've got a deal."

*****

When Jocelyn showed up at six o'clock with take-out Chinese, he told her about his visit with Sam. "I did as you asked and talked with Sam Baxter. I like him, Jocelyn. Thank you for suggesting him. I think we'll work well together."

"What did you decide?" Jocelyn took a bite of her dumpling and looked at her boss for an answer.

"For starters, I'm moving."

"You've got to be kidding me. You're going to sell this apartment? I can't believe it."

"No, no, no. It's only temporary. Just for a few weeks until we know more about what's going on. In fact, I'm moving to your old place. I talked to your father this afternoon and it's all arranged. For dramatic effect, my move will be done under cloak of darkness or some other nonsense."

"That's great. With Dad and Sharon in the main house, I'll feel a lot better about you."

"You're not getting off easy, my dear. A woman named," he hesitated. "I can't remember her name. Anyway, a woman will be with you for the next few weeks also. Sam will be in touch with more details this evening."

"Are you moving tonight?" Jocelyn's surprise was evident as she inquired.

"Most likely. I don't know yet, but my bag is packed and Sharon is expecting me whenever. She called an hour ago and told me that everything is ready for me."

"Okay. I've been assigned a bodyguard, but what about you?"

"Sam Baxter himself will be my constant companion for the next few weeks. I look forward to hearing his stories. I bet there's a new book in there somewhere."

"You're incorrigible, Lawrence. How many more books do you think you're going to write?" Jocelyn laughed and began to clear the table. "Which reminds me, do we clear your schedule for the next few weeks? You've got three or four book signings, and next month is the premiere of the new movie. Sam will probably want me to cancel your appearance at all of these events if he seriously thinks you're in danger."

"Honestly, you all are overreacting to all of this! We're not canceling anything, and that's that." Lawrence got up from the table in disgust. "I'm not a child and I won't have my life disrupted by this foolishness any more than I've already agreed to. Do you think at my age it's going to be easy for me to move? I like the comfort of my own home."

She walked over and put her arm around his shoulder. "We're just making sure that you have time to write all those new books. It's a minor inconvenience for our safety and if I can bear having a stranger watching my every move, you can put up with Sam for a few weeks. It'll work out and Sam and I will make sure you don't miss any of your upcoming events." She smiled as she walked with him to his favorite chair in the living room. "Besides, I think you'll like my old place and Sharon will treat you like a king."

*****

His bag was packed and he sat waiting for Sam to whisk him away in the middle of the night to his "hide-away." He thought of the hours of sleep he was missing and groaned. Intrigue wasn't meant for someone his age and every bone in his body was reacting to the stress. Smiling, he looked over at Jocelyn who was curled up on the couch asleep. He had told her to go home, but she insisted on being here to help him make this move.

Memories flooded over him as he watched her sleep. She was three or four years old the first time he saw her. He remembered her proudly climbing aboard the number-six city bus with her grandmother, bouncing up the steps, dropping her token in the box. Looking up at the driver of the bus, she whispered, "Hi, Daddy," and smiled when he winked back in response.

Over the years, as he rode the bus to town and back each weekday, he had watched her father, Carter, go through the many ups and downs of life and they had become friends. In fact, it was an observation he had recorded in one of his journals that had helped Carter clear his name when he had been accused of kidnapping Jocelyn as an infant.

The day he was called for a deposition, after Carter's arrest, was probably the day he went from thinking of Carter as a friend, to thinking of him as a son. There was no one in the world to help Carter defend himself against the charges—his mother, Gracie, had died the year before, and Jocelyn's birth mother, Rosanne, no longer lived in the area.

He and Rosanne had ridden the same bus for several years and he had observed her growing admiration for the bus driver. As a teenager, she rode the bus to school every morning—the number-six bus that Carter drove. During her senior year, he had observed her attempts to hide her pregnancy and he remembered feeling sorry for her—too young for such a task as motherhood. By the end of May, she was no longer on the bus and he remembered praying that she was going to be okay.

Years later, when Carter was arrested, with just a little bit of research, it wasn't difficult for him to put the pieces of the puzzle together. Especially since Jocelyn looked identical to Rosanne. All had ended well. Rosanne showed up at Carter's trial and told the judge that she had left her darling baby on Carter's doorstep because she knew that he and his mother would love and care for her.

It was a tough time for Carter and Jocelyn. She felt betrayed by Carter and Gracie—the father and grandmother she believed were her true family. And, she didn't know where Rosanne, her mother, fit in her life. Lawrence sighed when he remembered how angry Jocelyn was and the horrific situation she had been placed in when the court made Mary Ann Moss, a teacher at Jocelyn's school, her guardian. He had observed the unhealthy relationship that Miss Moss was trying to cultivate with her young charge and he had vowed to find a way to get Jocelyn out of the situation.

That's when he'd come up with the idea of hiring the teenager to assist him in writing his memoir. She was a freshman in college, majoring in English. It was a perfect fit and, it subsequently changed his life. He never thought that his attempt to write his memoir would turn into ten best-selling novels and two movies. Yes, Carter's arrest and trial were a nightmare, but it had ended with some pleasant rewards—Carter reunited with his high school sweetheart, Sharon, and they were now happily married, and he had gained Jocelyn and Carter as his adopted family. The one relationship that continued to suffer was the one between Jocelyn and Mark Sanders.

As he allowed his mind to wander, he pictured Jocelyn holding hands with Mark. The way she looked at that young man was the same way his wife had looked at him—eyes filled with tenderness and love. Alas, Jocelyn and Mark's faith had rules that prevented them from marrying and, while he understood the reasoning, it saddened him. Those two had fallen in love before they discovered that Rosanne, Jocelyn's mother, was also Mark's aunt. How unfortunate that two people who were so well-suited for one another could never marry because of the mandates of their church. Florida no longer had a law prohibiting first cousin marriages, but Mark and Jocelyn were Catholic and church law would not allow it if there was a possibility that children might result from their union. In his heart, he knew Jocelyn was still grieving over the break-up of the relationship even though she was trying to move on.

A quiet knock on the door brought him out of his reverie. It had awakened Jocelyn and she was already on her way to open the door for Sam. It was time to go. Lawrence took one last, long look around the room, picked up his small duffel bag, and followed Sam and Jocelyn out of his apartment.

*****

A tinted window, black sedan waited for them in the alley, and as he crawled inside Lawrence was aware of other people seated in the car. When the doors were closed, Sam quietly introduced Lawrence and Jocelyn to Claire McQuire and the driver, Joe Birdsong.

"Jocelyn, once we have Lawrence settled, we'll drop you and Claire at your apartment. We've already done a sweep of the place and Claire left her bags in your spare bedroom. Hope that's okay with you?"

"You all certainly move fast, Sam. When you told me I'd have someone with me, I didn't think you meant all the time." She smiled at Claire, "No offense. I just wasn't prepared. I'm glad you're here and I know we'll get on fine."

Claire nodded in response but didn't reply.

"Lawrence, Joe Birdsong is one of the best drivers and bodyguards you'll ever meet. He was raised in the Everglades and can tackle even the fiercest gator—man or reptile. He'll always be close to us. I'll be on the day shift with you and Joe will take over when I go home to sleep. How's that?"

"Joe and Claire, I look forward to working with you for the next few days. You can keep me entertained with all your war stories until this ordeal has been resolved." Lawrence was pleased that Sam was handling the details so well—things wouldn't be so bad for a few days.

They drove with the lights off until they were several blocks away from the alley behind Lawrence's apartment building. Once they were on the busier streets of the city, the driver turned the lights on, but he didn't take the shortest route to the McDeal's house in Coconut Grove. Lawrence knew the driver would continue to drive a circuitous route until he was sure they were not being followed. At that time of night, with so few cars on the road, it was very easy to determine if any of the cars behind them were tailing them.

Sam broke the silence in the car. "I've talked to Tom West at Miami PD and they haven't been able to come up with any clues about the threat. Of course, we didn't really think they would, but I was hoping they could give us something to go on." "I knew they wouldn't, but the incident had to be reported." Lawrence leaned his head back against the seat and yawned. "It's way past my bedtime, folks. So sorry."

"Once we get you to Dad's, are you going to be able to sleep?" Jocelyn knew that the long day of activity and stress were tiring her boss. Even inside the dark car she could see that Lawrence was fighting to stay awake. "I talked with Sharon earlier and they have everything ready for you. Dad is excited that all he'll have to do is cross the patio to have a visit with you. You'll probably have to run him off to get any peace and quiet."

"It will be a pleasure to spend time with your father. I can't imagine that I would ever get tired of talking to him."

The gate to the McDeal's driveway opened as they approached. "How did you manage that one, Sam?" Jocelyn was surprised. "There wasn't a gate or fence here before and now there's a gate that opens by itself. I'm impressed."

"Joe, show the lady the magic wand." Sam called to the man in the driver's seat.

"Your daddy gave me this." Joe held up the remote. "You've got a nice family. They've done everything they could think of to help us."

"I thought I was a detail person, but you guys have covered all the bases." said Jocelyn.

"That's our job. We have to be a few steps ahead if we're going to keep you and Lawrence safe."

The porch light on the guesthouse came on and Carter stood with the front door open in welcome.

Chapter Seven

Mark

He wadded up another sheet of paper and threw it in the waste basket. The song wasn't coming together and his deadline loomed. Standing, he began to pace. The melody raced around in his head, but he couldn't make the words fit. He had a contract for three new songs for one of the top country singers in the business—two of them had flowed out of his guitar and head like he'd known them all his life. So, why couldn't he make the third one do the same?

Picking up the guitar, he strummed the tune again hoping some new insight would wash over him. He sang the refrain and knew that part of the song was solid, but he stumbled every time he added the verse. It wasn't working.

"Mark, I've got lunch ready. Can you take a break and come eat?" Sunni called from the kitchen.

"Might as well. I'm not doing much good at song writing today." He knew he sounded like a two-year old, but he couldn't help it.

He walked into the small kitchen and watched her move from one counter to the other. She had a quiet beauty that calmed him and a smile that made him feel loved, yet, there were days when he looked at her and felt something was missing. Just like his song writing today, his relationship with Sunni Anderson had a good melody, but the lyrics never seemed to come together. Shaking his head, he laughed at himself and wondered where that crazy thought came from. He and Sunni had a great relationship.

"Smells good in here. What's for lunch?"

"The most fabulous BLT sandwich you have ever eaten!" Sunni held up a plate to show him her creation. "I may not be a gourmet cook, but I know how to put together a dynamite sandwich." The lilt of her voice and the smile on her face made him put aside his frustrations—at least for a few minutes.

"This lunch is a celebration," she exclaimed. "I've taken my last exam and turned in my final paper." She put the plate down on the table and hugged him. "Can you believe I graduate in three days? I can say good-bye to Sarah Lawrence." She let go of him and danced around the room. "No more studying, no more lectures, no more exams. What a great feeling!"

"That part may be over, but now you have to go to work."

"Yes, yes, yes, and I can't wait. I start in a month and I'm more excited about that than I am about finishing college." She sat down at the table and picked up her sandwich. "I know I'm starting at the bottom, but just to think about joining a major publishing house is a dream come true."

"There's one little problem." Sadness crept into Mark's voice. "You will be staying in New York and I'll be back in Miami. I had hoped you'd move back to Miami."

"Mark, we've talked about this. You're in New York so often—it would be so much easier for you to move here. What kinds of jobs are available in publishing in Miami? There's nothing there for me."

"Yeah, but how can we make plans for the future if you're here and I'm in Miami? You've always said you wanted to write children's books. You don't have to be in New York to do that."

"My job here will be like serving an internship. I'll learn so much about the publishing world and in a few years, when I'm established, I can quit and start writing. It's about knowing what I need to know and finding out who can help me. Besides, you can work anywhere, Mark." A scowl crossed her face. "You can move your studio here and then we can be together all the time."

"Sunni, you're not being realistic. Do you have any idea of the difference in cost between New York and Miami? It would cost me a small fortune to replicate the studio I have in Miami, and what about all the people who work for me? Their base is Miami." He walked around the table and took her hand in his. "I love you, sweetheart, and I want to marry you. But, right now, New York is out of the question for me. You know that."

Sunni shook her head. She looked at him, pleading, "Give me a little more time, please. I've already rented an apartment in the city and accepted the job. I can't back out now." She let go of his hand and picked up her sandwich again. "One year, Mark. Give me one more year?"

"Do you realize how many years I've waited?" All at once he knew he couldn't hide his frustration and disappointment any longer. "I'm going home, Sunni. Second choice just doesn't feel right to me." He saw the tears form in her eyes, but his need was so great he couldn't respond to hers. "I can't do this any longer. I'll be out of here as soon as I can pack."

She stood up from the table and tossed her napkin as far as she could throw it. "Do you know how much you're hurting me with those words? Do you know what it feels like to be pulled apart and torn in two by your dreams? How can you do this to me—to us?" She walked to the bedroom and slammed the door behind her.

"Yeah, Sunni, I know exactly what it feels like." He shouted after her. "I know only too well."

*****

He had hastily packed his bags and called a taxi to take him to the airport. There was no point in hanging around Sunni's apartment. No point in trying to convince her that their relationship should take priority. No point in having the same conversation over and over. This time they had backed themselves into a corner and neither of them could find a way out. It hurt that he would miss her graduation and he knew there would be questions about his absence. But, he also knew that staying would only drag out the inevitable. It was over and he'd have to live with it.

"What is wrong with me?" He shouted to the sidewalk, oblivious to the stares of the people passing by. His thoughts were all jumbled and he hurt. He didn't care if strangers thought he was crazy. Twice he had waited years on women he loved, only to have the relationships end in exactly the same way. First, it was Jocelyn. He had been willing to defy all the rules to marry her, even though they were first cousins. But she couldn't get past disappointing the family and having to leave the church. She had put him second for years. And, now, Sunni had just done the same thing. In one or two sentences, she had told him she was willing to put her career ahead of their relationship.

As soon as the taxi pulled up, he jumped in and didn't look back. He knew if he did, he would find a way to stay—to be her second choice. He leaned back in the seat and let the silent tears roll down his cheeks.

*****

The ringing phone broke his concentration and in the back of his mind he hoped it was Sunni calling to beg him to return to New York. It really surprised him that he hadn't heard from her in more than two weeks. Several times he had gone to the phone to call her, but something kept him from it. He had asked himself over and over if there was a possible way that he and Sunni could continue to make it work long distance, and always the answer was the same. For the past four years, now that he thought about it, the answer had always been the same.

When he answered the phone, at first he thought he was hearing Sunni's voice, but quickly realized it was her twin sister on the other end of the line. "Hey, Alli, big time rock star! How's it going?" He listened for a moment, then replied.

"Yeah, I'm back in Miami for good. I guess you heard that Sunni and I broke up?" He heard her out.

"No, Alli, I'm not going back to New York. It's over and it would only hurt both of us to drag it out any longer." He sighed.

"What can I do for you?" The longer he listened the more convinced he became that Alli was drunk. Her words were slurred and most of what she was saying didn't make sense.

"Alli, you fired me. Remember? And, no I'm not interested in going back on the road with the band."

It was three o'clock in the afternoon and she sounded like she had been drinking for days. "Alli, isn't it a little early to be partying? Don't you have a concert tonight?" He moved the phone away from his ear to protect his hearing.

"Yeah, Alli. It was nice talking to you. I'll catch you next time you're in Miami."

Hanging up the phone, he scratched his head, and decided that Alli must be following very closely in her mother's footsteps. He had spent years on tour with Margo and had put up with her alcohol, drugs and men. There was no way he would go back on tour and live the worries and heartache of that life. He would have to be homeless and starving before he'd even consider being anywhere around Alli.

He and Sunni had talked about the headlines they had read and rumors that were in all the gossip columns about Alli's wild life. He had tried to calm Sunni's fears by reminding her that the media always exaggerated and often fabricated the things they wrote about celebrities. But both of them were aware of Alli's tendencies to party too much and neither of them could deny the number of men that seemed to float in and out of her life. Mark had lost count of the names and faces of the men who had been linked to Alli. Singers, movie stars, wealthy business men, even a politician or two.

Alli trusted Sunni, but Mark knew the popular rock star wouldn't listen to her sister. So calling Sunni to intervene with Alli wasn't an option. In reality, he couldn't think of one person who might have any influence over her.

He tried to go back to his music, but he couldn't stop thinking about Alli's call. He couldn't help Alli, but maybe he could ease his own mind. He picked up the phone and dialed Sam Baxter's number.

"Hi, Lara, it's Mark. Is Sam at home?" When Sam's wife told him Sam was out, he decided to talk to her instead of waiting for him to return the call. Lara, Margo's long time assistant, had been on the tour long before he had joined the band, and he was sure that she knew all the secrets.

"Lara, have you heard any gossip about Alli lately? I hate to ask, but I'm concerned. She just called me and I'd swear she was either drunk or high or both."

Lara told him that she and Sam had been called several times by members of the band and the crew about Alli's behavior, but as far as she knew Alli had not missed a concert.

"Have you talked to Michael and Margo about the rumors?" He listened to her explain that she didn't feel it was her role to go to them. Sam had talked to Alli's manager and to Todd Madison, her bodyguard, and they assured him there wasn't a problem.

"I think they've put their heads in the sand, unless today is an exception instead of the rule. But you're right, the tour is almost over. Maybe when she comes back to Miami on hiatus, they can figure out a way to get her some help if she needs it," Mark remarked.

Lara told him she had missed talking with him and hoped he would stop by soon.

"Yeah, I agree. Tell Sam I called and I'll catch him later. Maybe we can have lunch one day next week. It's been too long since I've seen you guys."

He had always liked Lara and Sam. They were a stabilizing force for him all the years he had been lead guitar player for Margo. It amazed him that they had been able to keep their relationship a secret from everyone until Margo's addictions and cancer forced her to retire from the stage. Then they surprised everyone by getting married. Neither of them wanted to continue as part of Alli's team when she went on tour, so they had semi-retired, and he hoped—were living happily ever after. He knew Lara still worked for Margo, but he wasn't sure what Sam was doing now.

Ten minutes after hanging up the phone, it rang again.

"Hi, Alli, why are you calling me back?" As she rambled on he realized that she didn't remember that they had talked earlier.

"We just had this conversation, Alli. Nothing has changed. I'm not interested in coming back to work for you."

The tone of her voice became kitten-like and her next question really rattled him. Once he had collected his thoughts, he responded. "No, Alli. I don't have those kinds of connections. I wouldn't know how to go about buying cocaine for you." Deciding the conversation was going nowhere, he returned the phone to its cradle without saying another word.

Her problem was worse than he had imagined. Alli Anderson was in trouble and he didn't know of any way he could help.

Jeanne Moon Farmer

Chapter Eight

Elena

"Tell me again why we're handling these cases?" Elena Martinez was angry and her voice betrayed her feelings and her concern. "This isn't the direction we wanted to go with our practice, or at least, I didn't think it was. What's changed, Eric?"

Her husband and law partner, Eric Randell, lifted his head as she talked, but seemed to be looking beyond her. He listened to her questions and calmly replied, "We take the clients who come to us, Elena. It's always been that way. We defend people, for crying out loud, and most people who need defense attorneys don't walk in here with Harvard degrees and Boy Scout badges."

"There are differences and you know it." She took a seat across from his desk and continued to express her concerns. "The last three clients that Jeff has taken are known to have Mafia connections, and now you've agreed to defend someone who makes no effort to deny his connection to the cocaine cartel. I think, as a partner in this firm, I have the right to let you and Jeff know that I don't like what you're doing."

"I hear you and if you want to go have this same discussion with Jeff, then go right ahead. I'm busy, Elena. I'm due in court this afternoon and I've got work to do." He opened the folder in front of him as a way of dismissing her.

"You're right! I will have this conversation with Jeff. Even if he ignores me the way you're doing." She headed for the door, then turned back to Eric and asked, "Will you be home for dinner tonight?"

"I doubt it. I'm snowed under and I'll probably work fairly late. You and Jason eat without me. I'll grab something after court." He replied without taking his eyes off the papers on his desk.

Elena closed Eric's door and crossed the hall to her office. Her emotions were raw enough on a professional level and now her personal life was taking a beating, too. Eric seemed to be dismissing her more and more on every level, and it was getting to her. She sat down and swiveled her chair so she could look out the window at Biscayne Bay. The empty place in her heart was growing larger everyday and, as much as she tried, it was getting harder to move beyond her sadness. For some time she had sensed things were happening at the law firm that she wasn't being included in; now she was seeing the correlations to her personal life.

Jeff and Eric had changed. She couldn't put a time frame on when she became aware of it—call it woman's intuition—but months ago something shifted. The money was rolling in, their client base had suddenly expanded beyond their imagination, and they were busier than they'd ever been. In the last year they had moved into larger office space in a building she wondered if they could really afford, they had hired four new attorneys and the staff needed to support them, and they had increased their hourly rates to an astronomical amount. Jeff had purchased a new home on the Inter-coastal, a large boat, and was even talking about buying an airplane. When she had laughingly reminded him that he didn't know how to fly, he told her he was taking lessons.

She and Eric had also moved into a larger home near Coconut Grove—a home she had protested against. Their family of three didn't need a house that large and she didn't want to be tied down to a huge mortgage, but Eric had overruled her. Every time she tried to discuss their finances and budget with him, he shook his head and told her they could afford to enjoy the fruit of their hard work. She wasn't convinced.

Eric was never home, Jeff was dating women who acted and dressed in ways that made her blush, and, with all the violence in Miami, the thought of the new clients made her nervous. As Eric and Jeff's client load increased, her's was diminishing. True, she wasn't working full-time because of her son, Jason, but in the past there had been a more equitable division of cases. She hadn't been to court in the last six months.

Looking at the clock, she realized it was time for her to leave to pick Jason up at school. She would have to wait to have her conversation with Jeff.

*****

As she arrived at home, the phone was ringing. She hurriedly told Jason to go start his homework and grabbed the phone.

"Hi, Aricelli. I just walked in the door." She listened as her sister tried to convince her to join her for a 'girl's night out.'

"I don't know if I can get a sitter on such short notice. How are you planning to get away? What are Peter and the kids going to do for dinner if we go out?" Her sister excitedly explained that her husband was making it possible for them to have some sisterly time.

"Really? Peter has agreed to take your kids and Jason to the ball game, hot dogs included. Wow! How can I say no to this deal? What time do you want me to come over?"

*****

"We should do this more often." Aricelli said as they sipped a glass of wine before dinner. "I haven't had a chance to talk to you in weeks."

"I'm sorry, but work is crazy and life at my house is even crazier. Once I go home, I do what needs to be done and then I just crash."

"Well, my dear sister, I can't say that I blame you. If I had your new house, I wouldn't want to leave it either. Elena, did you ever think you'd live in a house like that?"

"It wasn't my choice and you know it. I agreed with Eric that we needed more room, but I feel like we live in a hotel. The house is too big, it's too modern for my taste, and I worry about where the money is coming from. We've built up a good practice, but I didn't think we were making the kind of money that buys million dollar houses. And, it's just not us, Aricelli. Jeff is spending money like his name is Rockefeller."

"I'm sure Eric wouldn't have made the move if he didn't think you could afford it. Stop complaining and enjoy it. When the money runs out, you can move back to the old neighborhood   and live like the rest of us."

"Am I complaining?"

"Just a little," she teased. "Let's change the subject and enjoy a couple of hours without kids or husbands." Aricelli picked up the menu and began reading aloud all of the options that she would love to order.

For the next hour, they acted like sisters. No complaining, no worries, no mention of responsibilities or concerns. They shared childhood memories and talked of vacation plans that might or might not ever happen. Laughing over some of the latest fashion trends, they decided they needed to spruce up their wardrobes and made promises to meet soon to go shopping. Lobster and two glasses of wine later, they paid the bill and headed arm-in-arm for the parking lot.

"This was fun! Thanks for making me do this tonight. I needed it." Elena had forgotten how much she enjoyed her sister's company. "You've made me forget all the things I was worrying about earlier." She was more relaxed than she'd felt in months and the wine had made her feel giddy. "Too bad we can't go dancing. I think I could cha cha cha all night."

Her sister stopped abruptly causing Elena to stumble. "Tell me that isn't Eric walking ahead of us? And, who the hell is that redhead?"

Elena looked in the direction her sister was pointing just in time to see Eric and Maddie Sonnett get in his car and drive away. "Dear God, I don't believe what I just saw." She felt her knees giving way beneath her and grabbed her sister's arm to steady herself.

"Who's that woman, Elena? I'm sorry, but the way they were wrapped around each other didn't look like they were having an attorney client meeting."

"She's an attorney that we've known for a number of years. But, I didn't think..." Suddenly, she couldn't speak. Her throat tightened and she couldn't form the words.

"I'm sorry, honey. But seeing him took me by surprise." Aricelli stammered over the words. "Are you all right?"

"I haven't been all right for months, but I never thought Eric was cheating on me." Turning to her sister, she tried to smile. "I've recovered from the shock, Aricelli, so stop looking at me like that! I'm fine. Really. I'm fine."

"If you say so. I know I'd be waiting for Peter at the door with a flame thrower!" Shaking her head, she hugged her sister. "Looks like there'll be a hot time at your house tonight. Why don't you leave Jason with me? I'll get him to school tomorrow. You need some private time to talk this out with Eric and you wouldn't want Jason to hear what you have to say." Aricelli was still holding on to her.

"You can let go of me, sis. I'm not going to fall over." Elena felt like she was being smothered and took a step back. "If you don't mind taking Jason, I'd appreciate it. I'll go home and wait for Eric. There has to be a logical explanation for this."

*****

She sat in the dark living room with one beam of light from the kitchen casting shadows on the wall next to her. She had thought about turning on the lamp, but decided it would take too much energy. In the light she would see a beautifully decorated room that, only this morning, had represented security, a happy family, love, the future. She would see the life she thought she was living and she would cry. In the dark she saw the shadows, the cracks in the foundation of her life, and the anger that was keeping her from falling apart. Yes, it was better to see the dark side. It would give her strength when she had to face Eric. Right now, the last thing she wanted to do was cry.

When the clock in the hall chimed eleven times, she realized she had been sitting for over an hour, yet she couldn't remember how she had passed that time. Maybe she had dozed off, but she doubted it. She felt suspended in slow motion—her movements, her thoughts. It was almost as if she was no longer inside herself, but had miraculously stepped out of the hurt, pain and confusion to a place that was empty of every feeling but anger.

She didn't know how much longer she sat there before she heard Eric come in through the kitchen door. She recognized the sounds of his briefcase being placed on the counter and the refrigerator door opening. She listened as he poured himself something to drink and wondered why these normal sounds added to her anger. As she listened to him walking across the kitchen floor, she thought about how many times she had heard the sound before and taken it for granted. In the quiet of the night, she was startled by how loud one small glass could sound as he placed it in the stainless steel sink. Then there was silence and for a few seconds she lost the sense of where he was and what he was doing.

Without warning, he turned on the living room lamp and jumped when he saw her sitting there. "What are you doing sitting in the dark? I thought you were asleep."

"And, I thought you were working late." Her voice was calm and she felt totally unattached to what was happening between them.

"Yes, that's exactly what I've been doing. I had to finish preparing for a trial that begins in the morning." He sat down in his favorite chair and reached for the newspaper that was on the table. "I'm surprised you're still awake."

"No more lies, Eric. I want to know how long you've been sleeping with Maddie Sonnett." The flatness of her voice should have alarmed him.

He closed the paper, leaned forward in his chair and stared at her for several seconds. "I don't know what you're talking about, Elena. What kind of craziness is going on here?"

"The craziness is over for me now that I know why you've been acting the way you have. You're never here—physically or emotionally. You've moved so far away from me and Jason, you might as well be living somewhere else." She heard herself saying the words, but there was no reality to them.

"Are you accusing me of something, Elena? If you are, you might want to be a little more specific." He was using his attorney voice now and it made her want to laugh.

"I've known something was different for a long time. I just couldn't figure out what it was until tonight. I thought I was doing things to irritate you or push you away. I tried everything I could think of to change in the hope that it would make a difference. But, now I know I was wasting my time. Wasn't I?" She averted her eyes from his face when his eyes began to reflect his guilt.

"This is a pointless conversation, Elena! I'm going to bed." He threw the paper down and stood up.

"I asked you a question that you haven't answered, Eric. How long have you been sleeping with Maddie?" She stood up and took a few steps toward him.

"What difference does it make? You've made up you're mind that I'm guilty, so what difference does it make whether I answer your question or not." His voice rose in anger. "What's your evidence, counselor? What have you got to back up your accusations?" His step toward her was menacing.

"I was at the Chart House tonight, Eric. I saw you in the parking lot acting like a love sick teenager. I saw you leave with her and I have an eye witness who will testify against you!" She was shouting now and suddenly all the hurt and pain of the evening came crashing down on her. "You've betrayed me. You've turned away from our marriage and our son." She felt her fingers curl into fists. "Don't stand there and try to turn this back on me. You may be a good attorney, but you have proved that you are one lousy husband! You are guilty, Eric. Guilty, and you know it. You just haven't been sentenced, yet!" Brushing by him, she fled down the hall to their bedroom. She didn't wait to hear his excuses or his rebuttal.

*****

He didn't try to come to their bed and she assumed he slept on the couch. All night long she lay in their big bed, wide awake. One minute she was angry and plotting her revenge; the next she was crying for her broken heart and broken dreams. Morning came too slowly and she finally rose, headachy and puffy eyed. As she entered the kitchen to start the coffee, he looked up from his cereal bowl.

"Where is Jason?" His tone was lifeless, but she caught a glimpse of rage in his eyes. "If you think you can keep my son away from me, you're wrong!"

"Why do you care where he is? You probably haven't spoken a dozen words to him in the past few weeks."

"Don't play with me, Elena! I want to know where he is."

"He spent the night at Aricelli's. She was afraid we might go to war last night and she offered to have him stay over." She sat down at the table and put her head in her hands. "I would never try to keep your son from you. No matter what."

"I want a divorce, Elena. I'll draw up an equitable financial settlement, you can keep the house, and we'll have joint custody of Jason. I think that's fair."

"You're joking, right? If you think it's going to be that easy, you better think again."

Eric's face turned red and when he stood up he towered over her. "Don't mess with me, Elena. Just. Don't. Mess. With. Me." He picked up his things and stormed out the door. In a few seconds she heard the squeal of the expensive tires on his very expensive car as he raced out of the driveway.

Knowing that he had to be in court, gave her a time to take care of some important business. She grabbed her purse and hurriedly left the house. She had to protect Jason and herself. First, she'd go to the bank and withdraw half of the money in their joint account, then she'd see their investment broker for advice, and finally, she'd call her father. He had been practicing law since before she was born and he would know what else she needed to do.

As she started the engine of her car, Eric's words hit her with the force of an avalanche. He had asked her for a divorce! In less than twelve hours she had lost her security and, if she wasn't careful, she could easily fall off the edge of the world. Hot tears formed behind her eyelids, but she banished them. Now was not the time to fall apart.

*****

She heard what she was saying, but as she recounted the events of the morning to her father she still couldn't believe what she had discovered. "The number of accounts that had my name on them was a shock. I have two accounts that I use—one is personal, the other is business—and I thought I had an approximate idea of the amount of money that was in each of them. I may have been a few dollars off, but Dad, I was thousands of dollars off."

"Elena, don't you check your statements? How could you not know the amount of money you have?" Eugene Martinez shook his head as he listened to his daughter.

"Our accountant handles everything. I never see the statements." She handed her father several pages of bank records. "Look at the records the bank gave me this morning and tell me what you think."

Shuffling through the papers, her father's eyes widened and then the furrow in his brow deepened. "First, I'd say you are a very rich woman. But, Elena, these records are frightening. Where did all this money come from? Do you have investments that return huge dividends? Did Eric inherit a large sum of money? What can account for this kind of money? There's several million dollars here."

"Like I said, I went to the bank to take out half of what was in my two accounts. They're joint accounts and I wanted to make sure that Eric didn't wipe them out. When I told the teller what I wanted to do, she sent me to the branch manager because of the amount of money involved. I laughed, but did what she asked. Can you imagine my shock when the manager started questioning me about why I'd want to withdraw so much money. When he showed me all these accounts, I was floored. There are ten accounts that have both of our names on them and five accounts with just my name. It makes me wonder how many accounts Eric has in his name."

"Elena, surely you remember signing bank cards for these accounts?"

"If I did, I wasn't aware of what I was signing."

"The papers you handed me just show balances. Did you ask to see the history on these accounts? Do you know when they were

79

opened? Do you know how active they are? What did the bank manager suggest that you do?"

"Slow down, Dad. The only thing he told me was to talk to my accountant. He was very aware that I was flabbergasted. The only thing he could do to help me was tell me he would begin monitoring the joint accounts and call me if there was any new activity on any of them. The accounts in just my name will be transferred." As she talked with her father, her reality shifted and she became afraid. "There is something very wrong here. What do you think Eric has gotten us into?" She hesitated. "Our firm is solid, but we don't make this kind of money."

"Don't jump ahead of yourself, Elena. Right now all you've got are questions, no answers." He walked over to her and put his hand on her shoulder. "Let me call my accountant. I trust him. He can look into this for us and give us some suggestions." His voice grew sterner. "For now, do not discuss this with Eric. Do you understand, Elena?"

"Oh, Daddy, I don't want to think that Eric is doing something illegal. But I can't get that thought out of my mind."

"Elena, let's get some answers to our questions before you start jumping to conclusions. I'll call Javier Ricardo and have him do some research on these accounts. You call the bank manager and give permission for Javier to access the records." His voice softened. "In the last few hours, you've had a serious shock and my heart is breaking for you and my grandson. But, you've got your family to lean on, Elena. Don't forget that."

Standing up, she let herself be engulfed by her father's strong arms. "I know, Daddy. I know."

Chapter Nine

Sharon

"Operator, this is Sharon McDeal at 1108 Hibiscus Road in Coconut Grove. I need immediate assistance. My house guest is missing and his body guard has been seriously injured." She tried to speak calmly, but her heart was racing and she was afraid. "Yes, his name is Lawrence Fitz and he's in his 80s. I'm not sure exactly how old he is. The body guard's name is Joe Birdsong and I think he just lost consciousness."

The emergency operator continued to ask her questions, but most of what the operator was saying was a roar in Sharon's head. "Wait. They told me last night if anything happened I was to get in touch with Tom West at Miami-Dade PD. After you've called for the ambulance, please call Tom West and tell him I need help." She listened to the instructions from the dispatcher.

"Yes, yes. I hear the ambulance. I need to go open the gate." Sharon dropped the phone and ran from the guesthouse down the drive to the new gate that had been installed very quickly yesterday. As she ran she tried to remember the code or where Carter had put the remote.

"Oh, God, help me. I can't remember." Looking at the gate, she realized the keypad was on the outside and there was no way she could get to it. Confusion stopped her until she remembered a keypad had been installed inside the door of the house. Darting in that direction, she tried to remember the four numbers that would open the gate. When she stood in front of the keypad, she took a deep breath to clear her head, but all she could think about was the poor man lying in a pool of blood in the kitchen of the guesthouse. The deafening sound of the ambulance jolted her and she quickly punched in the date of her anniversary, then she tried her birthday, finally she tried Jocelyn's birthday and the gate began to open.

"Go to the guesthouse in the back. Please hurry! The door is open and he's on the floor in the kitchen." She was running beside the ambulance, shouting as loud as she could.

She was about to follow the paramedics inside when several other cars pulled in the driveway and people were descending on her, the guesthouse and her garden. One man rushed up to her and called her by name.

"Mrs. McDeal? I'm Tom West. What has happened here?"

"I'm not sure I know. Lawrence and Joe were supposed to come to the main house for breakfast at eight o'clock this morning and when they didn't show up, I walked out to the guesthouse to see why they were late." Her voice quivered and her hands shook but no matter what she tried, she couldn't seem to calm down. "I'm sorry. Give me a minute and I'll be okay."

"I know you're upset, but I need to know every detail of what you heard and saw. Everything." He motioned for her to follow him to the chairs on the patio. "Sit down and let's start again." His voice was patient, but she could tell that he needed her to talk quickly.

"When no one answered the door, I took my key and opened it. The blinds were closed and the front room was very dark. When I switched on the light I nearly fainted. The place was a wreck. Furniture was turned over! Lamps were on the floor! My first thought was to run out of there but then I heard the groaning. I followed the sound to the kitchen and that's when I found Joe.

"He didn't respond when I called to him. I grabbed the kitchen towel and tried to stop his chest from bleeding, but all I could do was slow it down. I don't know whether he's been shot or stabbed. All I could see was the blood." The more she talked, the more quickly her words were coming. "I knew I had to see what had happened to Lawrence. I looked everywhere. He's gone! He's not there! Someone has taken Lawrence." She began to sob, fear-filled sobs. They shook her body and came so rapidly she almost lost her breath. "Joe...is...hurt. He's really hurt and Lawrence is gone."

The officer stood up and put his hand on her shoulder. "You've had an awful shock. Sit here and let me go see what's happening. I'll be back."

Standing up, she caught her breath and tried to tell him she would be all right. Her words were jumbled and a sudden pain behind her eyes made her fall back against the chair.

"Mrs. McDeal, sit here for a few minutes and try to get hold of yourself. Do you think I should call the paramedics to see about you before they leave?"

"No, no! I'm just so frightened. I'm fine, or I will be in a minute."

"If you're sure, I'll go check on what's happening in the guesthouse. When you feel okay, would you make two phone calls for me? I need your help." He emphasized the last sentence. His look told her that what he really needed was for her to calm down and this was the only way he could think to help her. "Call your husband and ask him to come home, and then, call Sam Baxter and tell him we're in crisis mode."

Before he finished the last sentence, he started walking across the yard certain that she would do as he asked.

Sharon wiped her eyes with the back of her hand and bit down on her lip to try and stop her hysterical behavior. "This is not the way I deal with things," she whispered. "I must be in shock." She forced herself to get out of the chair and walk into the house. Yes, what she needed was for Carter to come home.

*****

With Carter seated beside her, holding her hand, Sharon began to relive the ordeal of the morning. Sam Baxter and Tom West were firing questions at her so fast she barely answered one before there was another to think about. Unfortunately, what she had to recall was very limited and not very helpful. "No, I didn't hear anything out of the ordinary. No, I didn't open the gate for anyone before the ambulance got here. Yes, I glanced in all the rooms. No, I didn't actually go into any rooms except the kitchen and living room."

They kept asking her for details and she didn't have any. All she had were questions of her own. How could someone have gotten on the property without being heard? Who knew that Lawrence was staying at the house? How could they have ransacked the house without being heard? When did all this happen? And, oh dear God, where was Lawrence Fitz?

"What about Joe Birdsong? Is he going to be all right?" In all the chaos, Sharon had forgotten to ask about the condition of the man she had found on the kitchen floor. "Is he hurt as badly as it looked?"

"He lost a lot of blood, but he's going to survive. He'll probably be in the hospital for a time-bruises, a few cuts that needed stitches, a deep stab wound in his chest, and a bad blow to one of his kidneys." Tom West said. "I think whoever did this meant to deliver a message, not a death blow."

"Sam, I thought they would be safe here." Carter looked perplexed. "You all did such a good job of making it safe. What went wrong?"

"This is another example of how these people operate. They seem to have eyes and ears everywhere." Sam answered Carter and then turned to Tom West. "Are you going to tell me there's not a leak in your department? Someone knew our every move! Someone got to the guys who installed the gate! Someone knew we had moved Lawrence!" His anger was tangible.

"Hold on, Sam. I'm working on it as hard as I can. Everything you're saying is being checked out." The policeman was defensive. "Remember, Lawrence is my friend, too."

"Right now I don't feel reassured. How do you plan to keep this out of the newspapers?" Sam asked Tom, then spoke quietly to Sharon. "I'm sorry, Sharon. Once you called the operator, the information became public record. The media has access to everything."

"I was so shaken, I didn't think. I just knew that Joe needed an ambulance." Sharon felt terrible about the situation she had created. "What other choice did I have, Sam?"

"You made the best choice. I'm sorry if I sounded critical. I didn't know if you understood how the system works." Sam replied.

"We've got a little time before we have to worry about the media." Tom interrupted. "Right now we need to be concerned about finding Lawrence." The mood in the room became somber. "We're trying to get in touch with all our undercover guys. We've called in some favors, and we're talking to everybody we know on the street. So far, we don't have any leads."

Alarm crossed Sam's face. "Has anyone been in touch with Jocelyn?"

"I called her about an hour ago." Carter said. "She and Clair were okay. I told her to come here. Most likely they're on their way."

Tears ran down Sharon cheeks as she thought of what could have happened to her stepdaughter. "Are you sure this Claire person can protect her, Sam? After what I saw this morning, I want as much protection for Jocelyn as possible."

"Claire is a former intelligence officer in the Army. I can assure you she knows what she's doing. Jocelyn is in good hands." Sam's voice was encouraging. Then he looked at them as they sat holding hands, staring at him. "Listen, both of you. I honestly don't think Jocelyn's a target. But to be safe, I'll put on some added security at her building."

A policeman walked into the living room and told Tom that they had finished their investigation of the crime scene and the unit was leaving. "We've done everything we need to do here. We'll see you downtown."

Tom motioned to Sam. "Ride downtown with me. There are a few things we need to discuss. I'll bring you back to pick up your car."

"I'll follow you. There's no need for you to drive all the way back to the Grove." Sam nodded to Tom as he left the room. "Carter, we'll find him. I promise you that much."

"I don't doubt that, Sam. I just want you to find him alive." Carter patted Sharon's knee. "What can we do or not do now? Can I call someone to begin cleaning up the guesthouse? Do we need security here?"

"Don't do anything about the guesthouse until I've checked with Tom. And, even though I don't think there will be a repeat of any of this at your house, I've already called several guys that I work with to see if somebody is available to be here at night. I want Sharon to feel safe."

"Thanks, Sam. Keep me in the loop."

*****

"Carter, I don't think I've ever been as frightened as I was when I found Joe. It was gruesome and there was so much blood everywhere." Sharon still felt weak and she wondered how she would ever erase the memory of what she had witnessed.

"Honey, I'm so sorry you had to go through this. But, you're not sorry we asked Lawrence to stay here, are you?"

"Never. We did the right thing. I only wish we'd hear something about him." She stood up and started toward the kitchen. "Are you hungry? I just remembered I haven't eaten today and there are cold scrambled eggs still sitting on the kitchen table."

"Yeah, I'm hungry. But not hungry enough to eat those eggs!"

"Sometimes you're so funny." She grabbed Carter and gave him a quick kiss. "Thanks for making me smile. The eggs go in the trash and I'm sure I can find something more enticing in the fridge."

She made sandwiches and Carter poured them glasses of iced tea. "I'm worried about Jocelyn. I know she told us she's okay, but I could tell she's afraid. Maybe not for herself, but for Lawrence. She dearly loves him," Sharon said.

"We're all worried about Lawrence, and for the first time, I'm concerned for my daughter."

"They're not after her, Carter. Surely, she's not in danger." Sharon was surprised that she hadn't thought about that before. "Why would she be in danger?"

"I don't think she's a target, but she might get caught in something that's intended for someone else."

"That woman who's watching her looks like she can take care of herself and Jocelyn. Don't you agree?"

Carter chuckled. "I don't think I'd want to tangle with her."

"I wish Jocelyn had taken everyone's advice and stayed here today. Someone could have delivered her column to the newspaper office."

"She needed something to think about besides Lawrence. If she'd stayed here all she would do is worry." Carter hesitated. "She made good sense when she said we all have to try and act normal. This place will be a circus once the papers get hold of the news."

"Carter, you do believe Lawrence is alive, don't you?" Tears welled up in Sharon's eyes.

"I'm not going to lie to you, Sharon. These people are lawless." His words sounded hollow. "All we can do is pray for his safe return."

Jeanne Moon Farmer

Chapter Ten

Lawrence

He had a headache and he needed to go to the bathroom. Not a good combination for someone who had a hood over his head and was tied to a chair. If it weren't so serious, he would laugh at his predicament. No authors ever included that kind of information in their story. They never mentioned that a victim, tied to a chair in a strange place ever had personal needs. He made a mental note to remember that heroes got hungry and thirsty, and then, they had to go to the bathroom. It was humanly impossible to ignore the basic facts of life, but as an author he had never given them a second thought.

Ever since he had been awakened by the brute who forced his head into the hood, he had tried to remember every detail—sounds, movements, numbers of steps, smells—anything that might help him identify where he was taken. He knew they must have done something horrible to Joe Birdsong or they never would have been able to get to him. He only hoped the man wasn't dead. Whatever had happened in the house before they got to his room had been accomplished in silence. He had not been awakened by any noise. His first awareness of danger had been his head being snatched off the pillow and then the voice whispering, "Don't make a sound or your good buddies in the big house are dead." The man had pulled him out of bed, tied his hands behind his back and nudged him to walk. Lawrence had asked for his shoes, but the response was a grunt and a shove forward.

Now he sat in the dark in his pajamas and bare feet. Sore, bare feet. Somewhere between his bed and this chair, he had been made to walk over gravel and sand. He tried to estimate how long he had been in the car and how many turns they had made. He had listened for any sounds coming from outside the car. But it was all a blur now. He knew they had crossed a drawbridge—he remembered the sound of the tires on the metal grating—and he tried to think which bridges in Miami had that kind of structure. He could think of two, the Venetian Causeway and the Brickell Avenue Bridge, but there had to be more. If they had crossed Venetian, then he was somewhere on the beach. If it was Brickell, then he was north of the city. His senses led him to believe he was in a small, damp space that smelled like fish. Maybe he was in a shed somewhere near the river, but they had driven too far for it to be the Miami River.

He shook his head in frustration. He was an old man and his instincts were not what they used to be. Try as he might, he didn't have a clue to his location. Years of knowledge, skills, and experience, and he didn't have a clue. But at least all the thinking was helping him forget his bodily needs.

Without warning, a door creaked open. He sensed brightness and heard footsteps coming toward him. His body tensed and he waited.

"Other than looking like a clown, you don't look too uncomfortable." It was a woman's voice. A woman who wore an overwhelming amount of perfume. "You see, Mr. Fitz, you have made me very angry."

"How is that possible?" He asked. "I don't even know you."

"My sources tell me you have even written a book about me." Her voice was controlled and each word was spoken precisely. Then she began to shout. "You are a fool. You have put your nose in my business. Nobody does that! Do. You. Understand?"

He could feel her getting closer to him and instinctively he drew back against the chair.

"I'm not going to kill you, Mr. Fitz. At least not until you've done what I want. You call your editor and tell him to can that book." Once again she was talking in her controlled, precise manner. "And, I want the name of your informant. Who told you what you think you know? It has to be someone very close to me and you will give me the name."

"Madam, I don't know who you are or what you think I know. But I can assure you that my books are fiction based on actual FBI cases. There is no informant. You can read all the case files if you wish. But I don't have a name to give you."

She leaned in closer to his face. "What you said about me isn't in a case file and you know it! You don't exactly paint a flattering picture of me, Mr. Big-time Author. That was very stupid of you. If you had to write about me, you could have listed my good points. I'm a great business woman, I have power, and I have made a lot of people very wealthy. Don't you agree? That alone would have made a great chapter in your book. Or, you could have mentioned I'm a good mother. There's so much you could have written about. Why did you have to say all those bad things about me, Mr. Fitz?" Her hands came around his throat and she pushed her thumbs deeply into his flesh. "Make sure that book never gets published." She increased the pressure and he tried to gasp. "I get what I want and maybe you get to live." Her hands fell away, making him cough as he struggled to breathe again.

"And, let's see who else might get to live. I think her name is Jocelyn." When she spoke the name, it was almost in a whisper. "Yes, that's it, Jocelyn."

He choked again as he tried to reply. "You have no reason to harm that girl."

"Oh, but I do. She's my insurance that this book doesn't get published." She laughed a coarse, cruel laugh that was distorted by an echo created by whatever space they were in. "Did you really think I would leave this to chance? You are an old man and I know you would die rather than stop the publication. But, dear, sweet Jocelyn is young and very important to you. Her life is worth saving, don't you think?"

Lawrence's head fell forward and his shoulders slumped. She had trumped his ace and he felt beaten. "There'll be no need to hurt her. Let me out of here and I'll stop the book. But, it will take time. You'll have to give me time."

"How much time do you need to make one phone call?"

"It's a bit more complicated than that. But, I'll take care of it."

"I'm a generous woman, Mr. Fitz. You have two weeks to make sure." Her hands pushed against his shoulders. "I'll know every move you make. I'll know every move she makes. Two weeks and I better get a call from my man in New York that you have accomplished this little assignment. Then, I want your notes, your files. Every word that you have written about your so-called Scorpion." She slapped him hard across the face. "Two weeks, Mr. Fitz. You have two weeks."

His ears followed the sound of her steps as she walked away from him. Fifteen, then twenty steps until he heard the door slam and lock behind her. He wasn't that far from the door and if he worked the legs of the chair at just the right angles, he might be able to cover that amount of space. His mind was racing through the possibilities of his escape, and then he stopped. Why use all the energy to move to the door when she was going to release him at some point? He wasn't any good to her sitting in this chair.

Minutes, hours later, he couldn't tell how long he waited, he heard the door opening again and knew that his captors had come back for him. Roughly, he was untied from the chair and told to stand, but his hands remained tied behind him. As he tried to put weight on his legs they buckled and he crashed to the floor on his knees.

"What's the matter wid you, old man? Get up! We gotta go." The heavily accented voice bellowed at him, but the man made no attempt to help him.

The pain in Lawrence's right knee was searing and there was no way he was going to be able to stand without the use of his hands. "You'll have to help me. I can't get up on my own."

Rancid breath and the odor of an unwashed body went with the strong arms that reached under his and pulled him to his feet.

"Don't let go. I've done something to my knee and I can't walk." Lawrence said.

"You kiddin' me. I ain't your nurse. Walk or crawl, not my problem." The man cursed and walked away.

"Then take off this hood so I can see where I'm going." Lawrence knew the man would never let him see his face and hoped that would persuade him to come back and help.

"You loco, abuelo? Ain't no way you gonna point a finger at me." The man yanked him up off his knees and pushed him so fast that he barely had time to balance himself. The pain in his right knee was excruciating but he knew the small-time thug wasn't concerned about his pain. Without another sound, he dragged Lawrence across the floor and out a door. He clumsily pushed him into the back seat of the car.

Within a few miles, the driver stopped the car and pulled Lawrence out. He yelled to him as he was driving away. "Somebody'll find you old man. You can count on that."

Lawrence's bare feet hit the hot pavement and he could hear the sounds of traffic and people talking. What would they think when they saw a bare-footed man in pajamas with a hood over his head and his hands tied behind him? All he could think to do was yell for help and endure the humiliation.

"Hey! Somebody help me." He shouted as loudly as he could. "Help!" He wasn't sure if he was on a road or a sidewalk, so he was afraid to move too far from the spot where he landed.

"What the....! What happened to you, man?" The voice sounded young.

"I know I look like a lunatic, but I need some help."

When the hood was lifted over his head, he stood facing a teenage boy. "Somebody took me for a ride. Help me untie my hands and get me to a telephone."

The boy stood with his mouth open. "You still in your pajamas, man! Is this some kind of joke?"

"I assure you it isn't a joke. Let me use a phone and the people who come for me will reward you for helping me." Lawrence was having a hard time recovering his dignity and he was becoming annoyed at the teenager. "I know I look like a clown, but do as I ask. Please."

By then a small group of teens of various sizes had gathered around and were hooting and calling him names. Lawrence looked beyond the ring of boys and realized he was at the edge of some kind of playground or park surrounded by one of Miami's many housing projects. "Laugh if you will, but I need help. Isn't one of you willing to help me?"

"I'll do it, but I sure don't want nobody to see me. I don't wanna get shot because of a clown." The young boy pulled out a small knife and cut the ropes that had been binding Lawrence's hands. "You wait here and I'm gonna git my mama. You tell her what you want."

"Is there a place where I can sit down? I've hurt my knee," he asked as he tried to shake some life back into his hands. "Help me over to the bike rack and I can lean against that."

"Naw, there's a bench inside the fence. I'll hep you git there," one of the younger boys offered. "You sit and wait for Miz Collins. She'll hep you."

It didn't take long for a middle-aged woman to come running. "What you doin' scaring dem kids?" She yelled. "I'm a mind to call the police."

"That would be a wonderful idea." Lawrence offered. "I'll take any kind of help."

"Who you be?" she questioned suspiciously.

"My name is Lawrence Fitz. I'm dressed in my pajamas because I was dragged from my bed in the middle of the night and taken to God knows where. I don't have a clue why—or where I am now. I'm sorry to bother you. But, if you could either call my friends or the police, I'd greatly appreciate it." He was becoming annoyed.

"Gimme a number and I'll call. But you gonna pay me, right?"

"Of course, you and the boys will be rewarded for helping me." He thought for a minute before speaking again. "The easiest thing would be for you to call the police and tell them you've found Lawrence Fitz."

*****

94

Once he had been told that Joe Birdsong would survive and Jocelyn had not been harmed, his goal had been a steaming shower and a pair of bedroom slippers. His feet were blistered and his knee was swollen so badly that he had wondered whether his trousers would fit over it. Yes, he had agreed to see a doctor this afternoon, but soon his friends would understand there were more important things to do. The hot shower revived him and the feel of fresh clothes against his skin reassured him that the few hours of exile had ended. At least it had ended for the moment.

He had to figure out his next move. There was no way he was going to give in to the demands he had been given; there was no way he was going to let evil win. And, yes, he did believe the woman he had met this morning was evil. Her voice had reflected her demons and he knew she had to be stopped before those demons inflicted more damage. He had to think smartly to insure that her destruction was complete.

Friends and law enforcement were waiting to question him about his ordeal, but he wasn't ready to talk to them just yet. He needed time to sort through the details of the previous evening. His mind wasn't as sharp as it used to be and he didn't want the details of this story to be lost in his telling of it.

Sitting at his desk, he carefully wrote his recollections in his journal. That was always his process and it had served him well. His journal notes had been useful in solving crimes when he was an agent and were the foundation for the books he had written since his retirement. He listed what he could remember—sounds, smells, her words, his feelings and thoughts—and realized how disconnected things were when you could not see them. Being under the hood had heightened some of his senses, but had really disoriented him. One thing was for sure. He would never forget her words or the smell of her perfume. That fragrance, his wife's favorite, was burned into his memory. Yes, the Emperitza, if that was who she was, definitely loved Chanel No. 5.

Jeanne Moon Farmer

PART TWO

The mind is its own place,
and in itself can make a heaven of hell,
a hell of heaven....

Awake, arise or be forever fall'n.

—Excerpts from *Paradise Lost*, John Milton

Jeanne Moon Farmer

Chapter Eleven

Alli

Groaning as she turned over, Alli's head ached and muscles in her back felt like she had been beaten. *Where am I?* Whatever she was lying on was cold, hard and rough. She turned her head slightly and looked through bars to the open sky! *What the hell?*

She sat up too quickly which made her head spin and created a sharp pain across her forehead. Her hands flew up to cover her face and shield her eyes from the bright sunshine. *Ahh. It's still morning. I don't do morning.*

When she felt more stable, she took her hands away from her face and tried to get her eyes to focus. As she lowered her hands, she touched bare skin and knew she was naked. *Where did I leave my clothes this time?* She tried to remember, but the pounding in her head was too distracting.

Sighing in relief, she realized she was on the balcony of her parent's condo in Miami, and not in a jail somewhere. *Now that's funny*, she thought, *these are balcony bars, not a cell*. She had no idea why she was on the balcony or how long she'd been there. Thank God, her parents were at their house on the island of Eleuthera or she might have some explaining to do. *Michael and Margo would not find this amusing.* She was in Miami because her last concert of the current tour was at the Orange Bowl. She had planned to spend the month of June in her own condo on Miami Beach, but it was being renovated and the decorators were behind schedule. It probably wouldn't be ready before she left for the French Riviera where she was vacationing all of July. Her folks had offered their condo to her in the meantime.

I hope whatever I did last night was worth how I feel right now. She struggled to stand up, but her legs wouldn't hold her. *Great. I'll have to crawl if I want to get out of this heat and blasted sunshine!* Crawling took more energy and effort than she expected and her attempts to open the sliding glass doors would have been laughable if she hadn't felt so terrible.

On her third try, she was able to push the door open far enough to crawl into the living room. A rush of cold air hit her face and took her breath away. For a few seconds she was stunned. Then, as the initial shock wore off, the coolness revived her somewhat and she continued to crawl toward the closest piece of furniture. Pulling upright, she found herself face-to-face with the naked man sprawled on the couch. She looked at his face and tried to remember who he was. It didn't surprise her that he was there or that she didn't know him.

"Hey, you! Wake up! You've got to leave." As her voice got stronger, she knew she wanted whoever he was to go away.

"Huh. Leave me alone. I need to sleep," a groggy voice whispered as he made an effort to turn away from her.

"Get up and move or I'll have you thrown out!" She was finished with whatever he had offered and she wanted to be alone. "Find your clothes and get out of here." Where was Todd? Surely, he was somewhere around and could take care of this situation. Wasn't that what she paid a bodyguard to do?

Then she remembered they were in Miami and he was across town at his house. She had assured him she didn't need a security detail in this building and she hadn't planned to go anywhere last night. They had argued, but eventually Todd had agreed to take the night off.

"All I'm going to do is rest, Todd. I have the biggest concert of the year tomorrow night and I need a break. So do you. I'll be fine."

Todd wasn't happy about leaving her unprotected, but she finally won the battle and he agreed to leave. So, where did she find this guy? "Oh, god!" she groaned. She had been drinking when she decided she needed something with a bigger punch. She had called one of her contacts on the beach to bring her some cocaine and this must be the guy who delivered it. She had sunk to an all time low if she was having sex with the delivery guy!

She would never hear the end of it if she called Todd to get this guy out of the condo. For several months he had been lecturing her about the amount of alcohol and drugs she was consuming. He had even threatened to call her agent and her father if he didn't see a change. To keep him quiet, she had really tried to slow down. He knew the stress she was under; the number of concerts on this tour; and the pressure the fans put on her to make every show better than the one before. Why couldn't he be on her side? She had laughed when he called her an addict. She knew she could quit if she wanted to!

Nudging the sleeping man with both hands, she shouted in his face. "You've got five minutes to get out of here before I have you arrested as an intruder!"

*****

A sell-out crowd waited for her. The Orange Bowl was packed with concert-goers who were screaming her name. The air was charged with electricity and her fans were eager to catch a glimpse of her. This was her kind of night, but her hands were shaking so badly she couldn't pick up the water bottle on her dressing room table. Her throat was dry, her head ached, and her legs were still so weak she was afraid she wouldn't be able to climb on the stage.

All day she had looked for ways to pull out of the fog of last night's binge. This had never happened to her before—she had always been able to party all night. Alcohol, drugs, sex—she could handle it all and still be at the peak of performance. The only recovery time she required was a few hours of sleep. What was wrong with her today? Everyone had noticed and Todd had suggested that they cancel the concert. That thought outraged her enough to get her out of bed and had kept her moving to this point.

The warm-up band had been told to do an extra set and the stage manager was furious that he had already given her several "ten-minutes to show time" calls. Fear gripped her. Panic engulfed her. She wasn't ready; she couldn't do it; she couldn't make herself move.

People had been swarming around her for the past two hours—make-up, hair, costume—last minute details with the band, dancers and back-up singers. She sat numbly through it all; listening, nodding at the appropriate times, trying to keep up with what was being said. But, all she wanted to do was sleep. If she could close her eyes for five minutes, she'd be better. No, that wasn't what she needed and she knew it. It was too late to call Toro, her drummer, for help. Desperately, she tried to think of where she might have hidden one of the small packets. Surely, she hadn't used everything she had stashed away. *Think, Alli, think.* There's got to be a packet somewhere. If she could quiet her mind, she'd be able to find what she needed.

Frantically, she forced her body up from the chair and staggered across the room to her make-up case. Clutching the case, she recklessly began rummaging through the layers. Tossing jars and bottles in all directions, her urgency grew as she fumbled with each item. It wasn't there! She had been so sure she would find what she was looking for. Her hands grasped the last tray at the bottom of the case and as she lifted it, her eyes locked onto the small packet lying innocently on top of the velvet lining. She had found what she needed, what she wanted, what would help her do her job. It was only one small packet of white powder, but it was worth everything to her in that moment. She had hidden it away one evening long ago. Long before it had become so important. Her shaking hands caressed the packet. It was her savior. Now, she would be able to make it to the stage with more than enough energy to satisfy the waiting crowd.

Even shaking hands knew what to do. She drew the powder into her nostrils and closed her eyes. It wouldn't take long for her miracle to happen. Soon her hands would stop shaking and the sensations, the power, the blessed relief would be hers.

Chapter Twelve

Jocelyn

The seats were uncomfortable and her thoughts were jumbled. She sat between Ben and Claire and wondered how Ben had pulled off getting Claire a ticket to a sold-out concert. Somehow he had managed and Sam had finally agreed that she could attend. Everything was crazy now that she had a bodyguard for her shadow. Everywhere she went, Claire was there. *What a laugh! Insignificant Jocelyn McDeal needed a bodyguard. Now really?* But after the terrifying events of the past two days, Claire's presence did give her some peace of mind.

What kind of people kidnapped an old man and then left him in his pajamas on a street corner in Liberty City? The same people who nailed a dead chicken to his door and made threats against his life. The same people who demanded that he stop the publication of his new book, that's who.

She was afraid for Lawrence, not for herself. She wasn't a threat to these people. But, everyone else seemed to think she might be in danger—her father, Sam, and even Ben—so she was going along with the inconvenience of having a bodyguard for a few days. How did the celebrities handle the intrusion? How did they manage to have a life?

Claire had only been with her two days and she was already aware of big changes. Like having to ask permission to attend s concert. It had been too many years since she'd asked permission to go on a date. Remembering the look on Claire's face when she announced that she was going to the Alli Anderson concert with Ben, made her smile. The woman looked horrified and told her it was "out of the question."

They had been sitting in her cubicle at the newspaper office—yes, the woman had actually gone to work with her—when she casually mentioned she had a date that evening. After some irritating discussion, Claire told her that Sam would never give permission for that to happen. Jocelyn grimaced when she remembered her immediate reaction. "Are you kidding me?" She snapped at the poor woman. "You're actually saying that I can't go to the concert unless Sam Baxter gives me permission?" She had called Sam herself and been told the same thing.

"Sam, be reasonable. They're not after me. Ben will be with me the whole time." No matter how she phrased it, almost begging at times, the answer was the same until they finally reached a compromise. Sam had told her she could go if Ben was able to find a ticket for Claire.

"That's impossible! This concert has been sold out for months. That's a sly way of telling me no, isn't it?"

But Ben had worked miracles and the three of them were sitting in the Orange Bowl waiting for Alli to take the stage. She looked over at Claire who appeared to be utterly unfazed by the frenzied atmosphere. For Claire, this was work—she was on alert—she was on duty. Her eyes darted quickly from one side of the section where they were seated to the other and Jocelyn had even heard her give Ben some instructions on the ride from the apartment to the stadium.

The crowd was getting restless as the warm-up band started another number. Where was Alli? As Jocelyn scanned the crowds, she thought back on her few encounters with the pop star. She and Alli weren't friends, but their lives were tangled together because of the people they knew. Alli's twin sister, Sunni, and Mark were in a relationship; Mark had played in Margo's, band; Sam had been head of Margo's security until illness had forced her to retire. The list went on. She was surprised at how many connections she had to so many other people. All my life's a circle. Had she read that somewhere or heard it in a song? No matter, it seemed true. And, she had an advantage, something most of the thousands of others didn't have. She knew the rock star personally.

Yes, she mused, leaning back. *I am more than ready to enjoy this concert—and I'm going to ignore all the rest for one special evening. After all, I'm getting to see the world famous Alli in her first Miami performance in more than three years.*

"There must be something wrong." Ben leaned nearer to her and had to shout to be heard. "The warm-up band has been on stage for way too long."

"It's almost nine o'clock. Alli will probably start in a few minutes." She thought about her encounters with the very self-absorbed singer years before. "She's always done things her way, Ben. It's always on her own schedule."

"I'm tired of waiting!" grumbled Ben. "From the number of people who are shouting Alli's name, I'm not the only one who's ready for this show to start."

"Oh, Ben, relax."

*****

"That girl wore me out. Wonder where she gets her energy and stamina?" Claire yawned as she walked through the parking lot with Jocelyn and Ben.

"She was fabulous. Her songs, her costumes, the dancers, the band. It was great and I enjoyed every minute. Didn't you, Ben?" Jocelyn's face was flushed from the excitement of the concert. "I can't believe we were on our feet for most of it."

"I can," said Claire. "My feet are killing me."

"I agree, Claire. Standing for two and a half hours is not my idea of a good time." Ben sounded quarrelsome.

"Aren't you the grumpy ones tonight. Standing or sitting, I thought it was worth every minute." Jocelyn was trying hard not to let Ben and Claire ruin her mood. She had enjoyed herself even if they hadn't.

"Holy crap!" Ben yelled as they approached his car. "Look at my car! What have they done to my car?"

Claire moved between Jocelyn and the car and stopped Jocelyn's forward motion. "Stay behind me. Ben, don't touch anything and move away from the car."

Paint was splattered on the top of the car and all four tires had been slashed. "Ben! Move away from the car, now." Claire's voice carried more authority when she issued the command the second time. "You stay here with the car and don't touch it. Jocelyn, come with me!" She grabbed Jocelyn's arm and moved her in the opposite direction. "I've got to find someone in law enforcement who has a radio. Sam needs to know about this."

They walked several feet away from the car before they saw a policeman directing traffic. He was not happy when Claire rushed toward him and interfered with the line of cars trying to get out of the parking lot.

"Move out of the way, lady. I got work to do and you're going to get hit by one of these cars if you continue to stand where you are." The policeman shouted and continued motioning them out of the way.

"I've got a problem and I need your help." Claire pulled out some kind of badge and flashed it at the young man. "Call the dispatcher and tell Detective Tom West that Claire McGuire needs help. He'll understand."

"Lady, I can't leave this post. Do you see all these cars? These people want to get home tonight." He turned back to directing traffic.

"Maybe you didn't take a good look at my badge. I just gave you a direct order." Claire was determined to get his attention. "Give them our location in this parking lot and, then, lock this young lady in your patrol car and don't leave her."

Reluctantly, the young policeman strode over to his car and did as he had been instructed. "Tell them to send someone over to do crowd and traffic control. Your job assignment just changed." Claire waited until the call had been made and Jocelyn was safely locked in the patrol car before she walked back to where she had left Ben.

*****

It seemed like hours, but was probably closer to thirty minutes before the crowd had thinned and Tom West pulled his car into the parking lot behind Ben's and the patrol car. The policeman had driven his car closer to Claire and Ben when his replacement had arrived, but Claire wouldn't let Jocelyn get out of the car.

"Stay where you are until we have a better idea of what's going on." Claire's look confirmed that she meant what she said. "There's too much for this to be a coincidence. Vandals would never have taken the time to pour all this paint on the car. Slashing tires is one thing, taking a risk with the paint is another story."

The investigation at the scene didn't take long. In less than an hour a wrecker had towed Ben's car to a police warehouse for a thorough inspection, Tom West had asked his questions, and Sam had arrived.

"This is typical of the games they play when they're trying to intimidate somebody. I've seen it over and over again." said Tom. "Ben, we'll send your car on to a body shop once we've gone over it for evidence."

"Do you really think you'll find anything?" Ben questioned. "I'll bet there isn't a fingerprint on it."

"That's true. But our forensic teams are good at spotting things nobody else would give a second look."

"I'll call you tomorrow, Tom," said Sam. "Come on, guys. I'll take you home."

After Jocelyn, Claire and Ben got in the car, Sam's questions became more personal. "Tell me all about the concert. Did Alli wow everybody?"

"Oh, Sam, she was wonderful. It was a great show." His question took her mind off the parking lot scene as she remembered the electricity of the concert. "Alli had the Orange Bowl rocking with her first song and it didn't stop for hours. She's incredible."

"I can see Jocelyn had a good time. How 'bout the rest of you?"

"She was late starting. She kept her warm-up guys out there for way too long. That kinda' surprised me." Ben complained.

"What do you mean, Ben?" Sam questioned. "One thing I can say about Margo is she always tried to start on time. Too bad Alli's not following in her mother's footsteps on that one. Was she a few minutes late or hours?"

"Maybe I was just impatient, but the warm-up started at seven thirty and Alli didn't come on stage 'til almost ten o'clock. That seemed like a late start for the star of the show."

"Yeah, it's not a good idea to keep the crowd waiting that long for the main event." Sam's voice had an edge to it.

"If you asked me, that little gal was higher than a kite. She was almost frenzied. I wasn't impressed," offered Claire. She had spent time protecting Margo several years before and her impression of Alli was not a good one.

"Not your kind of music, Claire?" teased Sam. "Or a dislike of Alli."

"Sam, you know I don't think she treated her mother very nicely. But that has nothing to do with her show tonight. I like her music but I'll admit I like her mother's better. Alli has a different style—loud, energetic, and louder." The others in the car laughed.

Claire defended her opinion. "She's good at what she does, it's just not for me. Don't get me wrong, Sam. You know her better than I do. But, tonight, something didn't feel right to me."

"Your gut instincts are usually right, Claire. I'll give Todd Madison a call in the morning to see if there's a problem," said Sam.

"On this one, I'll agree with Claire," added Ben. "I've got all of Alli's albums and tonight's version of every song seemed different."

"I still think it was a great concert," said Jocelyn. "I'm sorry the prank with Ben's car changed my mood. I was having a good time until I saw his car." Jocelyn sounded concerned. "Sam, does this incident mean they're after me, too?"

"Jocelyn, you'll need to be very careful until this matter is settled. You're not the primary target, but tonight proves they'll use you to get to Lawrence. These are the kind of people that stop at nothing to get what they want."

"What should I do?"

"Claire will give you good protection, but you're going to have to watch and listen. Pay attention to your surroundings at all times." Sam reassured. "For the next few days, don't trust anybody. They don't know what Lawrence is going to do about meeting their demands and they'll keep trying to convince him to cooperate."

"I think Jocelyn should leave town. This isn't her fight and I don't want anything to happen to her." The anger in Ben's voice was evident.

"Don't think that will work, Ben. She'll be okay if she doesn't take any chances," said Sam. "That means no more concerts. I should have stuck to my guns about tonight."

"Sam, I feel bad about pushing you to let me attend. I'm sorry. And, Ben, it's making me crazy to think your car was messed up because of me." Jocelyn shuddered as she realized that she might be the only thing the Emperitza could use to make Lawrence do as she wanted. "I'll do whatever I can, Sam. You tell me and I'll do it."

"Stay put for the next few days. Make sure Claire is with you at all times. If anything changes, I'll let you know." Sam was emphatic, but kind. "And try not to worry. We're doing everything we can to keep you and Lawrence safe."

"You know he's not going to turn over his book, don't you." Jocelyn knew her boss well enough to accept that fact. "There is no way he'd do that."

"For you, he'd do it, Jocelyn. And, you know it." Ben's anger sparked again as he spoke. "I'd never considered that you might be used as a weapon. Sam, you can't let her stay here. She's got to leave town!"

"Calm down, Ben. Let us do our job. If we think she needs to leave town, we'll move her as quickly as possible."

The evening was taking a toll on Jocelyn. She was tired physically and emotionally. She wanted her grandmother. If only Gracie were still alive, she could curl up in her lap and know that everything was going to turn out all right.

*****

Tossing, turning. Jocelyn couldn't sleep. Sweat drenched her body and her muscles tightened with fear at the slightest sound. *These terrible people are everywhere; they know every move I'm making; I'm not safe. No matter what Sam or Claire tell me, if these people want me they'll get me.* She checked the clock every five minutes, tried to quiet her mind, and had even gone so far as to count sheep. Nothing worked.

She stared at the ceiling and watched the shadows created by the moonlight. They looked eerie and creepy, and only added to her anxiety. Finally she turned on the lamp beside her bed and picked up a book. Perhaps reading would make her drowsy enough to fall asleep. But, after reading the same sentence three times, she gave up. In a few hours it would be morning, so she tried to organize her day and think through everything that needed to be done. *What a joke! I'm confined to my apartment, so my list of "to do's" is very short. Number one, call the Herald and let my boss know I won't be at work for a few days; number two, edit my columns for the week and get them posted; number three, twiddle my thumbs.*

Pulling her knees up, she wrapped her arms tightly around them, making her body as small as possible. How many times had she tried to curl inside herself, wishing she could make herself invisible? She couldn't remember doing it before her grandmother died. Her life had felt safe and secure until that awful year when it unraveled. She had lived a wonderful lie until she was seventeen, believing Gracie was her grandmother and Carter was her father. They were a familyt. Then Gracie died and left an empty place in her heart that she hadn't been able to fill until Mark Sanders told her he loved her.

Remembering it all now brought back the sadness, loneliness, and insecurity that she was always trying to overcome.

Rosanne was a beautiful, sweet woman who had given birth to her and had tried to make sure she had a loving family to raise her. Even now it was hard for her to take it all in. She and her mother had worked hard since their first meeting to forge a bond, but it was more like a friendship, not a mother-daughter relationship. As an adult,

Jocelyn could accept that she and her mother, while sharing genes and some history, could never recoup her childhood years.

Yes—they were close in other ways—and, she had been accepted by Rosanne's other children and wonderful husband. She could think of them now with warmth and gratitude that they had finally found one another, thanks to her mother's courage. But, she certainly didn't want to drag any of them into the mess she was in now. So, once again, she felt like she was all alone, even though she wasn't.

Whenever she looked back on those troubled years, she could see how the pieces had fit together to bring her to her senses and teach her what love really looked like. Carter and Gracie had loved her enough to give her safety, to teach her values, to help her build a strong faith in God, and to see that problems were solvable. Carter had loved her enough to give her space to work through her anger and figure out that he was the only father she would ever need. He continued to love her enough to legally adopt her and make her feel part of a family once again.

And, when he married Sharon, she really found her place in their family. Her stepmother was kind, beautiful, loving, and wise. Sharon gave her so many of the things she had missed when she lost her grandmother and had brought laughter back in their lives. She could go to Sharon with her problems and never feel judged.

When her dad had moved to Sharon's house, Jocelyn had moved into the guesthouse behind their house and had spent hours around Sharon's kitchen table just like mothers and daughters might do. She had even gained three stepbrothers who accepted her as though she had been born into their lives.

Lawrence was the other meaningful person that had come into her life because of her father's trial. For one thing, Lawrence had noticed things years before that led her dad's attorney to search for Rosanne. And, for another, he had rescued her from an unbearable situation with her teacher by giving her a job. At the time she couldn't understand why he would offer her, a young college kid, an editing job. It was only later that the answer to that question became apparent and she had her first encounter with his uncanny ability to see clues that others missed. He had sensed something about Miss Moss that caused him to investigate her. The evidence he found suggested that the teacher's apartment was not a healthy place for Jocelyn to live.

She sometimes had nightmares about Miss Moss. The woman had been her teacher and had volunteered to be her guardian. But only Lawrence had seen that Miss Moss was in love with Jocelyn and had taken steps to prevent the inevitable. She had thought Miss Moss's behavior was suffocating and over protective until that horrible night when the woman had tried to physically force herself on her.

There were nights when she would wake up shivering at the memory of the woman's hands on her body. And, then she would relax and be thankful because it was the woman's action that had forced her to call her father for help. God had probably engineered that night to show her that blood lines or not, Carter was her father and she needed him.

Yes, most of her life had fit back together very nicely. The only relationship that couldn't have a happy ending was the one that meant the world to her. What were the odds of her falling in love with someone she would later discover was her first cousin? Mark's mother was Rosanne's sister.

Jocelyn and Mark had separated and come back together so many times, trying to find a way to make it all right for them to marry. But, the church would never condone their marriage and she had finally accepted that. She'd broken it off with him forever and had been trying to move on with her life ever since. *How do you turn off love? How do you make the hurt go away? How do you learn to love someone new when the person you love more than anything can't be a part of your life?*

She had tried hard to fall in love with Ben. At first, she'd been infatuated with him and had pretended that was enough. But it wasn't. In her heart she knew it would never be enough. She wanted a life with a man she loved and it hurt her to think she was being unfair to Ben. She knew she'd have to break it off with him. Perhaps the timing would be right when this thing with Lawrence was over. As soon as she and Lawrence were no longer in danger, she would tell Ben.

A noise from the kitchen alarmed her and she sat frozen in fear. She silently waited for some other indication of trouble. Her ears perked up when she heard the TV come on and knew that Claire was probably in the kitchen making coffee. When she looked at the clock she was surprised that it was ten minutes after seven and she hadn't slept a single minute all night.

Picking up the phone, she dialed her father's number at work. He was always at his desk by six-thirty, so she knew he would answer. After two rings, she heard his voice.

"Daddy, do you know what happened to Ben's car last night?" She listened to his response and heard the concern in his voice. "I know I'm safe. Everyone keeps telling me that, but I'm so scared." Again, she listened and felt her muscles slowly begin to relax. "Yes, I'll be all right. I just needed to say it out loud and hear you tell me not to worry."

Hanging up the phone, she felt more at ease. Her father had made her feel safe—almost. It was reassuring that he already knew all the details of what had happened last night.

*****

She was typing her column when the doorbell sounded. Jumping to answer it, she was stopped by the sound of Claire's voice. "Sit back down, Jocelyn. I'll get the door."

"Yeah, it's probably not a good idea for me to answer the door." How was she going to deal with her new reality?

"Come in, Sam. What's going on?" Claire seemed surprised that Sam was at the apartment. "It's awfully early for a visit."

"Got to make some different arrangements." He nodded at the women and took a seat on the sofa. "We just finished putting alarm systems in both houses over at Carter's and the guys will be here within the hour to install a system in your apartment. Jocelyn, we don't want any more surprises."

"What kind of alarm are you talking about, Sam?" Jocelyn didn't want some industrial looking equipment destroying all the work she and Sharon had done on the decor of her new place. "Where will it go and what does it look like?"

"You won't even notice most of it, Jocelyn. But there will be a small alarm on each door and window. The component for the system will be placed in one of your closets. The only thing you'll notice is the key pad that will be attached to the wall near your front door." His eyes scanned the room. "You'll use the keypad to activate and deactivate the alarm."

"What good is a lot of noise going to do if someone tries to break in?" "It's all wired to a monitoring company who notifies the police when the alarm goes off. It's not something that's commonly used in residences unless you live in a multi-million-dollar house. But, we thought, under the circumstances, that you, your folks and Lawrence needed to have this."

"Sounds more and more like an episode of Miami Vice, if you ask me." Jocelyn was incredulous. "Do you think it'll help me sleep better tonight?"

"Jocelyn, there's another reason I'm here." He walked over to the chair where she was sitting and held her gaze for a minute. "I need you to talk to Lawrence. He has got to stop the release of this book. We need more time and he's going to have to come up with some plausible reasons for stalling."

"Oh, Sam. You don't know him very well if you think I can change his mind."

"We've got to try, and we know he won't listen to us or the police." His voice changed to a deeper tone as he tried to convince her. "You're the only one who might have a chance. This morning he's already coming up with ways to work around the demands. He's scheduled a meeting with me and Tom West this afternoon to elaborate on his scheme and I need for you to be there."

"I'll be glad to be at the meeting. But, I know what he's going to say if I even mention a postponement." She nodded and began to twirl a strand of her hair around her fingers. "He'll never agree."

"How do you want me to get her to the meeting, Sam?" Claire asked. "Will you send a car for us?"

"I'll do better than that, Claire." He winked at her. "I'll pick both of you up at three o'clock and drive you myself. The installers should be finished by then and I don't want anyone in this apartment unsupervised. Claire, these guys are from a company we trust, but while they're here, don't take your eyes off them."

"How lucky can I get?" Claire laughed.

Jeanne Moon Farmer

Chapter Thirteen

Sam

"Lara, I need you to help me with something today. Do you have any time this afternoon?" Sam looked at his wife sitting across from him at the kitchen table.

"Maybe. Depends on what you've got in mind." Lara grinned suggestively.

"That's on my mind, but it'll have to wait." He laughed and grabbed her hand. "I got a call this morning that worries me and I'd like for you to call Michael and Margo. I'm wrapped up in this Lawrence Fitz business and I won't have time."

"I talk to Margo once a week, so what's going on that's so urgent I need to call her today?"

Sam sighed. "I got another call from Todd Madison this morning. He's convinced Alli is in trouble. It sounds like the same story we lived when we were on the road with Margo. I don't know Madison well enough to know if he's over playing this, but he's convinced Alli's drinking and drug use are way out of control. Even Jocelyn, Ben and Claire voiced some things about last night's concert that make me wonder what's going on."

"Honey, you know this is going to be a touchy subject with Margo. Don't you think it'd be better if you talked to Michael?"

"Todd is threatening to quit. He says if her behavior continues, he can't stay." He paused to think about the consequences of Todd leaving. "You know how hard it is to find trustworthy security for stars as big as Alli. But aside from that, if what he told me is true, then Alli needs to be in a treatment center before it's too late."

"You know," Lara was shaking her head, "it took Margo three times in rehab before she could get her act together. I was hoping when Alli went on the road it would be different for her."

"Alli should have been in rehab long before she went on the road and became such a sensation. How many times did I try to convince Michael and Margo that their daughter needed help?" He smiled at her. "You've always been able to say things to them in a way that they'll listen."

"They listened all right, but how often did they act on what was said? Margo brushed off anything I said about her daughters. Do you think she's changed her mind about motherhood? I don't."

"Give her some credit, Lara. She's worked hard on her marriage to Michael and I know she and Sunni have a fairly decent relationship now. Since her bout with cancer, she's changed."

"You're right. She's made progress. And, her forced retirement has made her change her priorities. It's wonderful that she finally realizes how much Michael means to her and she's made some overtures to Sunni that I think are sincere. But Sam, I think it's been years since she's had a conversation with Alli."

"Margo has lived the life that Alli's living. She knows the pressure and she understands the temptations better than anyone. You and I both know that alcohol, drugs and sex cost her almost everything. If anyone can talk to Alli with any credibility, it's her mother."

"I think there's someone else who might be able to reach her. Do you remember Dr. Lulu Sarsyn? She's the psychiatrist that helped Margo. What if we could get her involved?" She hesitated. "Okay, I'll make the call to Margo and Michael, but I'm going to suggest they call Dr. Sarsyn."

"That's a good idea. I know Margo stays in touch with Lulu. If anyone can reach Alli, it just might be the flamboyant doctor in the turban."

He laughed as he remembered the first time he had seen the psychiatrist who had helped Margo turn her life around. His impression of Lulu Sarsyn had been astonishment and he remembered doubting her credentials. But the doctor knew her stuff and he had quickly become one of her biggest fans. As unorthodox as Lulu looked, she had made a difference in Margo's life when no one else had been able to.

As they finished lunch, the call from Alli's bodyguard was still paramount in his thoughts. Todd Madison was a former detective with Miami Dade Police, who left the force to be head of Alli's security team when Sam had refused to take on that job after Margo retired. Alli had been a hell-cat all her life and Sam knew there was no way she was going to change. He had suspected that once she launched her own music career she would only get worse. For most of her growing up years, he had kept tabs on her but he had never been able to contain her. Alcohol and sex had been part of her life since her early teen years and even he was surprised at the extent of her escapades.

As a child or a full-grown woman, Alli Anderson seemed to know no bounds, and that worried him. He had been on the road with Margo for over twenty years and he knew all about the temptations and pressures. He also knew that unsavory characters were always out there waiting to take advantage of beautiful, successful women.

"Tell Michael I'll call him in a couple of days. And, let him know I'll do whatever I can to help. My ties to that family go back to when Michael and I were kids growing up. If he needs me, he knows I'll be there." Sam's concern was genuine. Michael Anderson had always been like a brother to him.

"We both care about that family. I'll call this afternoon."

"Just one more reason why I love you, Mrs. Baxter." He walked over and planted a kiss on the top of her head. "Thanks for lunch. I've got to run. This thing with Lawrence Fitz has the potential to blow up in our face." His tone softened. "I do have you and that gorgeous body of yours on my mind. Make sure to wear something sexy tonight. I've got plans for you."

"Promises, promises!" Lara rubbed her hand up and down his leg. "Don't be late 'cause I'll be waiting and ready."

Jeanne Moon Farmer

Chapter Fourteen

Maddie

Maddie Sonnett was in love with her professional life. She had finished law school with honors, passed the Bar, and landed her dream job with the State Prosecutor's Office. Pulling together witnesses and evidence that could put criminals behind bars made her feel like she was avenging her husband's death.

She loved courtroom drama, and presenting her case before the judge and jury was definitely an adrenaline high. Each case had challenges and that's why she loved what she was doing. Growing up as the daughter of an FBI agent and working as a police officer on the streets of Miami, gave her a solid background for the investigative side of prosecution work. And, when an aspect of a case stumped her, she had the years of experience of both her father and his partner, Lawrence Fitz, to fall back on. Fortunately, they never tired of her questions and her appeals for help. Yes, her career life was good.

The unresolved area of her life was Eric Randall. She had promised herself she would never get involved with a married man, but it had happened and now she was addicted to him. When they were together she could forget about his wife and son, but sitting alone in her kitchen in the darkest hours of the night, they haunted her. Elena Martinez didn't deserve a husband who would cheat on her, and Maddie was smart enough to know that Eric would probably one day cheat on her, too.

Despite her efforts to break it off, she always succumbed to his charm. Or was it the sex and cocaine that drew her in so strongly? How did she get in so deep? She had never done drugs. But the pull of recreational coke had enticed her. The man had taken her integrity. No, she had given her integrity away in order to be with him and she couldn't understand why or how she had allowed it to happen. Until she met Eric, she had been the kind of person she was proud to be. Now, she often wondered who she was but she wasn't very happy with that person.

She faked it during the day. She was the competent, organized, honest trial attorney she had worked hard to become. When she dressed in a power suit and high heels, she commanded attention and she knew it. She was tall, worked hard at the gym to keep her body firm and tight, cultivated a sultry smile to go along with her seductive eyes, and used her mane of long, curly red hair to gain an advantage over any other women who might be in the room. As a teenager, she had learned what worked for her and she developed the confidence she needed to use all of her assets for her gain. Her poise and striking good looks had served her well.

But, sitting at home in an old t-shirt and sweat pants, she couldn't hide from herself. Even the darkness could not cover the fact that she was an impostor. She had fooled the others in her world, but on nights like tonight, she couldn't fool herself. Inside, in that place that only she knew, there existed a Maddie who was as insecure as a wallflower or a teenager who was never chosen for the team. She knew she wasn't really pretty or sexy or smart. And all the years it had taken to create that kind of image disappeared as though they had never happened. She was a lonely, needy woman who had allowed herself to be manipulated by the desirous looks and flattering words of a married man.

Yes, Eric was attractive and he had a great body. Yes, he made her feel beautiful and sexy. Yes, she loved to spend hours lost in the way their bodies fed on each other and how dramatic sex had become. There were no words to describe the way her body reacted when she saw him, let alone how she radiated heat when he touched her. She craved the intensity of the feelings he stirred within her and was starved for the endless pleasure his touch provided. Yet, as much as she hated who she had become because of him, the hunger was always there. No matter her determination and resolve to walk away, all he had to do was look at her and it all melted away. She had relinquished control of her body to the man, and as she sat alone in the dark, the thought sickened her.

Earlier tonight, she had been so sure that she would say no. But the minute he walked in the door she became his puppet; a toy designed for his pleasure. She was his to do with as he pleased. Even now, long after they had finished with one another, her body still yearned for more. Hours into the night, they had pounded away at each other's need—sex was never gentle or loving between them—and they had brought each other to the heights of passion over and over again. It was always the same. Their first caress started out with a turbulent lust so powerful it took over all rational intent. Often the turbulence was satisfied quickly, other times they got lost in a storm that became more intense as it raged on and on, so powerful that pain became pleasure.

But even that was never enough and once they had satisfied that initial hunger, they resorted to a long line of cocaine to help create stronger sensations and cravings that sent them over the edge for longer and longer periods of time. With the drug, he could possess her with renewed intensity and more imaginative requests. No matter what he asked of her, she complied. Even when her body ached from his forceful touch, she wanted more and there was no shame. At least, not until it was over. Then she had a chance to think about what she had done to satisfy his desires and she wanted to hide from the memory.

What catalyst could force her to walk away? What more was she willing to give up of herself to continue the madness? Yes, it was madness! And, every instinct in her body screamed for her to run from him as fast as her legs would carry her. But, if she could, she knew she would pick up the phone and beg him for a repeat performance.

*****

She sat behind her desk the next morning and studied the case that had just been assigned to her. A punk kid in one of the city's crime ridden housing projects had gotten sloppy and had been arrested with a kilo of cocaine in his car trunk. He was contending that someone had put the drugs in his car when he wasn't watching and he didn't know anything about it. That was typical. The drug business was using young kids in poor circumstances as couriers and, eventually, the kids always got caught. And, they couldn't wait to scream to the world of their innocence.

This kid would probably spend some time in jail. Then he would be back on the streets willing to get involved again. The small amount of money that he was paid to deliver the drugs was enough to feed his own habits, or take care of his family. So, the few months in jail was a small price to pay. And, in some bizarre way, the jail time gave him bragging rights on the street.

Winning the case wasn't going to change the drug trafficking problem in Miami, and she knew it. But, there didn't seem to be much progress toward shutting down the big guns behind the problem.

Her mind wandered back to the phone call she had received earlier from her father. He had told her a harrowing story about Lawrence being kidnapped and threatened by a woman that Lawrence believed was the infamous Emperitza of the cocaine business in south Florida. Maddie was astonished by her father's story, but she knew her dear friend would never give in to the demands that his novel be destroyed and never published.

Her father had reminded her that this was an active case and she was not to discuss it with anyone in her office. She feared for Lawrence's life and wanted to help. But what could she do?

*****

At dinner that evening she was deep in thought when Eric asked her, "What has taken that beautiful mind of yours so far away from me? You've hardly said a word all evening."

"I'm sorry. I was just thinking about my father's former partner, Lawrence Fitz. Seems he's written a new book that has stirred up some trouble."

"I didn't know he had finished a new book. I'm a big fan." He settled back on the banquette seat and turned to look at Maddie intently. "What kind of trouble are you talking about?"

"I'm not really sure. The book's supposed to be published soon and some folks in this town don't want that to happen."

"How do you know that?"

"Oh, a few things my father told me today. I'm sure it's nothing, but it got me thinking about all the bad things that keep happening in this town because of drugs." She looked at him with purpose. "I need to stay away from drugs, Eric. I'm really uncomfortable about what we've been doing. You know we're both putting our careers in jeopardy. We could be disbarred if someone suspected we had ever touched cocaine." She was whispering—a sudden paranoia making her afraid of being overheard.

"You're kidding me, aren't you? There is no way that will happen." His voice grew sterner. "Unless, of course, you've started telling someone about it." A dangerous look in his eyes told her he was very serious about his question.

"No way. Why would I want to put my head on the chopping block?" She tried to lighten the mood. "I'm overly concerned about Lawrence, that's all."

"Everybody's using these days, Maddie. It's just for fun and nobody is going to get hurt. Stop worrying and think about how much fun we have." His hand caressed her leg under the table. "Baby, remember how much I love what you do when you're high and all this nonsense will float right out of your head." His hand rose higher under her skirt and as he fondled her she quickly forgot about Lawrence. "In case you've forgotten," he whispered breathlessly, "let's get out of here and I'll show you what I mean. It won't take long before you are begging me for everything I can give you."

*****

Later that night, as she lay in her bed in the dark, quiet house, she remembered the look she had seen in Eric's eyes when he had spoken to her at the restaurant. For the few seconds of that look, she had felt unsafe. What a silly thought. There was nothing about Eric Randall that should make her feel unsafe. She snuggled back into her pillow, closed her eyes and fell into a troubled sleep.

Jeanne Moon Farmer

Chapter Fifteen

Margo

"Do you think Lara is over reacting, Michael? Could Alli be foolish enough to fall into all the traps she witnessed me falling into?" Margo had listened to every word that Lara said, but didn't want to accept what she was being told about her daughter's present behavior. "Lara says she's been told that drugs are controlling Alli."

"Margo, you know how easy it is to give in to all that nonsense when you're on tour and everyone is telling you they want more and more from you. Alli's smart, but she's also vulnerable. From things Sam told me over the years, I know she has a long history of alcohol use, and there have always been way too many men in her life. But, up to this point, no one has mentioned drugs." He took his wife's hand in his and kissed it softly. "Let's wait and see until I've had a chance to talk to Todd and Sam. They would never lie to me about this kind of thing."

"I'll do whatever you think is best. But I'm going to call Lulu and let her in on what we've been told. I trust her, Michael. And, if Alli's in trouble, Lulu's the one we can depend on to help her."

"Do you think she would listen to you if you gave her a call?"

Apparently Michael wasn't listening to her. "What are you talking about? I just told you I was going to call Lulu and you know she'll listen to me."

"I'm talking about Alli. What if you called Alli?"

"Honey, I'm the last person Alli would ever talk to. She hates me, remember?" Margo sighed as she thought about the failure she had been as a mother and then, how hard she had tried to make it up to her daughters. Sunni had forgiven her and they had a good relationship today, but Alli wasn't like her twin. Alli wanted nothing more than to punish Margo for all the years of abandonment and loneliness she had felt when Margo was on tour and away from home.

It really was a nightmare when she allowed herself to think about it—Alli had been sexually active with the men in Margo's life since she was a young teenager. At every chance, she had betrayed Margo as a way of dealing with the pain of having an absentee mother who had never wanted to be a mother.

Margo tried her best not to think about it. But in those times when it overwhelmed her, she telephoned Lulu Sarsyn. It always helped to hear the calm, but often humorous, voice of her psychiatrist. Lulu was a different breed and her no nonsense manner of mental health therapy had helped Margo get back in touch with what was really important in life. Now, as she looked across the room at her husband, she still couldn't believe he had forgiven her for all the hurt she had caused him.

"Hey you. Would you like to walk with me on the beach? I know a romantic little cove where we can steal a few kisses and take a nice swim." She stood and reached for Michael's hand.

"Honey, that's the best offer I've had all day. Give me a minute to change into a swimsuit and I will be ready to follow you anywhere." Michael laughed and gave her a gentle swat on her bottom.

"What did I do to deserve a man who would follow me anywhere?" She sighed as she watched him walk away.

Her husband had stuck by her through all the years of their divorce and he hadn't abandoned her when her lifestyle and cancer ruined her career. When she remembered those years, she was grateful that he had stayed and she had been trying for the past few years to make it up to him. Loving him was so easy for her now.

She had managed to make amends to everyone in her life but Alli. The daughter that was most like her. The girl had tremendous talent—in fact she was more talented than Margo had ever dreamed of being—and she had inherited Margo's appetite for men and booze, and now apparently, drugs. Alli was now repeating all the mistakes she had made in ways that were more abusive than she could imagine. Yes, Lulu could definitely give them some good advice on how to deal with the situation.

Reaching for the phone, she dialed the private number and waited to hear the voice of the woman who had saved her life.

*****

"Michael, I had a long talk with Lulu this afternoon and she thinks Alli may be in real trouble. The sad part is the small chance we have of getting her in treatment." Margo wanted to snuggle closer to her husband as she talked, but the conversation didn't need any distractions. "I told Lulu everything we know and she agreed that we should be concerned."

"We got you in rehab by default, I guess. Each time you were so strung out you couldn't argue with us. I can't imagine trying to convince our wild daughter that she needs help. Can you?"

"She's in Miami, at our condo. Do you think we should leave the island and go see for ourselves what's going on?"

"Are you sure you want to get involved? It might be very painful for you to see." Michael moved closer and took her in his arms. "I can say from experience that it's not easy to watch someone you love self-destruct. I can go to Miami by myself. I'll understand if you'd rather stay out of it."

"Oh, Michael. I'll never know why you stayed or why you never gave up on me, but I'm so grateful that you didn't walk away." She rose up on her elbow and looked at his face. The moon shinning through the glass doors gave her enough light to make out his features. She loved the strength and gentleness that she saw reflected in his eyes. It amazed her that she could see both—there never seemed to be a conflict in Michael—and knew those qualities defined the man she loved more than her own life. For years she didn't understand who he was and she did hurtful things that should have destroyed the love he felt for her. She used alcohol, drugs, and scores of men to hide from the love that Michael offered, and now their daughter seemed to be following in her footsteps.

"Where did you go, sweetheart? You seem a million miles away." Michael pulled her closer and kissed her tenderly.

"I'm here and I want you. I want your arms around me and I want to feel every bit of your wonderful body. I want you to hold me until I regain a sense of myself." She moved her body on top of his. "I'm going to roll off this bed and I want you to undo my hair, slowly remove this nightgown that is separating me from you, and then I want you to kiss me into oblivion." She whispered in her most seductive voice. "And, when you've done all of that, I want to touch every inch of your body until I've driven you into a frenzy."

"Is that all, Mrs. Anderson?" Michael laughed. "You are one demanding woman. And, if you want all of that, we'd better stop all this talking and get busy." He pushed her off the bed and looked at her standing in the moonlight. "You are so incredibly beautiful, Margo. I never tire of looking at you." He stood up and began to undo the pins in her hair.

"Your hair grew back more beautiful than it was before you got sick."

As his hands caressed the silkiness of her long chestnut hair, she felt her body's reaction and she knew she would soon be lost in his touch. She twisted away and moved his hands from her hair to the straps on her gown.

"Now, Michael, now. I want you now."

*****

Much later, sated from their lovemaking, she ran her fingers across his sleeping body. Although he had taught her that love was so much more than the physical, his body showed her that he knew how to convey his feelings through their love-making.

She watched his chest move up and down as he drew in each breath and the rhythm of his breathing relaxed her. When she and Michael remarried, they made a commitment to work on their relationship every day and her goal was to never again lose sight of who he really was.

For years, she had taken him for granted, knowing that even in divorce he would always be there for her. She had abdicated the role of parent because she knew Michael would take care of their girls. She had relied on him as her manager to keep her safe, to protect her assets, and to always make sure that she had the best venues. He had kept her in front of the best audiences, had promoted and marketed her to her best advantage, and had helped make her a star.

Yes, she had talent and good looks, but there were hundreds of people with those qualities who never succeeded. She had made the big time because of Michael, and once she was there, she'd lost sight of who he was. She began looking for love in shallow relationships, alcohol and drugs. As her hand caressed the warmth of his body, she closed her eyes and swallowed hard. How could she have traded his steadfast love for the highs and lows offered by one-night-stands and the false gods of addiction?

She had been a fool, and now her daughter was repeating the pattern. Alli knew the pitfalls. She had seen Margo at her worst and, yet, she hadn't learned from the mess that Margo had created in all of their lives. She winced as she remembered her selfishness and the chaos she had brought into her life and the lives of Michael, Alli and Sunni. She had been on the verge of losing everything when Lulu Sarsyn helped her see what was truly important.

But, recognizing the mistakes she had made with her family didn't give her the credibility she needed to deal with Alli. Her daughter would probably laugh in her face if she tried to interfere. Michael might be the only person who could reach out to Alli, and Margo would support him in any way possible. Together they might be able to move Alli in the direction of Lulu; they might be able to save their daughter's life. They had to go to Miami. They had to try. Before it was too late, they had to try.

*****

After calls to Lulu and Alli, Margo and Michael boarded a private plane and flew the short distance from Eleuthera to Miami.

"I can't believe she said she'd be out of the condo by the time we arrived." Michael shook his head but was too upset to look at his wife.

"She called me back within the hour and told me that Todd and the security team had checked her into an exclusive, very private hotel on South Beach."

"Sounds just like her, Michael. Why are you so surprised?" Margo was resigned to the fact that her daughter didn't want anything to do with her, but she never thought Alli would give her father the brush-off. "She wanted the use of our condo, but that clearly didn't include us."

Looking out the window of the small plane, she marveled at the blue of the sky and ocean. It looked so perfect, so untouched, and she wished her life could be the same. Then a slight smile crossed her lips. Since she and Michael had remarried, her life was becoming more like that image. Every day there was a new sense of peace. She could count her blessings; she could walk on the beach without mobs of people demanding something from her; and she could look in Michael's eyes and see his love for her. These days, she didn't need or want much. As a pop singer, she always thought she needed more—fame, money, adoring fans and men who could make her feel special for an hour or a day.

But, there was always an empty place inside her that she kept working hard to fill. Alcohol, drugs and sex were not the answer and the more she craved those things, the emptier she became. After her suicide attempt, she was moved to a residential treatment center where she met Dr. Lulu Sarsyn, a most unorthodox psychiatrist.

"You divorced a wonderful husband, totally ignored two beautiful daughters, and convinced yourself you were living the good life, right? If you had the life you wanted, why did you decide it wasn't worth living?"

Lulu's question had helped her see the truth of who she was, and eventually, the truth of who she wanted to be. During her months of treatment, she had learned that life could be wonderful and exciting without the highs and lows she had experienced when she was on the stage. And, most of all, she had opened her heart to love, genuine love, and the realization that Michael had loved her through all her craziness.

She closed her eyes and reached for his hand. "Did I ever tell you how much I love you?"

Michael laughed, "Let's see now. I think I can honestly say that you've told me a million times."

"Do you ever get tired of hearing me say the words?"

"Sweetheart, I will never get tired of the words or all the ways that you continue to show me that you mean them."

"We can help her, can't we? Together, we can help our daughter get through this awful place in her life." Her eyes were still closed and she heard herself sigh. "Success happened too quickly and too easily for her, didn't it?"

"I won't lie to you, Margo. Alli's at the top of her game right now. She's adored by millions. Her concerts are sell-outs and her latest album will go platinum very soon. It isn't going to be easy to convince her that she's headed for a crash if she doesn't change her life style. Look how long it took for you to realize you were hurting yourself."

"We've got to reach her before she hits bottom like I did." Tears welled up in Margo's eyes, but she didn't bother to wipe them away. "I didn't get the message until it was too late to save my voice. You'd think she would have learned something from all my mistakes."

"She's young, Margo. Nobody that young ever thinks it will happen to them. Besides, Alli doesn't have your heart or your basic goodness. I know that's a hard thing for me to say about her, but it's true."

"I'm not going to give up on her." She snuggled against his arm. "If I can see the light, then I'm sure she'll come around, too."

"You went through several interventions before you were ready to move forward. Remember that. At some point, I know it will work for Alli. But this may not be the time."

"Let's change the subject. This is too depressing." She looked out the window at the passing clouds. "Did you let Sunni know that we're on our way to Miami?"

"I talked to her just before we got on board. She's worried about her sister and if we need her she'll be on the next plane from New York."

Margo smiled. "That sounds like our Sunni. She is so much like you." It frightened her sometimes to think that her twin daughters had such different personalities. Poor Alli had all of Margo's worse characteristics and Sunni had all of Michael's best. "Has she talked to you about her break-up with Mark?"

"The only thing she's said to me is their lives are taking different paths. He wants to be in Miami and she loves New York. Looks like neither of them are willing to compromise."

"Has she mentioned Dr. Phillip Doyle? I think he may be the new man in her life."

Michael groaned. "Don't get attached, Margo. Wait until she mentions him in every other sentence before you get your hopes up."

"And I thought you were the romantic one!"

*****

"Look at this place! What in the world has she been doing? I can't believe she walked out of here and left this mess." Disgust and anger combined in Margo's tone of voice. "Who does she think she is?"

Michael stood in the doorway and stared at the unsightly wreck that his daughter had made of the living room. "Did she have a wild party here or something?"

There were glasses, empty bottles, dirty dishes, clothes, and turned over furniture everywhere.

"It's worse than we thought." She gasped. "Look on the table, Michael. She didn't even make an effort to hide the fact that she's been snorting cocaine!" Margo was yelling and her words reverberated across the room. "Where is the cleaning service? I know we hired a service to take care of things while we were gone. Well, they surely did a bang up job, didn't they?" She stomped into the kitchen fighting tears. "I thought it couldn't get worse, but this kitchen is …" She stopped. There were no words to describe what she was seeing or how it made her feel.

"I'll call the service and get them over here immediately." Michael focused on what needed to be done as he regained his composure. "Then we'll go out to eat or over to visit Sam and Lara until this place is cleaned up." He turned to use the phone and saw that it had been torn from the wall. "Let's get out of here before my blood begins to boil. I'll use the phone in the management office to make those calls."

*****

"Just how bad is it, Sam? Alli doesn't owe anybody money, does she?" Margo's thoughts jumped to the trouble that Tomas Labato had caused her because he owed money to some bigwig in the drug cartel. Tomas, the cousin of her then fiancé Paolo DaSilva, had tried to extort money from her by threatening to harm her family and had ultimately been responsible for Paolo's murder. She cringed as she remembered the horror she felt the night she was to deliver the money to the deranged man. "Sam, I don't think this family could survive another Tomas situation."

"As far as I can discover, she's not in over her head financially. But, I can't find out who her supplier is and that worries me." Sam said. "Tomas was a whole different story, Margo. His major debt was from gambling. The drug thing was minor in his case. But, he did owe money to the cartel."

"Do you need to get Eduardo DaSilva involved in this? He seems to have some connection to somebody." Margo wondered why she had brought up Tomas and Paolo's grandfather. "Once he got involved in the extortion issue, it sure got resolved in a hurry."

"Eduardo has connections in a lot of things, but this has nothing to do with him, Margo." Sam changed the subject. "We don't know enough about Alli's situation, yet. All I know is she's using very heavily and Todd is worried." He studied Margo's face as he spoke. "I wasn't at the Orange Bowl for her concert, but people who were there and know her personally have told me it was obvious that she was out of it."

"I've talked to Lulu and she's willing to help us. We've just got to figure out a way for her to get to Alli. I thought we could get them together at our condo, but from the looks of the place I can't imagine Alli will want to face us any time soon." Margo was still seething about the condo. "It's obvious she doesn't have any regard for other people or their things."

"My connection to Todd is fairly solid. Let me try to work through him." Sam suggested. "I know she is planning to travel to France in a few weeks, so time is not on our side." He looked over at Michael. "How long are you all planning to be in Miami?"

"As long as it takes, Sam." Michael's voice broke as he spoke. "Margo and I will be here as long as we're needed."

Chapter Sixteen

Lawrence

He was worried. Not so much for himself as he was for those around him who were being impacted by his decisions. There was no way he was going to let the Emperitza tell him what he could or couldn't publish. Yet, he knew he was playing with fire. He ran down the list of people that he was putting at risk—Jocelyn, Carter, Sharon, Sam, Claire—and the man who was already paying a high price—Joe Birdsong. He was worried, and he knew he was too old to be in the middle of this kind of intrigue. His instincts weren't as sharp and his defenses were no longer reliable. Over and over he asked himself, "How can I get out of this situation without collateral damage?"

Walking over to the liquor cabinet in Sharon's guesthouse, he hoped to find a good, strong brandy stored there. Something had to calm the queasiness in his stomach and help him settle down so he could think. He smiled when he recognized the label on the bottle of brandy and silently thanked his friends for enjoying some of the finer things in life. The familiar fire in the drink warmed his throat and, whether it was psychological or not, within minutes he began to feel his body relax.

"Who can understand the magic that a sip of brandy holds when one is tense and tired?" He mused as he sat at the kitchen table and stared at the notepad in front of him. Not too long ago, he was good at finding clues, hidden meanings, relationships that others missed. But, tonight he was empty of ideas. He needed someone to brainstorm with him; to listen to all the odd bits of information that kept bombarding him. There had to be someone who understood and yet, was impartial. After a few minutes, he picked up the phone and dialed Maddie Sonnett's number. He trusted her. She knew law enforcement and had grown up in an FBI household. She had insights that others might miss.

"Hello, my dear. I hope I'm not disturbing you, but I need a favor. Would you mind coming over to see me tonight? There's something I'd like to discuss with you."

******

Lawrence looked over the rim of his glass and spoke intently to the young woman seated across from him. "Maddie, I have to find a way to make this all work without anyone getting hurt. You heard what happened to Joe Birdsong, the man who was trying to protect me, didn't you?"

"I'm sorry, I don't know what you're talking about. But judging from the security they've got around this house, it must be something big."

Maddie's look confirmed that his last few hours had not been made public. So he began to fill her in on the events of his kidnapping and meeting with the Emperitza. "Joe Birdsong is still in the hospital and will probably require an extensive stay. They really worked him over. The poor man took a beating for me."

"My God, Lawrence! I can't believe what you're telling me." Maddie leaned forward in her chair with a look of concern. "I'm surprised that you're alive. From everything I've read about this woman, she shoots first and doesn't care who gets hurt. Now you've made me very concerned for you."

"She knows, to get what she wants, she needs me alive. I'm the only one who can keep this book from hitting the streets." He jumped up from his chair and began to pace. "She won't win this one! I won't let her censor the press and control me or this book." His voice was hard and steely as he spoke and his steps were forceful.

"How can I help?" she offered.

"I've always been so good at figuring out what to do in situations like this. But, that was when I was giving advice to others. Now it's me and I'm not sure how to handle it." When he turned to look at her, softness crept into his voice and his shoulders slumped forward.

"There are others to be considered. I have no doubt that she would hurt anyone she felt thwarted her wishes." He returned to his chair and looked at her beseechingly. "Maddie, I need you to strategize with me. There has to be something I'm not seeing; some clue that will turn this ordeal into a peaceful solution without compromise."

"Okay, you've made up your mind that the book will go forward. You're not backing down, right?"

"That's the one given in this situation. If I stop the book, she does more than win. She gains control of freedom of speech and I can't let that happen."

Maddie squirmed in her chair. "Lawrence, I understand the principle, and I agree with you. But, you only have a short time to come up with a way to save your life. You do understand that she will kill you if you don't do what she says? And, after you comply, she'll kill you anyway."

"I know, I know! I'm not worried about me. We have to figure out how to save the book and make sure that no one connected with me is hurt." His frustration was returning. "I don't care for myself, Maddie. But, I do care about Jocelyn and the others who have helped me. And, after this conversation that will include you, also, my dear. I'm sure she already knows you came to see me tonight."

"We need more information, like the name of her plant in the publishing industry? How can we get to her before she gets to you again?" Maddie's mind was racing. "She surprised you once. How can we make sure she doesn't surprise you again?"

"You've worked with Sam Baxter before. Perhaps the two of you can come up with some new ideas." He took a long look at the beautiful woman he had just placed in jeopardy and wondered whether he had done the right thing by pulling her into the fray. "Oh, my dear, I shouldn't have gotten you involved in this mess."

"That's what friends are for. You and my dad go back half a century and I grew up wanting to be just like the two of you. I'm not afraid to get involved and you know it." She smiled tenderly at him. "You know I like Sam and we worked well together on the Anderson

139

case." She stopped for a moment, deep in thought. Then her face brightened.

"I'll talk to Sam, but I think I've come up with an idea. Do you remember Eduardo DaSilva? You know, the Brazilian oil baron whose grandson was mixed up with the cartel?"

"Of course I remember. Tomas Labato, one of his grandsons had a gambling and drug habit that was responsible for the death of his other grandson, Paolo DaSilva. And then, Tomas tried to extort millions from that singer, Margo. But, I don't see the connection here."

"Lawrence, when I confronted Eduardo with all the information I had about that case, he took care of the situation! He has some kind of connection to that woman. I'm sure of it. Within a few hours of my meeting with him, the person we thought was a threat was found dead."

"You think DaSilva is involved in the cartel?"

"No, I don't think that at all. But, I know there's something between him and that woman."

"And, you're basing your assumption on what evidence, counselor?"

"My woman's intuition." She laughed. "It's one of those 'gut' things, Lawrence. Remember, you're the one who told me to rely on my instincts, and that's all I've got to go on here. If you're agreeable, I'll see if Eduardo will work with us. It's worth a try." She scribbled something on the pad of paper she'd been holding. "First, I'll have to talk to Sam. We can come up with something, I'm sure of it. Then we'll see if Eduardo will talk to me."

"Do what you need to do, Maddie. Just be careful." He sighed. "Now, on another issue. What's this I hear about you and Eric Randall?"

"What did you hear?"

"I know he and his wife have separated and I heard that you're the reason."

"You're right about the separation, but I hardly think I'm the reason." Maddie's face reddened and her words had an edge to them. "Whoever told you that is trying to stir up something that isn't real."

"What you do is your business, Maddie. Again, for very different reasons, I'm asking you to be careful. A man who cheats on his wife may also cheat in other ways, you know. Be sure you can trust this man before you lose your heart to him."

"Eric's a good man, Lawrence. He's trustworthy." She walked over and kissed the elderly gentleman on the top of his head. "I hear you and you can stop worrying about me. You have too many other things to worry about." She picked up her things and started for the door. "I'll call you after I talk to Sam."

Jeanne Moon Farmer

Chapter Seventeen

Maddie

"Where were you earlier? I thought you were going to be home all evening." Eric looked impatient. "I called several times, then decided to come over and check to make sure you were okay."

"I was visiting with Lawrence Fitz. He's in trouble with that woman who allegedly runs the drug trafficking operation and he wanted me to brainstorm with him."

"What kind of trouble?" He asked cautiously. "How does a retired FBI agent get himself involved with the Emperitza? If I may ask." He laughed. "I'm sorry, but it's ludicrous for an old man to think he can take down an operation the size of the one she runs."

"Oh, really?" She didn't like his tone. "He may be retired, but don't count him out. He's as sharp as ever. All he wanted to do was talk to someone he can trust."

"You're not going to get involved in this, are you? I would think it's out of your element, too."

"Aren't you the judge and jury tonight? This man is my friend and I'd do anything to help him. Aren't there people in your life that you feel that way about?"

"Maybe. But I wouldn't get myself involved in anything that might lead to my premature death." He laughed and pulled her close to him. "I don't want you to get in the middle of a fight that's not yours. Besides, all the man has to do is turn over the book and it will all be over."

"How did you know about that?" She gave him a puzzled look. "Who told you that the problem was his latest book?"

He stumbled over his words. "I just made an assumption, that's all. The guy's a writer of crime stories, so I figured he must have written something that made the woman mad."

"It's strange that you would assume his troubles were about a book."

"My darling, the last thing I want to do is talk about your friend, Fitz. Forget about it and make love to me." He grabbed her around the waist and began moving her down the hall toward her bedroom. "I have only one thing on my mind and that's your beautiful body. No more talk tonight about anything but what you're going to do to me once I've got you undressed."

"You do have a one-track mind. But, so do I when we're together." She started pulling off her clothes as they walked down the hall. "I'm always ready for you."

"I brought you a little surprise. A couple of snorts of this good stuff and we'll both be ready for a few hours of unbelievable pleasure." He pushed her to the bed and hastily laid out a line of coke on the bedside table. "I want you crawling all over me tonight, begging for more. The wilder you get, the more I love being with you."

As the cocaine began to take effect, Maddie felt powerless to control her desire and her emotions. All she wanted was to feel Eric's body and every sensation they could experience together. He could bring her to heights that she never imagined she was capable of achieving and he used every part of his body to banish her inhibitions.

*****

Hours later, trying to quiet her mind, she went over her earlier conversation with Eric and wondered how he knew about the trouble with Lawrence's book. Maybe she was making too much of it. People around the courthouse talked. Yes, that was it. He must have heard a police officer or someone mention it at the courthouse.

*****

The next morning, as she sat in the café waiting for Sam to join her for coffee, she reviewed the page of notes she had jotted down since her meeting with Lawrence and tried to fit what she knew into her checklist.

Really it was Lawrence's checklist that he had shared with her years earlier when she took her first job in law enforcement. He had shown her the importance of using what she knew to point her in a direction that might help her solve a case. Usually, when she used the method he had taught her, she could see where some events intersected with others; where times and places didn't match; and where the gaps were in everyone's stories. He taught her to look for patterns, to look between the lines; to let go of the obvious until she could hone in on that one small detail that didn't fit the overall picture. And, it had worked for her until today.

The only given in this case was a woman who was afraid of exposure. The Emperitza was a crafty businesswoman who had amassed a large fortune and seemed totally impervious to the fact that everything she did was illegal. She also happened to be cold-hearted, unethical, and extremely dangerous. The motive in this case was simple—prevent Lawrence's book from being published.

"Good morning, Maddie. It's been a long time." Sam smiled as he took a seat opposite her at the table. "I can't wait to hear what intrigue you are working on and how I can help."

"Sam Baxter. Gallant white knight. I'm so glad some things never change." Maddie gave him an appreciative glance. He was a nice looking man and well deserved her admiring once over. "Glad you could join me on such short notice. Seems like every time we work together we have some overwhelming life or death issue hanging over us that has to be solved in a matter of hours." She laughed. "Maybe our friend Lawrence will write a book about us someday."

"Spare me from that. But tell me why I was honored with your call."

"Short and simple." She stopped for emphasis. "I think Eduardo DaSilva can help Lawrence."

"That's a long shot, if I've ever heard one. Strange, but just yesterday Margo asked me something about him." Sam puzzled. "How do you figure him into this problem?"

"Sam, think about it! All we had to do was ask and he seemed to have a pipeline directly to someone inside the cartel. In a matter of hours that crazy thug who was trying to extort money from Margo was permanently removed." She slapped her hand down on the table. "I have a gut feeling that he has a connection to the Emperitza. He can help us find a way to get to her before she gets to Lawrence again."

There was a heavy silence between them before Sam finally spoke. "I agree with you on one point. He certainly has the means to move quickly and he knew someone who was willing to take Dario Vincetti down. But, I'm not so sure that his reach includes the head of the cartel. I think he was simply trying to settle the score for the murder of his grandson, Paolo."

"My gut tells me there is more to it than that. How did he know the guy to target? How did he get to him so quickly? I know money can work miracles, but he had to have some insider kind of information."

"Wait, Maddie. Are you implying that he is somehow part of the cartel?"

"I don't think that at all. I just feel a connection between him and that awful woman."

"You feel a connection? You're basing this on a feeling? Are you kidding me?" Sam scoffed.

"Go ahead and make fun, mister ex-Navy SEAL. I bet you went with your gut more often than not when you were one of the elite." She was surprised at Sam's attitude.

"I'm not making fun of you. And, yes, I understand where you're coming from when you say you have to trust your instincts. But, you'll have to let me digest what you're saying."

"Just think about it, Sam, and let me know whether you think we should try to get in touch with him. We don't have a lot of time, you know."

"Okay, how do you propose we approach DaSilva? We don't have time to go to Brazil." He frowned. "What do you hope to gain by asking this man to help? I'm curious."

"I was hoping you could help me figure that out. I know I can't pick up the phone and call him. I can imagine his response to, *'Hello, Senhor DaSilva, it's Maddie. Remember me? I'm the American redhead who barged into your office and told you about the antics of your crazy grandson, Tomas Labato. Yes, I know he's in prison because of our last conversation, but I was wondering if I could ask you for another favor.'* How's that?"

Sam clapped his hands at her performance and laughed. "Not bad for starters. I can see the dignified old gentleman now. *'Uh, tell me again who you are, my dear?'* Yes, friend, if we're going to approach DaSilva, we'll need a better plan than that and we'd better brush up on our Portugese."

"Are you saying you agree with me?"

"I'm not sure I see any value in trying to contact DaSilva. But, who knows. He just may have some insight that will help us. Did you try to talk Lawrence out of publishing the book?"

"Not at all. I agree with him! This woman thinks she can control everything by having her henchmen use their guns. If she doesn't like someone or something, she has one of her goons kill them. It's got to stop, Sam. One person has turned Miami into one of the most dangerous cities in the world. How can we sit back and continue to let this happen? Corruption, murder, mayhem. I can't believe this city I love has become a haven for crime."

"Not to mention the increase in illegal drug use."

"Yeah, that too." She whispered and avoided looking in his eyes. She felt the color rising in her cheeks as she remembered the cocaine she had shared with Eric no more than twelve hours before.

"Maddie, let me talk to Lawrence again and I'll be back in touch with you this afternoon. I've got a tight net of security around him but I don't know how I'll be able to protect him if that book goes to press."

*****

The ringing phone disturbed her concentration and she snatched it up in frustration. "Hi Eric. I'm really busy right now. I've got a brief to finish and I'm waiting on an international call from Brazil. Call me later."

She hung up the phone and tried to bring her attention back to the work she had been doing. Instead she kept thinking about how she was going to approach Eduardo DaSilva. Earlier in the day, Sam had called her and given her the 'go ahead' to try and make contact with the Brazilian oil magnet. With more confidence than she really felt, she placed the call and left a message with his executive assistant who told her that Senhor DaSilva was out of the country but she would get a message to him.

Out of the country might mean anything. Most likely it meant she would never get a returned call. She sighed as she looked across her desk at the books, files, and papers that needed her attention. When she had chosen to go to law school, she was certain that this was the right niche for her, but all the paper work was daunting and somewhere inside her she itched to get back to the more exciting work she had done as a private detective.

The phone rang again and she had to bite her tongue to keep from yelling at Eric that she really was busy. "Hello." The Portuguese accent of her caller surprised her even though she had been praying that he would call.

"Senhor DaSilva, thank you for returning my call. I know it's presumptuous of me, but I have a friend who has a problem and I thought you might be able to help me." She listened as the elderly gentleman explained that he would help her if he could and then she carefully presented a general picture of Lawrence's problem.

"My friend has only a short time until he has to meet the demands of the Emperitza and you can imagine our concern for him since he has stubbornly decided that he will not stop publication."

She listened as DaSilva asked her why she thought he might be able to help.

"I'm going to be honest with you." She took a deep breath before continuing. "Something in our last conversation leads me to believe that you might be able to help me contact this woman."

The silence was heavy and she wondered if he had hung up on her. Finally, he spoke and she listened carefully.

"Yes, I understand. Yes, I'll wait to hear from you." Before she could say thank you, the line went dead. DaSilva had said what he needed to say and had hung up on her.

Hurriedly, she dialed Sam's number. "He's in Miami and he's agreed to see us. Can you come to my office now? He's sending a car for us."

*****

He looked older than when she had last seen him three years ago. His face looked tired and the sadness in his eyes grabbed her heart. She wondered if a new tragedy had fallen on him or whether she was seeing the heartbreak of losing his grandsons. Paolo was dead and Tomas would most likely spend the rest of his life in prison for extortion and attempting to murder Margo Anderson.

As soon as she and Sam were seated in the back of the limousine, she thanked him for seeing her and reintroduced him to Sam. "Senhor DaSilva, I appreciate this time you are giving us. We know you have many other very important matters to attend to here in Miami. But we are desperate."

"Ms. Sonnett, we meet again. Although the circumstances do not bring a crisis to my world, I understand that for Senhor Fitz the matter is urgent." He nodded. "You honor me with your trust, but I am not certain that I can provide what you want and need. Mr. Baxter, tell me what you and the authorities know and how you plan to stop the execution that we both know will take place if the demands are not met."

Sam spoke for the first time and there was hesitance in his voice. "I don't know what law enforcement is planning. My role in all of this is to protect Lawrence. We do know that the woman Lawrence met with meets every description that law enforcement has of the head of the drug business and she gave Lawrence enough information that convinced him he was dealing with the Emperitza herself."

"If I could help you, exactly what is it you think I can do?"

"We need the name of the inside person at the publishing house. We need to know how we can get to this lady. And, we need to know how she is planning to get to Lawrence when she finds out that he isn't going to comply."

DaSilva began to laugh. "Is that all? Surely you don't think I have that kind of access to this woman."

Maddie looked from Sam to DaSilva. "I think you do. That's why I called." Now that she had directly confronted him, her hands began to sweat and she felt tension across the top of her shoulders. "A good man's life is at stake, yes. But more than that, this woman is terrorizing Miami and she has to be stopped. I know you can help us."

They rode across the causeway toward the beach in silence. Each person in the car seemed to be struggling with thoughts that couldn't be expressed. Out the window, Maddie could see the white caps on the bay as storm clouds built over the ocean. She looked back at Miami's skyline and then cast a worried look at Sam. Her Miami, her beloved city, was losing the war. The shadows of greed, deception and evil were engulfing all that was beautiful and good about this tropical paradise. She wanted to cry as she felt their chances with DaSilva slipping away.

The driver made a loop around Collins Avenue before turning the car back the way they had come. The car pulled in front of her office building and the door was opened for them to exit. She and Sam were already out of the car when DaSilva broke the silence.

"Ah, senhorita, I am flattered that you think so highly of me. Someday I would like for us to meet when you aren't bringing me trouble." He closed his eyes for a moment and then he smiled. "This time, I have no promises to give you. I'll be in touch."

Before they could respond, the chauffeur closed the door and drove away. Sam scratched his head as he watched the car disappear. "Well, damn, Maddie. Looks like you were right."

Chapter Eighteen

Jocelyn

There was no reason for her to be afraid. Claire, her protector, was across the hall asleep with one eye open, the Miami police were making routine checks around the neighborhood, and the building had a doorman and security guard. Yet, she couldn't sleep.

Tossing, turning and imagining the worse was wearing her out and she couldn't lose the sense of dread that held her in its grip. Every time she tried to close her eyes, she startled herself with crazy thoughts of the Emperitza and her henchmen, and her eyes would fly open. Even with the air conditioner pumping icy air into her room, her body felt warm and sweaty. She was losing her battle for sleep to the demons in her own mind. Looking at the clock, she was surprised that it was only midnight. Surely, she had been tossing and turning longer than an hour! In frustration, she threw off the sheet and sat on the side of the bed. With her face buried in her hands, she took a few deep breaths. Memories of the house where she grew up and the long forgotten fragrance of an apple pie baking in the oven, drew her mind to the one person who had always made her feel safe—Gracie.

Her grandmother, Gracie McDeal, had been dead for almost ten years. But, she would always be Jocelyn's 'safe haven.' When she closed her eyes, she could almost feel Gracie's arms around her: Pulling her into comfort, cocooning her from the scary things of the night. The sensation of being rocked in those loving arms was working its magic on her. She could feel the tension and frustration that had kept her awake ebbing away when the mood was abruptly shattered by a knock on her bedroom door.

"Jocelyn, are you asleep?"

Claire's voice jolted her back to reality and she jumped off the bed.

"What's wrong, Claire?" She inquired as she opened the door and looked at her bodyguard.

Claire, who was still dressed in street clothes, stood in the hallway looking sheepishly at her. "You have a visitor." She whispered. "I heard a light tap on the door and when I went to investigate there was a young man pacing up and down in the hall. He says he's your friend and he needs to see you. The doorman called Sam to check him out and Sam's okay with him being here as long as it's okay with you. If you think I need to talk to Sam, I will."

"Who in the world would need to see me in the middle of the night? This is crazy. What's his name?"

"Mark Sanders." Claire spoke and then waited for a response. "But, you don't have to see him if you don't want to. I can send him away."

Jocelyn's eyes lighted up at the sound of the name, and then, as quickly, they grew dim. "Did he say what he wanted? Did he tell you why he's here?" she whispered as she tried to gain some composure. For a moment she had allowed herself to forget that she and Mark had broken up. They no longer had a connection, except as cousins.

"All he would tell me is he would like to talk to you. Do you want me to ask him to leave?"

The years disappeared and she wanted Mark's arms around her. She wanted to hear him tell her that everything was going to be all right. As vulnerable as she felt tonight, how could she see him without exposing her heart and letting him know how much she missed him?

Instead of asking Claire to tell him she was asleep, she heard different words fall from her lips. "Please, ask him to wait while I change."

Watching as Claire walked down the hall, she wondered if she was losing her mind. And then she heard his voice. Longing coursed through her and she prayed she would be able to keep her resolve. She prayed for the strength to behave like his cousin and not the woman who was still in love with him.

*****

"You're still a night-owl, aren't you? What brings you to my door at this hour of the night?" She had taken her time changing clothes and hoped that her voice didn't reveal the emotional battle she was waging with herself. She made up her mind not to look at him and to keep the conversation very light. Then it dawned on her for the first time that something must be very wrong if Mark was in her living room after midnight.

"I'm sorry, but I had to come." Mark's voice was ragged and when she looked him in the eyes, she knew that something painful had happened. "Sit down, Jocey. I have some bad news."

"Just tell me, Mark. What's happened?"

"My mom had a call earlier this evening from Aunt Rosanne and I'm afraid something has happened to your step-father. I don't have all the details, but I know he's been shot and is in the hospital."

Tears sprang to her eyes as she thought about her mother's husband. Paul Donovan was one of those rare law enforcement gentle giants who could tenderly cuddle with his kids one minute and then round-up violent criminals with fierce determination in the next. Over the years, she had grown fond of him and often sought his advice. He was grounded, funny, devoted. One of the nicest men she had ever met.

"Dear God. What happened?"

"He was at home and had walked out to the mailbox when a car drove by and someone shot at him. When the kids heard the gun, they ran out front and found him lying in the driveway. Mom says he's in the Emergency Room and they're waiting to take him to surgery. Aunt Rosanne is a mess, but she told Mom not to worry about her. She's holding herself together for the sake of the kids."

"Oh, Mark, how awful for everyone. Does your mom think I should go to LA? Does Rosanne need me?"

"I don't think that would be a good idea right now. You can make your decision after we know the extent of his injuries." Mark took her hand and tried to offer some comfort.

"What am I thinking? How can I go to LA now? There's no way I could leave Miami with all this craziness going on with Lawrence." She threw off Mark's hand and stood up. "This is horrible!" Her tears had turned to sobs and she wrapped her arms tightly around her waist.

"Okay, I think I missed something. What are you talking about?" Mark grabbed her hand and pulled her down on the couch. He reached over to the box of tissues on the table and handed her several. "What's going on with Lawrence?"

At the sound of Jocelyn's sobs, Claire walked into the room with concern. "What's going on? Jocelyn are you all right?" She positioned herself as close to Mark as possible in case she needed to defend the young woman who was crying hysterically.

"There are too many things going on." Mark tried to explain. "I've just given her some bad news about her step-father and, apparently, something is happening to her boss that I don't know about." He stood up and looked at a woman he had never seen before this evening. "And, by the way, I know you answered the door, but who are you and how do you fit in this picture?"

"Let's get her calmed down and then we can talk." She turned from Mark to Jocelyn. "While I'm getting her a glass of water, try to get her to take a few deep breaths. She's had some tense moments over the last few days and I was wondering how long it would take for the dam to break. Those tears will help her get through all this mess. She's been wound tighter than a drum trying to show everyone that she's okay." Claire shook her head and headed for the kitchen.

Mark put his arms around Jocelyn and drew her to him. "Jocey, I know you need those tears, but try to take a breath. Whatever's going on, you'll survive it. I promise." He tenderly rubbed her back with one hand and continued to hold her steady.

Gasping between sobs, she slowly felt the hysteria subside. As Mark held her, she relaxed into his arms and held on to his strength. It felt right to be snug against his familiar body and she accepted the comfort he was offering.

"Take a few sips of this water and then wipe your face with this cool rag. It'll make you feel better." Claire offered. "Then I'll leave you alone so you can talk to Mark. Since Sam said he could be here, I guess it's all right to tell him what's going on." As she was leaving the room, she looked hard at Mark. "I'll be in the next room, and my one purpose is to protect Jocelyn," she hesitated, "from any kind of harm."

Jocelyn settled back against the soft cushions on the couch and tried to pull her thoughts together. Bad news was coming faster than she could handle and but all she wanted to do was ask Mark to hold her again. There was so much to tell him she scarcely knew where to start.

"It's about the new book. Lawrence's story is about a fictional character that closely resembles the Emperitza. Apparently it comes too close to reality and the lady wants him to pull the book. She had him kidnapped the other night! Can you believe that? And, then she threatened him, me, Dad and Sharon. She's ruthless and means business."

"Unbelievable! Is Lawrence all right?"

"He was shaken, but you know him. He thinks this is high adventure. It's made him forget how old he is and he's ready to take her on." She looked at Mark in exasperation. "He's not going to let her tell him what he can write about. So we're at war with the dragon lady of drugs and her henchmen."

"That's the reason for the bodyguard and everything being cleared through Sam." Mark shook his head and pointed down the hall toward Claire's room. "If Sam's taking care of things, I can breathe easier. When I was on tour with Margo, I always knew that Sam would make sure we were safe. He's a good man, Jocey. You can trust him."

"There've been a few minor incidents and then, when they kidnapped Lawrence, someone nearly killed the guy that was assigned to protect Lawrence. He's in such bad shape that he'll be in the hospital for weeks."

"Surely, Sam's gotten Lawrence out of the area."

"Well, not exactly." She hesitated.

"He's not at his apartment, is he?"

"No. But, Mark, he wasn't at his apartment when he was kidnapped. This woman seems to know everything!" Her voice was getting more animated as she spoke. "She found him! Only a few people knew where he was and still, she found him!"

"Why do you have to be in the middle of this? All you did was edit the book. I suddenly think going to LA to help your mom sounds like a great idea."

"Sam seems to think that she'll use a threat to me as a way of getting to Lawrence and that might be the way they'll catch her." She looked perplexed. "You're right. I should leave Miami until this is all worked out. But, Mark, I'm all Lawrence has and I can't leave right now. Rosanne will understand." She stood up and walked toward the window where she could see the lights of the city and the reflections on the Bay. "Paul will be okay, won't he? Promise you'll let me know as soon as you hear something."

He followed her across the room and gently placed his hands on her shoulders. "You know I will. As soon as she calls us, I'll let you know."

Slowly, she turned and faced him. "Mark, I … Never mind." She wanted to ask him to stay. She never wanted him to leave and the old sadness she had struggled to overcome swept through her like a wave of scalding water. She stumbled against him, but quickly recovered and pulled away. "Thank you for coming to tell me." She took his hand and started walking toward the door. "Call me. No matter what time."

His eyes held hers and seemed to reflect the same regret and sadness she was feeling. She knew there would only be more heartbreak if she asked him to stay.

*****

At six o'clock the next morning, she answered the ringing phone and heard an unfamiliar, heavily accented male voice. "Your stepfather didn't make it. He died in surgery. Make sure you tell your boss."

Jeanne Moon Farmer

Chapter Nineteen

Alli

"Wait one minute! If you think you can barge in here and tell me what to do, think again." Alli's rage was mounting and her animosity toward her mother seemed to have no limits. "I don't play by your rules, Margo. I never have and I never will." She whirled around and threw the glass she was holding across the room. "I'll pay for a damn cleaning service." She realized she was screaming when she saw the shocked look on her mother's face. But, she didn't care. "Now get out of here and leave me alone." Storming toward the door, she threw it opened and motioned for Margo to leave.

"You have certainly shown yourself this morning, Alli dear. Now that I've seen for myself how you're behaving, you'll have a hard time convincing anyone that you are in control of your life."

Margo's voice was dramatic and Alli remembered that same tone from her childhood. Even now, it could immobilize her. Motionless, she stood in the doorway and fought hard to regain a sense of her own power. After all, she was no longer an intimidated five-year old. She watched as her mother walked away. Margo held her head high and never looked back.

Alli almost swooned; feeling weak, lonely and abandoned once more. Then she threw her head back and began to laugh. The sound came from her gut, floating through the air with an hysterical cadence. She bent double as her triumphant laughter became a familiar pain. When the laughter subsided, she stared down the empty hallway and whispered through her tears, "You have no power over me, Margo."

Closing the door with a bang, she grabbed a napkin from the table and tried to dry her face. The task was impossible as the tears continued to flow. She tossed the napkin on the floor and walked into the kitchen to fix herself another drink. Looking around at the disarray, she wondered why she had left the hotel in South Beach and come home.

She knew her condo wasn't ready for her. How long could she live with the renovations before she completely lost her mind? The carpet was being replaced in most of the rooms so the floors were bare, wallpaper rolls were stacked in the corner of the living room and dining room, and there was only minimal furniture in most of the rooms. What's all my money for if I have to live like this?

She charged over to the phone and dialed her decorator's number. "I can't live like this!" She shouted. "Get this place cleaned up or I'll start deducting money from your bill for every day I have to look at this mess. I don't care what you have to do to get it done."

It was always the same—she had money, she had fame—but no matter what, she still had to deal with incompetent people like her decorator and hurtful people like her mother. Life was so unfair! And, her glass was empty.

Stumbling to the liquor cabinet, she grabbed a quart of vodka and hastily removed the top. Since she intended to drink the entire bottle, here was no point in finding a glass.

Within the hour, she was passed out on the floor of the kitchen.

*****

Slowly she felt herself coming to life and knew she was going to be sick. "Oh, God." She groaned and pushed up off the floor. Trying to stand and not being able to feel her legs was becoming a pattern and she thought of how often she was finding herself on the floor these days. Through blurry eyes she caught the shadow of an image and fear coursed through her.

"Who are you?" She demanded lamely. "I see you! Tell me who you are."

Waiting for a reply, she looked around to see if she could find something to use to defend herself. She struggled to get to her knees, but it wasn't working. Her legs kept sliding out from under her and she couldn't get close enough to a cabinet that she could use to pull herself off the floor. Feeling helpless, she called out again, "Answer me! Tell me who you are?"

In the silence, her vision cleared somewhat and she realized she was yelling at the refrigerator. There was no one in the room with her, only the shadow cast by the refrigerator. *"Oh, God. What is happening to me?"* She rolled over on the cold floor and wondered if she was losing her mind.

*****

After an agonizing hour, she remembered she had promised to sing at a charity benefit that evening so she tried once more to sit up. She rolled on one side and braced her arm against the floor. It took all her strength but she was finally able to pull herself up. On very shaky legs, she staggered to the bathroom.

"Oh my God! Look at me! There's no way I can do the damn show." She eased down on the edge of the bathtub as she felt the nausea rising in her throat. When the retching subsided she screamed in the silence. "Get with it, Alli! You've been in worse shape than you are today and you've never missed a concert." Self-talk had gotten her through on many occasions and she wasn't going to let a little hangover stop her now. She turned on the shower and let steam fill the room. All she had to do was let the hot water wash away the thoughts of her mother that she hadn't been able to forget with an entire quart of vodka. She had never let her mother defeat her and she wasn't about to start today.

Holding on to the sink for support, she shouted. "Take a good look, Margo. Nobody remembers your name any more. But, I'm Alli Anderson and I'm on top of the world!"

*****

Later, seated in the dressing room of the Jackie Gleason Theater, she tried to remember why she had agreed to sing at the benefit. It was not her style to give away her talent and she couldn't imagine why she had allowed her manager to book this performance. It had been years since she'd appeared at a venue this small and on top of that, she was not the headliner. She was one of ten performers who would take the stage tonight. She vowed she would never let this happen again.

Her hairdresser and make-up man had worked miracles and she looked better than she thought possible after the bender she had been on earlier in the day. In the mirror, she watched Todd who was seated on the couch behind her. He hadn't had much to say to her since he and the driver had arrived at her condo to pick her up. By then, she had managed to take a shower and put on fresh clothes, but she was still hung over and it showed. No wonder he was angry with her. But, that was his problem not hers and she was tired of his nagging.

"You're very quiet tonight, Todd. What's going on with you?"

"I'm fine, Alli, but I'm not so sure about you. You looked like hell when we picked you up." Todd was still irritated and his tone of voice was unkind. "Are you sure you can handle this show?"

"Why do you keep harping at me? Have you ever known me to miss a performance?"

"Alli, when's it going to stop? Will it stop when you can't go on stage and hide that you've been on a binge?"

"Why are you freaking out? I only had a few drinks to settle myself." She turned to face him. "My darling mother paid me a visit this morning and gave me the 'you're out of control' lecture. I don't need to hear it again from you!"

*****

After the show, Todd tried to convince her to go back to her condo. "Come on, Alli. We can stop and pick up some Chinese from that place you like at the beach. I'll bet you haven't eaten all day."

But being on stage had energized her. She was wound-up and wanted to party.

"I'm going to the after-show party! You seem to have forgotten that I'm the boss and you weren't hired to be my jailer. Stop treating me like I'm a two-year old." Her voice was edgy and she wanted to get away from her bodyguard as fast as possible. "Now tell the driver to take me to the party!"

"You know what, Alli. You're right. You can take care of yourself." Todd turned to the driver. "Let me out on that corner. I'll call a cab. Take Miss Anderson wherever she wants to go." When the car came to a stop, he got out and didn't look back.

"Where do you think you're going, Todd? Get back in the car!" Alli yelled out the window at her bodyguard's receding back. "Forget you! I'm going to have some fun." She rolled up the window and told the driver to go on.

*****

A prominent Miami attorney was hosting the after-show party and she expected it to be an extravaganza. As the car drove through the gates of the large estate located on the Inter-coastal Waterway, she was reminded of MarGrove, the bay front home her mother once owned. She stepped out of the car and looked appreciatively from the house to the gardens. This was her world—opulent, over-stated, created for self-indulgence—and she knew she would find her kind of people here. The Todd's and Margo's of the world were dim memories as she lost herself among the pleasure seekers. Champagne and drugs flowed freely, a tropical breeze and full moon invited playfulness, and the music seductively mimicked the siren's song.

People sought her out, complimented her performance at the benefit, and lifted her spirits even higher with their blatant adoration. She greedily took it all in and wanted more.

"You look like you're enjoying yourself." He was tall with elegant good looks and obvious wealth. His blue eyes commanded her to look at him and his sensual smile was irresistible.

"Nothing like a good party to revive one's spirit, I always say. And, whoever is hosting this one knows how to keep his guests happy." She finished one glass of champagne and grabbed another off the tray of a passing waiter. "I don't think we've met."

"No introductions needed for me to know who you are, Miss Anderson. Your performance tonight was unequaled by anyone else at the theater." His smile made her feel like she was the only woman in the room. "And, thank you for the compliment. I'm Jeff Cannon, the host who knows how to keep his guests happy."

She studied him carefully. His face was familiar—somewhere they had met before. "You look familiar, Mr. Cannon. Have we met before?"

"We met years ago under very different circumstances. I hesitated to mention it, but my law partners are Elena Martinez and Eric Randall."

"Yes, mentioning that I was once accused of murder could change my festive mood, couldn't it?" She remarked sarcastically. "I knew I had seen you before." She tried to hide her embarrassment at not remembering him. "You have to admit, that wasn't my finest hour. But, I was wrongly accused and I guess I never thanked you for being part of the team that helped prove that."

"Enough of that subject! The past is best left in the past." He took her hand and kissed it. "Tonight is all about having fun and celebrating a successful charity benefit. Here's to you, my dear, for making it happen."

After the toast, he turned to greet other guests and her eyes followed him as he made his way across the room. *That is one good-looking man. How did I miss seeing that before?* Her mind was made up in an instant. Tonight she would focus all of her charm on Jeff Cannon.

She made her way to where he was standing and slipped her arm through his. Without excusing herself to his other guests, she whispered in his ear, "Why don't you show me your garden?" Seductively, she smiled up at him and pulled him toward the French doors. "I can't wait to see the view."

Once outside, he steered her to a gravel path that led through the garden to the dock. "You'd probably like my yacht better than the garden. Follow me." They walked quickly toward a moderate sized cabin cruiser tied up to the dock. "This is reserved for private parties." He said as he helped her aboard and they entered the salon.

His gentle manners disappeared quickly as he sought her mouth and hungrily kissed her. She moved away from him and stepped out of her dress with ease. Finding the sliver of moonlight that cast a silver line of illumination across the cabin, she showcased her body for his admiring eyes. It had been weeks since she had lured a lover with the seductive movements of a dance. More and more her encounters with men had been sex without any passion, but this man made her feel like dancing and she swayed to the music in her mind.

As she moved from side to side and twisted her body in the moonlight, she felt free and joyous like she had once felt with Paolo DaSilva, her mother's lover that she had been accused of killing. The memory of her conquest over the man her mother planned to marry carried her higher and she began to dance with a frenzied intensity that wiped away thoughts of her morning encounter with Margo. She was caught up in celebrating herself and lost sight of her desire for the man who was watching her with unabashed lust.

She was totally absorbed in a world of her own making when he grabbed her with such brutal force that she almost lost her balance. Within seconds his mouth and hands were devouring her and her soft moan in response promised him everything he was craving. His body covered hers as he pushed her down on the settee.

When the fire of their passion was ebbing, she allowed him to cradle her in his arms. "You are an incredible lover, Mr. Cannon. Who would have anticipated such ardor from an upstanding pillar of the legal community?" She teased and playfully moved against him.

He laughed. "What man could resist your dance?" He ran his hand through her hair and looked into her eyes. "That was Act I, Alli," he whispered. "I know how to make it even better." He stood up and walked to a nearby cabinet. "I save this for special occasions." He waved a large packet in front of her and waited for her reaction.

"I hope that's all for me, Jeff. Between that and your prowess, this will be a night to remember. You must be trying to wipe away all of my inhibitions."

"Didn't I already do that?" He leered at her.

"Oh, counselor. I've got so much more to offer. Why don't we see if we can finish off that bag tonight?" She got off the couch and began to dance once more. With every move, she touched him with a different part of her body. Teasing, pleasing, building a new tension between them, she wanted him to respond to her eagerness.

"Hold on sexy lady! Give me a minute to get this ready." He was breathless as he pulled away from her.

In the moonlight, she watched as he prepared the white powder. "This, washed down with champagne, will take us where we want to go." He uncorked the bottle and poured her a large flute of the golden liquid. "Now you can join me for Act II?"

For hours, they repeated the pattern. Every time she thought he was sated, he came at her with more intensity and she wondered who would be the first to call a halt to this love fest. Her body was bruised and sore. She had been bitten, pinched and prodded relentlessly, but his abuse made her appetite stronger and she begged for more. What possessed her? What siren song called her deeper into the debauchery? Never before had she submitted so willingly to the demands of any man. And, he was demanding more from her than she had imagined possible.

"You never quit, do you?" Panting, he exclaimed. "Well, if it's more you want, then you've found the right man. I can give you more!" His voice sounded harsh and cruel.

She thought she had asked him to stop, but maybe not. He was pushing her body beyond its limits, but she kept responding. The alcohol and drugs continued to fuel her hunger. Her mind had stopped functioning but her body was not sated. She couldn't remember the last time she sat up to draw in a line of coke as she felt him forcing it in her nostrils over and over again. The pounding never seemed to stop as he continued to ride her body—turning her front to back and back to front without stopping. *No more!* She thought she cried out but it was only a whisper as she spiraled deeper and deeper into the darkness.

*****

The dock light shone through the porthole onto the lifeless body of Alli Anderson. He grabbed both her shoulders and shook her. "Wake up!" He shouted several times but she didn't move or respond to his words.

"There is no way I'm taking the rap for this."

Quickly he dressed and stashed her clothes in one of the compartments. He started the engine of the powerful boat and expertly steered it down the Inter-coastal toward Biscayne Bay. He had to take care of her before the first light of day and then make sure some of his other guests could give him an alibi. As the boat plowed across Biscayne Bay, he remembered that MarGrove had a deep water dock and he headed in that direction.

Jeanne Moon Farmer

Chapter Twenty

Sharon

One more visit to this house and my job is finished. Thank God. Sharon breathed a sigh of relief as she pulled into the driveway of the Moreno estate.

Today, she would do a quick walk-through and sign-off on the decorating and renovation project that had almost given her an ulcer. Every time she dealt with Mrs. Moreno, she walked away with either a stomach or a headache—the woman knew how to push all Sharon's buttons. But, that was nothing compared to how she felt when Mr. Moreno decided to put in his two-cents. Just the sight of the man made her feel like she was she was working with someone straight out of a 1930's gangster movie. She laughed at how she had described this couple to Carter. *She's a well-paid call girl and he thinks he's Al Capone.*

The housekeeper opened the door and told her Mrs. Moreno would be joining her later and suggested that she begin the walk-through without her. Sharon smiled in relief and hoped she could complete her work without the company of the home's owners. Walking from room to room gave her a sense of pride and accomplishment. Her designs worked, even with the constant interference and changes made by Mrs. Moreno. Each room made a statement of casual elegance and that had been her goal.

The room she liked least was the dining room, but she had made it work even when Mrs. Moreno had insisted on changing the color scheme. As she studied the room's new look, she knew it didn't make the dramatic statement she wanted, but it had its own appeal. As she turned to leave she heard Mrs. Moreno call to her.

"Good morning, Mrs. Moreno. I'm just finishing my final check and so far, everything seems to be in order. I hope you're pleased with the results."

"There are a few things I wish we could change. But it will do for the time being." Ava Moreno walked into the room dressed in her signature outfit—bikini with jewelry to match. "I saw a picture in a magazine of a bedroom that I want you to copy. But Jose says I can't spend another dime on this house." She smiled at Sharon and winked. "I'll give him a few weeks and then I'll call you. I'm sure I can change his mind."

"I'll look forward to your call." Sharon said, a little too brightly. "I think you've created a lovely home. I'm sure Mr. Moreno likes what you've done."

"He doesn't care what it looks like as long as I'm happy." She shrugged and the straps of her bikini top fell off her shoulders. "He'll get over the money thing, but he was real upset when he seen your bill."

"He had signed off on everything. Why was he surprised?" Sharon puzzled.

"Oh, he probably never really looked at what we showed him. He's a very busy man. He's not mad at you. He just told me I couldn't spend any more on the house."

"I see. Please let him know he received value for every penny he spent. Good taste often costs more than we expect." Sharon tried to smile.

"How much longer will you be? I'd like to take a swim." Ava tossed her hair back to show off her very large diamond earrings.

"Please go ahead. I'll only be here a few more minutes." Sharon picked up the clipboard she was using and started to walk out of the room when she noticed a wrinkle in the wallpaper. "I need to check the wallpaper on the other end of the room, then I'll be on my way." She watched the young woman walk to the patio and wondered, not for the first time, what kind of life Ava lived in this showpiece of a house.

170

*****

She returned the clipboard to her briefcase and started to leave the room when she heard Jose Moreno's voice coming from the patio. Since she knew she would never take another job from this couple, she decided to make one last attempt to be polite and tell the man she had enjoyed working on his house. But, she froze when she heard parts of the phone conversation he was having.

"What about that cop in LA? I told you what the boss lady wanted!" There was a pause before he exploded. "I told you to make sure he was removed. Now you tell me he's not dead."

Sharon gasped and began walking as fast as possible toward the front door. There was evil in this house and she wanted to get as far away from it as possible.

*****

Driving across the causeway, she gazed at the changing Miami skyline. Her beloved city was growing too fast and the streets seemed filled with hostility and fear. People walked quickly and no longer stopped to greet one other. The tourist havens were begging for customers and several had gone out of business.

Her heart longed for the way it had once been; the Miami where she always felt safe. From the time she was a young teenager, she could hop on the bus and go almost anywhere in the city without fear. The front door of the house where she grew up was only locked at night. She and her girlfriends could go to the mall or Bay Front Park and not wonder if they would get caught in the middle of a gun battle between rival drug factions. In her wildest dreams, she could never have imagined the horrendous events that had occurred in her guesthouse—Lawrence kidnapped and Joe Birdsong nearly beaten to death.

As she turned onto Biscayne Boulevard and headed south to Coconut Grove, anger overtook fear. She was angry at law enforcement and the customs officials who looked the other way. She was angry that one woman was running Miami into the ground for profit. She was angry with people like the Moreno's who flaunted their new wealth—wealth that she knew came from drugs and the devastation of so many lives. "Who will step up and stop this madness?" she shouted into the silence of her car.

Jose Moreno's words kept coming back to her. Did she overhear him correctly? If so, then he had ordered the murder of a policeman in Los Angeles and was angry that someone had botched the job. Could it be possible that he was talking about Paul Donovan? Was there a chance that Jocelyn's stepfather was not dead? She needed to talk to Carter. He would know what to do.

*****

"I overheard something today that I need to tell you about. I know you're going to think I'm crazy, but hear me out on this one."

"I won't think you're crazy. If something is bothering you just tell me." Carter said as he tried to eat his dinner.

"You know that couple I've told you about before. The ones who have given me such a hard time about the decorating I'm doing. Well, today I was signing off on the job when I overheard part of a telephone conversation that Mr. Moreno was having. Carter, he was furious with someone who was supposed to kill a Los Angeles policeman. Apparently, the job was botched and the man wasn't dead." She stopped to see if her husband would have some reaction. "Didn't you hear what I just said? I think this man ordered someone to kill Paul Donovan!"

"Sharon, that's a big assumption. First, the man wouldn't have that kind of conversation if he thought he could be overheard, and second, I think you're letting your imagination get the best of you. I know you don't like these people, but accusing someone of ordering a murder is a little bizarre, don't you think."

"I heard what I heard, Carter. Something about the Moreno's has always made me feel uneasy, but today those are the words I heard. Please call Roseanna and see what you can find out. Jocelyn thinks her stepfather is dead. Wouldn't it be wonderful news to tell her otherwise?"

"I'll think about it, Sharon. This is not the time to bother Roseanna."

She looked across the table at her husband and wondered if he could see her indignation. He was acting like what she said was insignificant. He was calmly eating his dinner and all she could think about was her anger and the events of the past few weeks. "This drug war is creeping into our house, into our lives. Doesn't that bother you?" Her words were thrown at him like darts.

"Calm down, honey, you know it bothers me. It's no longer out there somewhere and I feel like I have to look over my shoulder every minute." He sighed. "My daughter is caught up in this and I'm afraid for her. But, it is what it is, Sharon, and I don't see that there is much we can do to change it." He picked up the basket of bread and offered it to her. "If there was something I could do to make it go away, I would."

"I'm angry! And, I'm tired of being afraid." She threw her napkin on the table. "I'm tired of living with armed guards in front of our house!" She stood up and stomped to the kitchen. "Would you like a piece of cake?" she yelled at Carter.

"No, but I would like for you to calm down." He laughed. "I don't think I've ever seen you this angry. Thank God, you're not angry with me."

She walked back in the dining room and sat down in his lap. "I needed to vent and you got caught in my little tantrum. I'm sorry, but it's important that you call Roseanna." She looked at his face and felt her anger being dissipated by the love in his eyes.

"If it will make you feel better, I'll call her." He sighed. "This is not about the Moreno's and no matter what Roseanna tells me, you are not to go near that house again. After I talk to Roseanna, I'll call Sam and let him know what you suspect."

She snuggled closer to him. "I can't stay angry with you. Do you know that? I needed for you to hear me and it felt like you weren't taking me seriously. Thank you."

"I love you and I know how frightened you are. I wasn't laughing at your fear." He stroked her back and whispered. "I'm scared, too. But, somehow, we'll get through all this craziness."

"You're right." She could feel her body relaxing as he held her. "Keep reminding me and don't let me go for a few more minutes." She smiled. "Then, go make those calls."

She leaned against her husband and tried to get Jose Moreno's voice out of her head. Since the ordeal began she had worked hard to keep her fears under control, but this thing with the Moreno's was wearing away her attempts to cope with all she had witnessed.

It was the stuff that happened in the movies, not to her or anyone she knew. *How can one woman cause so much damage? How did Miami lose its way? When will it end?* They were questions without answers and all she could do at the moment was try to calm down and take care of her life. She didn't know how to fight this kind of war. She stood up and started toward the kitchen. But new thoughts rushed at her. If someone was trying to get to Lawrence by attacking the people Jocelyn loved, were she and Carter going to be next?

"Oh my God, Carter, do you think we're safe?"

Chapter Twenty-one

Lawrence

"Maddie, do you think DaSilva will work with us?" Lawrence tossed out the question as calmly as he could.

"I'm convinced he'll do something. It may not be what we want, but he'll do something." she said with conviction.

"Sam, what's your take on this? Do you agree?"

"Lawrence, the man is a mystery to me. But, I think I have to agree with Maddie on this one." Sam scratched his head. "Damned if I know how he'll do it, but I think he'll give it his best shot."

Looking from Sam back to Maddie, he decided they made a good team. He knew they had done all they could to convince the wealthy Brazilian to intervene. "If DaSilva has some connection to the Emperitza or the cartel, he certainly won't risk showing his hand. My guess is his help will come in a very unexpected way. Something that can never be traced back to him."

Lawrence leaned forward in his chair and continued to analyze the situation. They might have placed DaSilva in a compromising and dangerous situation. How would he react if the tables were turned and DaSilva had asked for his help?

He knew he would start with his contacts within the cartel. His questions would have to be carefully phrased in order to obtain information he could use. He couldn't ask direct questions about the Emperitza. All he could do was engage his contacts in a conversation and then listen carefully. If he was lucky he might be able to link together something that would show him where she might be vulnerable.

"Hey, Lawrence," Maddie called. "You seem a million miles away. What's going on in that head of yours?"

"Process, my dear. I'm thinking, process." He sat back. "I know a few things about this woman. She ran a very successful drug distribution business in New York before she was indicted. She may have even served some prison time before a technicality set her free. There was a period of time when she was off the radar of the FBI and then she was discovered in Miami.

"She's wicked. I understand she did her own killing before she gained the power to have it done for her. She's supposedly got a stable of trigger-happy henchmen to do her bidding. And, she has made most of them very wealthy. Apparently, she spares no expense with those who please her and turns lethal on those who don't. There is no way to estimate an exact figure, but the last information I had showed she brings about $80 million dollars of cocaine into the country every month. Most of it comes in through Miami." He paused for effect.

"Wait until you read my new book. I think you'll be shocked at the sophistication of her operation and the extent of the corruption in Dade County. She has myriad ways to control her business and she's good at it. There's no doubt in anyone's mind about who's running the show in south Florida. She's got ties in the Bahamas, Panama, and Mexico. As well as a direct link to her native Columbia." He sighed and then grinned at Maddie and Sam. "I'm really surprised she didn't have me killed."

"I thought the feds were cracking down all over the country? How does she keep slipping through the crack?" Sam questioned. "How did she get so organized?"

"Sam, people follow the money. She's made it almost impossible for anyone to say no to the amounts of money she promises. Look around you, my friend. How do you think all those new high rises are being financed? The banks can't handle the amount of money people want to deposit, so it's going into real estate. All of a sudden, this has become one of the richest areas in the world. Miami has turned into a playground for the nouveaux riches. We've gone from a city of Chevrolets and Fords to one of Ferraris and Mercedes."

"You're right. I see it everywhere I look." Maddie stumbled over the words.

"What's the matter, Maddie?" Lawrence looked with concern at the young woman.

"It's nothing, really. I just started thinking about all my business acquaintances who seem to have struck it rich. It makes me wonder." She smiled at Lawrence and changed the subject. "Sam, what do you want me to do next?"

"Maddie, if you're talking about Eduardo DaSilva, all we can do is sit and wait." Sam stood up and motioned to her. "I think we need to go and let Lawrence rest."

"Young man, if I weren't so tired, I'd argue with you on that one." Lawrence laughed. "But this ordeal has taken some of the wind out of my sails."

"As soon as we know anything, we'll let you know. In the meantime, I'll walk Maddie to her car and check a few things with Sharon McDeal. I won't be gone long." Sam rested his hand on Lawrence's shoulder. "You rest and then I'll take you on in a new chess match. You've beaten me the last two matches, but today I feel lucky."

*****

It was an hour before Sam walked back into the guesthouse and took a seat in the living room. "Is everything all right?" Lawrence asked. "You were gone longer than I thought you would be."

"Sharon overheard a conversation today that upset her and I spent a few minutes trying to reassure her that she and Carter are safe. It may turn out to be nothing, but I made a call to Tom West to check out a name. We'll see what comes of it."

"Can you be any more mysterious, Sam?" There was a hint of sarcasm in Lawrence's voice.

"I'm sorry. Sharon thinks she overheard one of her client's accusing someone of botching a policeman's murder in LA. Carter and I thought she was overreacting. But Carter made a call to California and found out that Jocelyn's stepfather is going to live.

177

He's still in ICU, but the doctors are fairly certain he's going to survive."

"That's great news. But, it's concerning that this client of Sharon's may know his conversation was overheard. Can you tell me who the client is?"

"His name is Jose Moreno. He and his wife bought a mega-house on the beachside and Sharon has been doing all the renovations. She's had her doubts about them from the beginning, but this conversation frightened her, particularly after we found out that Paul Donovan was still alive."

"She's not planning on returning to their house, is she?"

"She's finished with the work, so I don't think there's any reason for her to go back there. Like I said, we've talked to Tom about it." Sam's facial expression and voice changed as he continued. "Tom also told me some bad news. I don't think it's related to your situation, but we'll keep tabs on the development."

"What in the world, Sam? You look like you've lost your best friend."

"Not exactly. But, this news is going to impact some people I care about." He stood up and walked to where Lawrence was seated before he spoke again. "This morning Miami-Dade PD found Alli Anderson's body on the dock at MarGrove."

"My God, man. What happened?"

"They don't have a lot of details, yet. And, nothing has been released to the media. But, she was found on the dock in what they think maybe an accidental overdose. The mystery is why MarGrove? It's been years since her mother owned that place."

"I had heard rumors that Alli was quite the party girl. But this doesn't add up." Lawrence frowned. "Anything else unusual about this?"

"God, I hate to think about how this is going to hit Michael. He's going to be devastated when he hears all the facts." He turned and crossed the room. "Lawrence, she was nude and apparently her body had been abused pretty badly. All the worst signs—bruises, bites, cigarette burns." Running his hands through his hair, he closed his eyes. "Even from an early age, she always seemed to be pushing the limits. But, the kid had talent." He stopped and looked over at Lawrence. "I could tell you some wild stories about her, but, damn, she didn't deserve to die like this." There was an aching sadness in Sam's voice.

"My friend, I'll be all right here. You go to Margo and Michael. They'll need your support."

"Sorry, Lawrence, but I can't walk out of here and leave you alone. I've called Clair, and she and Jocelyn will be here soon. I've also called Maddie and she's coming back over. They'll stay with you while I'm gone," he explained. "You're right. I do need to see Margo and Michael. I'm stopping to pick up Lara and I asked her to call Lulu Sarsyn. You remember her, don't you? She's Margo's psychiatrist."

"You've taken care of everything. But, I'm getting very tired of having a babysitter."

"Just think, Lawrence, for several hours you'll be surrounded by all those lovely ladies." Sam tried for levity with his teasing note, but it wasn't working. "I've known Michael since we were kids and I traveled with Margo for almost twenty years. They're part of my family." His voice broke. "When I think back over my years as Margo's body guard, I thank God she didn't end up like her daughter. She had her demons, but somehow managed to find her way out of the darkness. I can't tell you how many times I thought we'd find her dead somewhere."

He paused as if he was searching for the right words. "There's a difference between them. Alli was reckless and always looking for the next high. She could never get enough. I've always been afraid for her because she never thought or cared about the consequences. Men, booze, drugs. It was all a game that she never thought she'd lose."

"She and her twin were direct opposites, weren't they?"

"Yeah, you could say that. Poor Sunni is going to be devastated. As different as they were, they were close. With show biz parents, they had to depend on each other. Michael and Margo were always gone, but I will say Michael tried to make time for them. Not Margo, she was an absentee mother from the beginning."

Lawrence's face began to redden and he clapped his hands together. "This is a homicide, Sam. No matter how reckless Alli was, someone did this to her. Some monster did this to that poor girl! Good God, that makes me angry."

"You're getting ahead of yourself on this one. Tom didn't say a word that leads me to believe this is anything but an accident."

As Sam turned to the window to watch for Jocelyn or Maddie's cars, Lawrence grabbed his arm. "I've just had another horrible thought, Sam. You don't think this is connected to me, do you?"

"Nothing surprises me anymore. But, I don't think so. Alli's family and you are acquaintances. If that woman is going to get to you, she'll pick a more direct target. Someone you care deeply about."

"I don't know about that theory, Sam. That woman feels so threatened by my book, I think she'd go after people who have nothing to do with me."

Sam seemed to consider that statement. Slowly he nodded. "She's paranoid and, she's trigger-happy. Apparently, her answer to every problem is a show of her power. Lawrence, she's crazy or she's using what she's selling, and that makes her very dangerous. We'll have to wait and see." Sam turned back to the window. . "The second team is arriving. Stay safe, my friend. I'll be back after I've talked to Margo and Michael."

*****

Lawrence listened to the sound of voices coming from the kitchen and wondered how the three women could keep up with each other. To his ears all the words, and occasional laughter, were running together in one strange symphony of noise. Every now and then, he could distinguish one voice from the others, but he couldn't hear the distinct sound of words being spoken. His mind wandered away and his thoughts hurled back to his problem like darts being thrown at a board. Was he making the right decision about publishing his book?

Was he doing it for the right reasons? Was he letting his ego place others in danger?

The questions kept coming, but he knew the answer would always be the same. The book wasn't about his ego. It was about a city that was being torn to pieces by drugs and corruption; it was about the murder rate and the destruction to human dignity caused by cocaine. It was a wake-up call that just might play a part in rescuing Miami and other cities that were being held hostage by the few who were gaining more wealth and power every day. If he backed down now; if he gave in to the demands of the Emperitza, then, he was guilty, too.

Over and over, he looked at the pieces of the puzzle. He examined everything he knew about the drug trade in Miami and he wondered what strategies needed to be put in place to win the on-going war. President and Mrs. Reagan had launched an offensive that was making some headway, but something more specific needed to be done if Miami was to survive.

He knew that the County Commission had petitioned the federal government for help, but so far there hadn't been a positive response. Drug violence was destroying tourism, the life-blood of the city, and it was making the streets unsafe for the residents. On one hand, Miami development was booming because of drug money. New buildings were being constructed everywhere, the ports were busy, and symbols of wealth were more evident than they had ever been. Opulent mansions, luxury condominiums, extravagant cars, over-sized yachts, furs and designer clothes were making the newly rich greedy for more. He wondered, *who needs a fur coat in a city where the temperature rarely dips below seventy degrees?*

Where was the key to solving the problem? What was he missing? Criminal kingpins had always existed and law enforcement had always been able to stop them. But, Miami's law enforcement was imploding. Cops and custom agents on the take had become the rule rather than the exception. He was becoming fatigued thinking about it and frustrated by his inability to make a difference. Yes, that was the reason for the book in the first place – he was hoping to make a difference.

Suddenly, he was startled from his thoughts by someone calling his name.

"Lawrence, we've made some lunch. Come and eat." Jocelyn invited. "It's not the Fontainebleau, but it looks edible." She joked as she helped him out of the chair. "You looked lost in thought. Anything you'd like to talk about?"

"No, my dear. I'm just an old man pondering life. I wasn't thinking about anything in particular."

It would be too hard to admit that his worries were getting the best of him.

Chapter Twenty-two

Margo

When Todd Madison appeared at their door, Margo knew he was bringing some kind of bad news. She had no idea that it was going to be the worst possible news they could receive. Had she known, she probably wouldn't have been so glad to see the young man. Her first thought was that he was going to confirm their suspicions about Alli's over indulgences and was going to ask for their help in getting her in a rehab treatment center. But, instead he told them that their beautiful, vibrant daughter was dead.

She hadn't been prepared to hear those words and for days afterward all she would remember was sitting in a stupor trying to comprehend what he had said. There had been no tears, no screams, no way for her to even acknowledge that her larger-than-life daughter had been found dead on the dock of their former house. She remembered Michael's voice asking all kinds of questions, but she couldn't remember any of the answers. And, then suddenly his arms were around her and she could hear his sobs.

"Michael, don't cry. Please don't cry." She held him tightly and felt his body spasm as he cried without embarrassment.

"God, why?" He whispered over and over. "Why did this happen to my little girl? I should have been able to help her."

"Michael, listen to me. You couldn't have stopped whatever happened." She looked over Michael's head at Todd and tried to read the look on the young man's face. "Todd, please forgive us."

She moved her arms from Michael and pushed his head so she could see his face. As kindly as she could she spoke softly to her husband. "Darling, we've got to know everything Todd has to tell us.

183

There will be time for tears after he's gone. Okay? I know it's hard, we've had a big shock."

Her husband's reaction surprised her. He was always the calm one who knew how to handle even the toughest situations. It saddened her to see the pain in his eyes, but it frightened her that she wasn't feeling anything.

Slowly, Michael crossed the room. "I'm sorry, Todd. This news has really shaken me." His voice broke and tears welled up in his eyes again. "You'll have to excuse me. I think I need to be alone."

Margo watched as her husband walked out on the balcony and sat down facing the ocean. "He's going to be all right, Todd. We need to give him some time to collect himself. If you don't mind, could you start at the beginning and tell me again what you said. I think I stopped listening once you told us that Alli's body had been found."

"They think it was an overdose, but they can't figure out how she got to MarGrove or why she would go there."

"You look terrible." It was the first time she had looked at the young man who had brought them the unthinkable news. His face was drawn and his usually neat appearance was disheveled. There were dark circles under his eyes and she could tell that he hadn't taken time to shave this morning. "I'm sorry, Todd. I didn't think how this must be affecting you."

"I was very fond of her, Margo, and I let her down." He leaned forward and put his head in his hands. "It was my job to protect her and I let her down. I wasn't there when she needed me."

The regret in Todd's voice was almost as painful to hear as Michael's tears were to see. These men had loved and cared for a daughter that she had ignored and barely knew. How sad that her emotions were for them and not for Alli. *Dear God, am I that shallow and uncaring that I have no tears for my own daughter? She tried to think of a way to comfort him.*

"I know that's what you think, Todd, but I hope you'll talk with Sam. He'll tell you this could very easily have been my story." Saying the words aloud made her shiver and she turned to look at Michael.

When she finally spoke there was anguish in every word she said. "When I think of how carelessly I treated Sam and Michael, I'm ashamed."

She turned back to Todd. "Please believe me. There was nothing you could have done. My daughter was in trouble a long time ago. Long before she went on the stage and long before she even met you. She thought she was larger than life and was always searching for something she didn't realize she already had. That lifestyle is always on the verge of spiraling out of control. And, believe me, Todd, I know what that downward spiral feels like." She was surprised by her words until she thought about how far she had come and how hard she had worked to get where she was today.

"We were trying to get her some help, but we were too late. We didn't realize how desperate she really was." She could tell by the look on his face that he wasn't convinced. "Do you know how many times I was in rehab before I finally decided I wanted to live a different life?"

Todd's voice was barely audible. "You're right, I know that. But right now I can't get past all the questions I have. I can't stop thinking about how many times I saw her wasted and did nothing about it." His shoulders dropped and his voice began to quiver. "I let her go to a party last night without me! Don't you understand what that means? I didn't do my job and now she's dead." He stood up and started for the door.

"Todd, wait! You can't leave like this. Please sit back down and talk to me. Somehow I've got to help you understand how little you could have done to stop Alli's destructive behavior."

"Maybe later, Margo. I've got to go. I've got to see if I can find some answers."

Before she could reach him, he had bolted out the door and was gone. *I've got to do something before everyone comes unglued.* The haunted look in the young man's eyes was frightening and she wondered if there was a chance that Todd might do something to harm himself. She whispered a prayer for his strength and comfort.

There were two people she knew who could help. First, she picked up the phone and dialed Lulu Sarsyn and asked her to come right away. Next, she called Sam and told him how concerned she was about Todd Madison.

She leaned back in the chair and took a deep breath. All she wanted to do was crawl in bed and forget that this day had ever happened. In her old life, she would have drowned her thoughts in alcohol and drugs. *I taught my daughter well. God, forgive me. I was the perfect role model for Alli's self-destruction.* In that moment of confession, she felt a stirring in her heart and knew there were tears very near the surface. But, she wasn't ready to cry. She wasn't ready to open herself to the grief. She wasn't ready to experience a mother's loss.

She shook her head and tried to clear her mind of those thoughts. Staying busy was the only way she was going to out-run the emotions that she didn't want to face. She would have to make a list of all the things that needed to be done in the coming days. It was then that she remembered she had another daughter who was going to be devastated by this horrible news. She thought about asking Michael to make the call, but then decided that he was too emotional. It was up to her to tell Sunni. She would have to dig deep within herself to find a way to be there to comfort Alli's twin. And, then she would have to tell Mrs. Davis and the rest of the family before they read it in the newspaper.

*****

Later that day, she sat in living room and tried to recall the events of the day to her psychiatrist. "Lulu, you've got to help me deal with all of this. Michael and Sunni have fallen apart and Mrs. Davis hasn't stopped crying since I told her the news. On top of all that, we've had police detectives here all morning asking us the same questions over and over." Margo tried to ignore her exhaustion, but it was obvious that she was drained. "It's overwhelming and I don't think it's going to stop anytime soon. There's so much to do. We've got to plan a funeral, deal with the media, and help with the investigation!"

"Margo, slow down and let's take it one step at a time. I didn't drive down here from Boca Raton to watch you get yourself all worked up for the wrong reasons." Lulu walked over and took Margo's hand. "My friend, we've got to talk about some of those feelings you're working so hard to hide. That young woman was your daughter. No matter the history between you, she was first and foremost your child. You've got to deal with that before you can attempt to deal with the other things."

"I never had a relationship with her and you know it. That's my fault and I take the blame for most of the things that went wrong in her life." She looked at Lulu for understanding. "I'm not ready to think about it right now. Can't you understand? Michael needs me to be strong and Sunni will be here this evening. How am I going to be here for them if I'm busy beating up on myself for neglecting Alli?" She pushed Lulu's hand away and started to pace up and down the length of the room. "How do I pretend that I'm the grieving mother when I didn't take time to be her mother?"

"Sit down, Margo. You're wearing me out with this craziness."

"Lulu, you are the most unsympathetic person I've ever met."

"You don't believe that for one second and you also know that I'm not going to let you get away with any of your high drama. Sit down and let's get to work. You called me to help you and that's what I'm going to do." Lulu's command startled Margo and she stopped walking. "Good, you've stopped trying to walk away. Now come over here and quiet yourself. I want you to tell me what's going on inside that head of yours instead of trying to make me feel sorry for you because you were a lousy mother."

After Margo had taken a seat, Lulu continued. "You're scared that the adoring fans are not going to see you acting like a distraught parent and from all I've heard in the last few minutes, you called me here to teach you how to pull it off."

"That's not fair! I need you to help me through this difficult time, that's all! My daughter is dead. How do you want me to act?"

"I don't want you to act, Margo. I want you to feel." There was no softness in Lulu's voice. "If you feel angry that this has happened, it's all right. If you don't feel sad, that's all right, too. But, you've got to feel what's happening in this moment, not all that claptrap about the past. There were times when you hated your daughter and times when you didn't want her to be in your life. But, two days ago you called me to try and get Alli some help. Why? Isn't it because somewhere deep inside you she meant something to you? Go to that place, Margo. Go to that place where Alli Anderson meant something to you."

At first she sat and stared with eyes that didn't want to see. She didn't want to hear Lulu's words and she certainly didn't want to allow her own feelings to bubble to the surface. Then slowly, she began to feel her shoulders relax and the tautness in her face began to loosen. The first tears to run down her cheeks felt alien and she hurriedly brushed them away. But they were coming faster now and her hands couldn't keep up with them. Tears fell in her lap and ran down her neck. There were no sobs, just silent tears filled with regret, and she was helpless to stop the flow.

Lulu sat quietly and let her cry.

With tears streaming down her cheeks, Margo raised her head and whispered, "I never sang her a lullaby. She was my baby and I never sang her a lullaby."

Chapter Twenty-three

Sam

"Margo, you know I'm here to help. Whatever you need, Lara and I will be around to give you support, to run errands, to help with anything. How's Michael?"

"He's not good, Sam. This has pulled the rug out from under him and he's having a hard time dealing with his emotions. He blames himself for not getting her help earlier and he is beating himself up for even letting her get into the crazy music business." Margo pushed a strand of hair out of her eyes. "I've never seen him like this. We've got to make plans and I can't get him to even talk about it."

"Let her manager and agent take care of the media circus. You and Michael concentrate on taking care of yourselves and Sunni. When will she be here from New York? Do you need for me to make arrangements for someone to meet her?"

"She'll be here this evening. Thanks, Sam, but I've made arrangements with our driver. He'll pick her up at the airport and bring her to the condo. She's as bad as Michael. I couldn't get her to stop crying when we were on the phone. The only thing I know to do for both of them is have Lulu come and be with them."

"What about you, Margo? You seem too calm. Are you really all right?"

"You know that my relationship with Alli was very strained. She never forgave me for neglecting her and she wouldn't let me back in her life after I realized the horrible mistakes I had made as a mother. She didn't want me in her life on a personal or professional level. As late as yesterday, she pushed me away. We had one of our famous shouting matches yesterday morning and she made it clear that she wasn't in need of a mother. She was hateful, but I deserved everything she said. It will take me some time to put it together in my head and heart. I know my grief will sneak up on me and I've already talked to Lulu. She helped me get to a place where I could cry and that seems to have helped. With everyone around me falling apart, I have to be calm."

He walked over and gave her a hug. "It doesn't get any easier, does it? Hang in there, Margo. We've weathered a lot of storms over the years, and you'll get through this one, too. I'm here if you need me."

*****

After an hour with the Andersons, Sam was exhausted. The pallor of grief was hanging heavy and Michael was so upset that Lulu had given him something to help him sleep for a couple of hours. Even though Sam was used to crisis situations, the emotions of his friends had touched him deeply. As he and Lara walked to the car, he suddenly stopped and pulled her close to him.

"I need a hug. This has been one of the hardest days of my life. I know it's the strain of everything that's going on, but seeing Michael's pain was tough."

"I know. Alli was too young, honey. It always hits us the hardest when someone young dies. That's not the natural order of things and it's going to take time for all of us to process this. To make it harder, Alli's death comes with so many regrets; so many things left unsaid and unresolved. Lulu will have her hands full dealing with Margo and Michael. And, what about poor Sunni? I can only imagine what she's going through."

"Maybe you need to see what you can do to help her. She trusts you."

"I'll call her this evening and see if we can meet for lunch tomorrow." Lara sighed. "I feel like I woke up in the middle of a very bad soap opera. Any chance you're coming home with me or do you have to go back to Lawrence's?"

"I would love to come home, but with things happening like they are it may be days before I get to come home. You'll be all right, won't you?"

"Sure. But I can wish, can't I?"

After he dropped Lara off at their house, he tried to map out in his mind all the events of the past few weeks. Each thing taken by itself was a problem, but when looked at as a whole was reaching crisis level. For the next few days they would have to be extra vigilant and his concern for Jocelyn and her family was growing. Lawrence was not going to give in to the demands and the Emperitza would surely begin applying more pressure. His job kept getting more complicated.

He used his remote to open the gate and drove down the driveway to the guesthouse. Sitting in the car, he glanced around at the peaceful scene. The gardens were beautiful and both the main house and guesthouse looked serene. To a casual observer, this would look like Eden. But behind the door of each house, there were people whose lives might be in real danger and they were depending on him to keep them safe.

*****

"You're not going to like my new plan" Sam said as he looked at Jocelyn and Lawrence. "But for the next few days we've got to tighten up security. Jocelyn, call in sick and let your boss know you'll be out the rest of the week. If you need groceries or anything, you'll have to call Lara. She'll handle any errands on your list. I know it's an inconvenience, but this is the way it will be until you hear differently from me. Claire told me you and Ben sort of called it quits, so I expect your only visitors will be your dad or Sharon. Right?"

"What's happened that I don't know about? And, what about Lawrence?"

"He's under the same rules. I think it's best to take some extra precautions. In the morning another security person will be added at your place, Jocelyn."

"What? This is too much, Sam. Isn't Claire enough? And, where am I going to sleep another person?" Jocelyn looked exasperated. "Until now I haven't been too worried about my safety, but you're scaring me."

"If there was another way to handle all this, I'd do it. The only thing I can do to make sure you're safe is to confine you and add extra people around you. It won't be for long." Sam looked around the room at the faces looking back at him.

"If someone else is moving to my apartment for a few days they'll want some privacy. I only have two bedrooms and two baths. Claire and I have pretty much filled up my whole place."

"It's going to get a little more crowded. I'm positive you'll manage." He ignored her complaints. "Claire, I'm sending over Patsy Sharp. I think you've worked with her before. She's on special assignment from Miami Dade PD and will be with you as long as we need her."

"Jocelyn, Patsy's a great gal. We'll do fine. She and I can work it out so we leave you alone most of the time." said Claire. "We can divide the time so one of us is sleeping while the other is on duty. It'll work out."

"Claire, I don't know what I'm expecting to happen. All I know is my gut is telling me to double up security on Jocelyn and Lawrence."

"Sam, we'll be fine. What have you got on the perimeter of Jocelyn's building?" Claire asked.

"The doorman has a list of who can come and go and Miami Dade has two squad cars making rounds. One call to Tom West and he'll have an army descending on the building. Call him first, then call me." Turning back to Jocelyn, he tried to reassure her. "We've got you covered with people who know how to keep you safe. Hopefully it's only going to be for a couple of days."

"I'm sorry I'm complaining. I know everything you're doing is for me and I'll try hard not to be a grouch. Claire and I have managed well, and I know Patsy will fit in fine."

"Good. Lawrence will be getting extra coverage, too." Sam stopped and looked at the perplexed faces of Jocelyn, Claire and Maddie. "Something has happened that may be totally unrelated to our situation, but I've got to make sure you all are protected. Jocelyn, I'm doubling up the protection on this entire property. Even your dad and Sharon will be covered."

"What haven't you told us, Sam?" Maddie asked.

"It'll be all over the news tomorrow and that may be the reason I'm feeling overly protective. This morning they found Alli Anderson's body on the dock at MarGrove. An apparent drug overdose, but they'll know more when they get the medical examiner's report."

"Oh, Sam. That's awful. Her family must be devastated." Jocelyn walked over to the door where Sam was standing. "Surely you don't think this has anything to do with Lawrence! Is that the reason we're getting double security?"

"I don't think there's a connection, but I'm not taking any chances. Alli's life was a mess before the book thing started and she has no direct link to Lawrence. I think whatever happened to her was an accident."

"I know how close you are to her family, Sam. This has to be hard on you." Jocelyn's voice was tender and caring. "Is the funeral going to be in Miami? Is there anything I can do?"

"Thanks, Jocelyn. I'm okay but Michael and Sunni have fallen apart. Margo is holding the family together and trying to make some sense out of this. There's so much to be considered before arrangements can be made for a funeral. This will be a media field-day event before it's over."

"Please, tell the family how sorry I am. What a shame this had to happen now. Margo was just beginning to develop a relationship with her girls." said Claire and the others in the room echoed her sentiments. "Jocelyn, why don't we head back to your place before it gets dark? Sam's got things under control here."

Claire and Jocelyn said their good-byes and walked with Sam to the door. "Are they sure it was an overdose, Sam? I know that girl was wild, but for this to happen at this time seems too coincidental."

"I've got my own suspicions, Claire. But, I don't think her death is connected in any way to what's happening to Lawrence."

"I feel sorry for the sister. Those two girls were so close. Well, goodnight, Sam. I look forward to working with Patsy. And, you can give Mr. Fitz my word that we won't let anything happen to Jocelyn."

"Sam, thanks for including my folks in your new plan. Daddy will balk, but I know Sharon will rest easier. She's feeling the stress." Jocelyn gave Sam a hug and followed Claire to the car.

When Sam had closed the door, Maddie began her interrogation. "Okay, mister. What's really going on that has caused you to add extra security?"

"Maddie, I feel like the Emperitza is about to close in on all of us. You've been seen coming and going at this house, so you better look over your shoulder, too. What do you know about Jeff Cannon?"

"He's a player, Sam. He has money, likes expensive things and beautiful women, and doesn't socialize much with people like me. His idea of fun usually costs more than my yearly salary."

"Did he inherit his money?"

"I don't think so. When I first met him, he drove a VW and lived in a small apartment in the Grove. He must have developed a client list with big bucks."

"I'll look into it. Is he the one that's bringing in the money to the law firm?"

"Both he and Eric are moving up the financial ladder. I think that's part of what's causing the rift between Eric and Elena. You know they're getting a divorce?"

"It's none of my business, but I want you to be careful. I know Eric is a friend of yours."

"I hear you." Maddie laughed. "You are a funny man, Sam. Mister tough-guy with a big heart. Thanks for caring."

Chapter Twenty-four

Lawrence

"How do you think this is connected to me, Sam? I've already told you this isn't an accident." Lawrence had listened to Sam and Todd discussing the death of Alli Anderson and continued to be convinced that it wasn't a drug overdose.

"Alli was a victim of the drug business. She had easy access to anything she wanted and she had the money to buy it. She was heavy into alcohol long before she became a star and it probably progressed rapidly after she became a headliner. Her parents came back to Miami from the islands just this past week to see if they couldn't get her some help. She's the "Miami" story that you've built your latest book about—excess, grand scale pleasure-seeking, and thinking that the worst only happens to the other guy. No, Lawrence, I don't think there is any connection between what's happening to you and Alli's death." Sam replied.

"It doesn't add up that she would be at MarGrove. Todd, where was she going when you left her last night?" Lawrence wanted answers as he tried to make sense of the events that kept unfolding.

"She did that big charity event at the Jackie Gleason Theater and then some big-shot lawyer was throwing a party for the performers and invited guests. She was in no shape to go to a party and I tried to convince her to go back to her condo. But she wouldn't listen. The driver said he took her to the party and waited for her but she never came out of the house. He checked at 6:00 this morning and was told she left the party with somebody around 3:00am. But, he said from where he was parked, he would have seen her leave."

"The driver has given a statement to the police that she never came out the front door." Sam added.

"Who owns the estate, Todd?" Lawrence asked.

"It belongs to Jeff Cannon."

"The same Jeff Cannon who is partners with Elena and Eric?" Lawrence was surprised.

"The same." Replied Sam. "My question is how did he finance that house and that kind of party? I know the law firm has been growing and Maddie's hinted that Jeff and Eric seem to be making good money, but she can't figure out how Jeff went from an apartment in Coconut Grove to an estate on the Inter-Coastal. Apparently he paid several million for that estate and all the trimmings."

"What do the police have so far?"

"Right now they're treating this as an accidental overdose. They're waiting for the coroner's statement and the toxicology reports. I know they've had crime scene investigators at both places looking for clues, but they haven't declared MarGrove or Cannon's house a crime scene."

"We've got a troubled mega-star at a private party. We know she'd been drinking and probably doing drugs before she arrived at Cannon's gala. And, we know she was found dead on a dock that was once owned by her mother. We also know the two locations are miles apart, separated by a bay." Lawrence turned from making notes and pointed his finger at Todd. "And, why was she at the party without a bodyguard?"

"I've been on the verge of quitting the job for months and last night was the last straw. I know I wasn't very professional about it, Lawrence. But, I'd had enough and in a moment of anger I left her. The driver dropped me off on a corner somewhere off Collins Avenue and she went to the party on her own. I caught a cab and went home. She called my bluff on it this time."

"Any witnesses to what you're telling me, Todd?"

"What do you mean? I can call the cab company and have them verify that they took a fare to my address around midnight. But other than that, I don't know that anyone could corroborate my story." Todd frowned. "Wait a minute! Do you think I had something to do with this?"

"It doesn't matter what I think. But you better prepare yourself for an inquiry. And, once this hits the papers there will be bedlam in Miami! She had millions of fans who will want to know where her bodyguard was and why he left her alone."

"Lawrence is right, Todd. You're going to be scrutinized and questioned by the media, the fans, and the authorities. We need to make some plans for your protection."

Todd was taken off-guard. "Are you serious, Sam?"

"The minute you left law enforcement and began working for Alli, your life was no longer your own. I know you've encountered the dark side of being connected to a celebrity, but I think you're in for a media frenzy like you've never imagined. Unless you've got other plans, why don't you take over for me with Lawrence and stay here for a couple of days. We've got enough guard power around this house to waylay the most insistent reporter or photographer."

Todd stammered. "I think you both are going overboard with this. But, it will give me something to think about beside Alli and the role I might have played in her death."

"I was her mother's bodyguard through some dark times and I know from experience there was nothing I could have done to change the things Margo did. I could talk her out of some things, but when it came to men, booze and drugs, she was on the same destructive path her daughter was on. Luckily, Margo got a scare before her addictions got the best of her or she would have been the one on that dock."

"The two of you have had the worst jobs imaginable." Lawrence sighed. "I thought being an FBI agent was dangerous, but I never had to deal with the kind of women you were duty-bound to protect. Todd, whenever you have your bag packed, I'll be looking for you to become my next roommate. I know Sam's lovely wife will be glad to have him home for a few nights."

*****

When Maddie knocked on the door several hours later, it surprised Lawrence to hear her say that Eduardo DaSilva wanted to talk to him.

"Of course, Maddie. I'll be glad to meet with him. But, whatever does he want to discuss? Do you have any idea?"

"He needs to tell you something and he wouldn't even begin to discuss it with me. All I know is he wants me to clear it for the two of you to meet later this evening. He'll have a car pick you up and he doesn't want anyone else to go along for the ride. He'll call me back later this afternoon to find out how we can make this work."

"Call Sam and get it cleared. If DaSilva has something to tell me, it's got to be urgent and important. I wouldn't miss this meeting."

"That man is used to having people do what he says." Maddie laughed. "That's what I like about him. He takes command, he's smart and he's got some incredible connections. Somehow Sam and I will make this happen."

She turned to Todd. "This is going to take a team. Put your thinking cap on and help us come up with some way to get DaSilva and Lawrence to the same place at the same time."

"I'll call Sam and have him get in touch with Tom West. You're right when you say this will take a team." Todd walked out of the room to use the phone.

"Whatever is motivating DaSilva has nothing to do with me, Maddie. Remember, he lost two grandsons because of this drug madness. I think he's been waiting for the right opportunity to make his own statement to the Emperitza."

"I guess you're right. But my woman's intuition tells me there is more to this story and I'd like to know what his connection is to that crazy woman."

"The odds are against you ever knowing the answer to that, my dear. There are some things that gentlemen never tell and my guess is Eduardo DaSilva is first and foremost a gentleman."

*****

198

The group took seats around Lawrence's kitchen table and tried to map out a workable plan before DaSilva called back. They tossed ideas back and forth, but someone always found a flaw in what was being suggested.

"Do you guys really trust this DaSilva?" asked Tom West. "Are you willing to just turn Lawrence over to him?"

"We have every reason to believe that he's helping us. We have a history with him and he has a very painful history with the Emperitza. Several years ago, she was behind a tragedy that cost him the life of one of his grandsons and she was indirectly responsible for his other grandson's incarceration. Information he provided at that time saved the short life of Alli Anderson." Lawrence explained. "Yes, Tom, I trust this man and will gladly meet with him."

"Sam, call Carter McDeal and asked him to come over here. I think I've just figured out a way for this to work," Tom offered.

From the time Sam called the main house until Carter walked in the door took less than five minutes. "Sit down, Carter. We need your help." Sam pointed to the empty chair at the table.

"Carter, would it be possible for us to get someone in the bus barn without detection?" asked Tom.

"That depends. Tell me what you're thinking and I'll let you know whether it'll work or not."

"We have to arrange a very secret meeting between Lawrence and another party. If we hid Lawrence in your car, could you get him to a place in the barn where he could have a private meeting?"

"That part would work. How would you get the other person there?" Carter looked perplexed.

"I want you to drive a bus and pick up this other person."

Carter's couldn't hide his surprise. "Wait a minute. You want me to drive a bus and bring the other person to the barn?"

"Yes. I think that would work. We choose a place that isn't too obvious for the pick-up, you turn on the "Out of Service" sign, and when the bus stops, our other person gets on. Then, you drive the bus back to the barn and get that person to the place you've designated for the meeting. Simple, right?"

The room was quiet as everyone around the table thought about the new idea.

"Our other person may feel too vulnerable with this plan. Nothing is in his control." Maddie suggested. "I know he trusts us, but the barn may be too confining."

"Okay, I see your point. What if Lawrence is on the bus when the pick-up is made and Carter drives them around while they talk? I'd be in an unmarked car following the bus and we'd choose a route where each of you could be staked out. I don't think this meeting will take long, so the route might only cover a few blocks. When the meeting is over, Carter takes the other person to a designated spot and drops him off."

Sam looked at Carter. "What about it? Do you think it's possible?"

"You work out the particulars and I'll drive the bus. I could stop anywhere along South River Drive and pick up a person without that person being seen. If we stay close to the bus barn, we'd attract less attention with an "Out of Service" bus."

"Timing is everything. Maddie, do you think you can get our person to agree to this plan?"

"All I can do is try."

*****

At nine o'clock, Carter pulled his car down the drive and stopped beside the guesthouse. The lights were off and he didn't get out. Within minutes Lawrence had crawled in the car and crouched down in the back seat. Slowly, the car moved away from the house and proceeded to take the route that Carter followed every day to the Miami Transit bus barn.

"It's all right if you're being followed, Carter," Lawrence said quietly from his position on the floor behind Carter. "When they see that you're going to work, they'll back off. Just do the same thing you'd do if you were going back to the office to finish some work."

Once they arrived at the bus barn, Carter pulled around to the back and parked next to the bus he had prepared for their adventure. The bus was parked in an area where Lawrence could board without being seen by the night crew of mechanics. It wasn't often that Carter drove a bus, but tonight he was prepared to tell the night guard several reasons why he'd been asked to take this particular bus out for a check ride. As soon as Lawrence was seated in the back of the bus, Carter started the drive that would take them to the pick-up place near one of the junkyards along the Miami River. He watched for the flashlight beam that would signal him to pull over.

Once he saw the light, he maneuvered the bus to the shoulder of the road and quickly opened the door for the mysterious passenger. The man climbed aboard and walked to the back of the bus. So far, all was proceeding according to plan. The roar of the diesel made it impossible for Carter to hear the conversation, so he turned all of his attention to making sure he followed the route that had been plotted out earlier that day.

*****

"Mr. Fitz, please let me speak quickly and without interruption because what I tell you cannot be repeated or acted upon. You have made a formidable enemy and she will not be easily dissuaded concerning your book.

"You have become a threat to the security of her operations in south Florida and she will stop at nothing to prevent its publication. I wouldn't be surprised at anything she might be planning for you; whether you comply with her wishes or not. However, you are just a small part of the problem. She has taken control of this city and the corruption she has engendered is more wide spread than you could imagine. She owns judges, lawyers, jurors, law enforcement, and the Port Authority. Her reach is extensive and her influence on the heartbeat of this city is massive. Alas, she has friends in very high places. Do you know that her operation takes in millions of dollars every month? Of course, you do. And you can guess that with that kind of profit, she is not about to let you hurt her business. The banks can't process or protect the money that flows here and now much of it is being used to build a new Miami.

"Take a look in any direction and you will see new office buildings and condos, new upscale housing developments, marinas filled with yachts that look like they belong to kings, and the streets are overflowing with luxury automobiles. People who couldn't afford the rent in the ghetto just five years ago own most of these things. They are loyal to the money and will fight by her side to protect the source. They do not want you to expose them and once she has that book stopped she will put out the word that you are fair game. Then you are worth nothing to her and a great deal to whomever can take you down."

The man stopped talking for a few seconds and Lawrence wondered if the conversation was over. So far, he had not heard anything that he didn't already know or suspect. But, he did as DaSilva requested and kept quiet. His eyes had adjusted to the darkness and he was able to see the body of the man seated to his right even though he could not see his face.

"I also have influence in high places, my friend, and a personal score to settle with this woman. Two things will be happening in the very near future. First, the president of your country has become extremely concerned about the problem in Miami and the endangerment that the drug trade has caused the citizens of this area. It will be announced very soon that a Drug Task Force headed by the Vice President has been formed for the sole purpose of breaking the back of drug trafficking in and out of south Florida. Federal troops and special agents will be deployed to this city to clean it up. If you listen to the news, you will hear that announcement within the next twenty-four hours. The plans for how this will be accomplished have been on the drawing board for several months, but in recent days the President has been shown the urgency of expediting this sooner rather than later.

"Second, I have information that leads me to believe that the state attorney has enough evidence and witnesses to put a case before the grand jury for the arrest of the Emperitza. She will be in custody before the week is out. But that does not mean that you are no longer in danger. In fact, once the task force is announced, she may move more quickly in your direction."

The darkness was swallowing up DaSilva's words as fast as he was speaking them and Lawrence found himself holding his breath and biting his tongue. He had questions to ask; he had issues to clarify. But he knew that his host would not give him more information than he was willing to reveal.

"Since your adversary has eyes and ears everywhere, she will know of these things before they become public. Do not drop your guard and you must continue to protect the young woman who is your assistant. The Emperitza will not let up on you until she is stopped by the plans that will be actively in place within days. I have told you all that I can and I expect that nothing you have heard will be repeated. I will inform Senhora Sonnett that I have honored her request and then I will be leaving your country before the morning. I am needed in Brazil."

There was a moment of hesitation before he continued. "What I have shared with you is vindication for the ruin that the Emperitza brought upon my family. I lost both of my grandsons because of this woman—one to death and one to prison. You see, my friend, that woman held a grudge against me for many years. She does not forgive or forget when she cannot have her way. I have done all I can to destroy her and the evil that surrounds her. God will take care of the rest."

Without another word, DaSilva stood up and started to walk toward the front of the bus.

"Senhor, I am honored by your assistance and deeply in your debt," Lawrence said. "Perhaps someday I will be able to show you my appreciation."

By the time DaSilva reached the front of the bus, Carter was pulling over to let him off. As the bus pulled away, Lawrence caught a glimpse of the car that had been waiting for DaSilva's return.

Carter pulled back into the bus barn and assured the guard that the bus was ready to begin its normal run the next day. As they passed under a light, Lawrence looked at his watch and saw they had been gone less than thirty minutes.

*****

As Carter parked the car next to the guesthouse, Lawrence sat up and saw that Maddie, Sam and Todd were waiting for him at his door.

"You got back to the house in a hurry. Are you sure you were out there covering me?" Lawrence joked.

"Well, what did he have to say?" Maddie ignored his question.

"I'm afraid you will have to wait and see. I'm not at liberty to disclose our conversation. Just know that the man has fulfilled our request. Not in the way we thought, but in a way that may result in the dismantling of drug trafficking in south Florida." He walked through the door and then turned back to the stunned faces.

"Maddie, he will be calling you shortly to tell you good-bye. He's returning to Brazil in the morning. Sam, for the next few days we must be extra vigilant. I need to know that Jocelyn has reinforced protection. Between you and Todd, I feel secure. But, I have concerns for her safety."

"I've already taken care of that. Is there anything else?"

"No. I have no doubt that you'll be able to handle any situation that comes up. Now if you will excuse me, I'm going to bed."

"Wait, you can't leave us hanging. There must be something you can tell us!" Maddie was emphatic in her demand for information. "Why are you so concerned about Jocelyn?"

Sam touched her arm. "Let him go, Maddie. He and Eduardo have worked something out and we'll have to trust that if we're needed they will let us know."

"I can't believe you aren't the least bit interested in what just happened!"

"Oh, Maddie! I'm more than interested. But Lawrence isn't going to budge on this, so I'm not going to spend any energy worrying about it. He looks like the cat that swallowed the canary. So, I'm assuming whatever is going to happen is to our benefit and will probably take us by surprise. Todd, since you're staying here tonight, I think I'll go on home and call Claire. How about you, Maddie? Isn't it time for you to be headed home? I don't want you to miss that call from DaSilva."

"Since you put it that way, I guess I'll be on my way. But I'm not happy about it. Perhaps Senhor DaSilva will be a little more forthcoming when he calls."

"Don't count on it, my friend. I think we'll have to just wait and see what happens. Todd, you lock up. I'll stop at the main house on my way out and thank Carter for his help."

*****

The ringing phone shattered the silence at three o'clock in the morning. Todd, who had fallen asleep on the couch, roused himself and ran to Lawrence's bedroom in time to hear part of the conversation.

"I don't understand what you're saying. Slow down so I can understand you." A wide-awake Lawrence was speaking to the caller. "When and where is this going to happen?"

He nodded to Todd and motioned for him to pick-up the phone in the hallway.

"Let me get this straight. You want all the notes and research files for my new book, you want all my sources named, and you want it today. Is that what you're saying?" He listened to the screaming voice on the other end of the line. "I've told you before, there are no names for me to give you. But, if you want my notes, you'll have to come and get them."

Todd walked back in the room and whispered, "Set up a meeting."

"Here's the deal. I'll have my assistant gather everything together today and we'll have a package ready for you by late afternoon. Come to my apartment on Biscayne Boulevard at five o'clock."

"If you want the notes, that's the deal. I will not bring anything to you! Take it or leave it. And, yes, I understand that we should be the only ones in the apartment when the courier arrives." Lawrence was finding it difficult to control his anger. "You want something that belongs to me, you'll have to come and get it." He hung up the phone before the screaming stopped.

"That woman is beyond crazy, Todd. We'll talk when the sun is up. I'm going back to sleep." He waved Todd away and turned over.

"Lawrence, if this meeting is going to take place, we've got to make some plans. That woman can't walk into your apartment building without us being prepared."

"Todd, I've got a plan and we'll put it in place at breakfast. Now go back to sleep."

*****

At the first light of dawn, Todd stopped tossing and turning and called Sam. "He got a phone call several hours ago from the Emperitza and she wants all his notes. He set up a meeting for this afternoon and I think you better get yourself over here." Todd listened.

"No, he wouldn't talk about it. As soon as he hung up the phone, he turned over and went back to sleep." He waited to hear Sam's next question.

"Sam, I was listening on the other line. That woman is a lunatic. There's no telling what she's going to do next. But, I'll be damned if Lawrence was going to let her disturb his sleep." He managed a tired smile at Sam's reply.

"Right, I'll see you in half an hour."

*****

"Sam, it's simple. I'll go over to the apartment this morning and gather up everything. I'll have Jocelyn meet me there and she can organize it and make copies. Then, I'll send her home. I don't want her there when the meeting happens. You and Todd can be with me when her courier arrives. I know she won't come herself. She'll know that she's walking into a trap. In fact, it wouldn't surprise me in the least if her courier arrives hours early to take us off guard." Lawrence sat in the kitchen with Todd and Sam calmly drinking a cup of coffee. "I told her the first time we spoke that I'd give her my notes. I can't imagine why she thinks having my notes is going to stop me from publishing the book."

"She doesn't want anything left after she's destroyed the book. She's convinced it won't be published." Sam listened to Lawrence's plan and shook his head. "I don't know if this is going to be as easy as you're suggesting. Let's think it through, one step at a time."

"I've got something the Emperitza wants and she knows she just can't send someone into my apartment to find it. It will take me some time to gather all the materials together and I'll need help. Jocelyn's the one who knows where everything is, not me."

"Before I left the house this morning, I got a call from Tom West. He wants me to be at a meeting at police headquarters at eight o'clock. He says something big is coming down and he needs for us to be aware of it."

"Looks like Eduardo DaSilva wasn't kidding. I'll be eager to hear what the good detective has to tell you. But, let's get back to our issue. Since you don't like my idea, how should we handle delivery of the notes?"

"You and Todd finish your breakfast and we'll talk after my meeting. Call Jocelyn and let her know that we might be in need of her help. I'll be back in an hour."

Jeanne Moon Farmer

Chapter Twenty-five

Sam

When Sam arrived at police headquarters, he was taken to a conference room where Detective West had assembled a team to discuss the possibility of new developments.

"I've asked you all to meet with me because there are rumblings that something big might be coming down the pike and we need to be prepared. My boss received word this morning that the President will be making some kind of announcement today regarding drug trafficking in south Florida. I know there've been rumors before that a federal task force might be formed, but until today I don't think any of us believed it would happen. If it's true, then Miami Dade PD will soon look like a different place. The chief knows that the corruption extends throughout this organization, but no one knows how deep it goes. Starting today, we're all on a 'need to know' basis about everything. We're most likely going to be playing second fiddle to agents from DEA and the FBI because we've got some cops who aren't clean. From now on, watch your back and check with me before you do anything. You're dismissed until I know anything further. Sam, I need to meet with you for a few minutes."

The gathering of men and women broke up and Sam followed the detective down the hall to a small office. Tom motioned for Sam to take a seat and shut the door behind them.

"I'm not sure what's about to happen but whatever's coming down is above our pay level. The chief told me his directive came from the President's office and announced a press conference for this afternoon. I know the FBI bureau chief in Miami received the same directive."

"This is going to be a busy afternoon," Sam muttered to himself and then looked up at Tom. "Lawrence and Emperitza had a middle middle-of-the night phone conversation. She is demanding all his notes and research and he agreed to give it to her at five o'clock this afternoon."

Tom groaned. "What is he thinking? Doesn't he realize that he's setting himself up?" He swiveled the chair around and looked out the window. "Okay, what's your take on this?"

"I think we should go for it. Do you know what time this press conference is supposed to take place? We've got to do this before the President's news is released. My hunch is the news is going to change things in this town and we want to make this deal before she gets wind of it."

"Sam, we can't allow Lawrence to be part of this. I know you don't think so, but he's liable to take matters into his own hands. Yes, I know he's retired FBI. But, this is too close and personal for him to be objective."

"I agree. That's why I think we let Jocelyn open the door to whomever is being sent to pick up the papers. You know as well as I do, the lady won't do this herself. She'll send one of her henchmen; probably someone who's pretty high up in her organization. As soon as he's inside, we take him in custody and she gets hit with a one-two punch. We'll have one of her top dogs and the President will shake her up with whatever he's got planned."

"This sounds like a good plan, but she's not going to send someone into a trap. We have to be ready for all-out war if her courier feels threatened. I'm surprised she didn't set fire to the building and be done with it." Tom picked up a paper on his desk and ran his fingers down a list of names. "Do you see this list? I confess, Sam. I don't know which people in this police department I can trust. We know there are huge leaks and she's got some major players in her pocket. Our whole justice system is compromised." He put the paper down before he spoke again. "We've got to have people we can trust."

"If that's the case, then let me handle it. I've got Todd Madison, Maddie Sonnett, Claire McGuire, Patsy Sharpe, and myself. If you come with me, I think we can pull it off. Keep the regular patrol on duty. She probably knows exactly when they make their rounds and will make sure her people know when it's safe to enter the building. I'll let the doorman know that Lawrence is expecting a guest at five o'clock so there won't be a scene in the lobby."

"What about Lawrence? How are you going to deal with him? She has someone watching that guesthouse day and night."

"Lawrence told the caller that he would get with his assistant and have a package ready for her to pick up. I think we take him to the apartment and find a place where we can move him within the building. If she doesn't see him leave, she'll think he's there. She's after him, not Jocelyn."

"So, who is on the 'need to know' list? You, the people you named, Jocelyn, Lawrence, and myself. I'll talk to the chief and then the two of us can figure out how we move people in and out of that building without arousing suspicion."

"If we make a big deal out of getting Lawrence and Jocelyn in the front door, that might cover the others going in the back and using the freight elevator. I'll check it out. The Emperitza knows that both Lawrence and Jocelyn have bodyguards, so Claire and I go in the front door. The rest of you use the back."

"That's too easy. We need a big diversion if we're going to get anyone in the building unnoticed. And, we've got to figure out how to get Lawrence out of the way." He laughed. "I just had a funny idea. What if we call the emergency operator around four o'clock and have an ambulance pick Lawrence up. Emperitza will see that and think the stress was too much for the old man. She'll know that Jocelyn is alone and that will work to her advantage. It'll make it easier for her man to get in and out without apprehension. While the ambulance and paramedics are making noise and causing a distraction, we send everyone in the back door."

"Whoa! I'll let you tell Lawrence about this new plan. There is no way he'll agree to leave Jocelyn in that apartment," said Sam.

"I'll make him see it my way. I'm not as concerned about him as I am Carter McDeal. He's going to go ballistic when he finds out we've used his daughter as our decoy!"

Sam nodded. "I agree, but I'll talk to him after it's over. On another issue, what have you got on the Alli Anderson overdose?"

"We're still waiting for the medical examiner, but there is some very suspicious evidence. One, the location of the body; two, there are some markings on her body that suggest she may have been in some kind of struggle; and three, we know there is evidence of recent sexual activity. Right now, my guess is she was involved with an over zealous lover who force-fed her too much booze and drugs. When things went south, he decided to dump her body. What better place than her old homestead? That means he had access to a boat. It was easy in and easy out. We're following up on everything. I've already talked to Todd Madison and he's in the clear if he can control his own conscience. He's pretty distraught about leaving the lady unprotected. We've got people going to interview Jeff Cannon about that party he threw last night. Do you know Cannon? I think he's an attorney."

"I know him through his partners, Elena Martinez and Eric Randall. But I've never said more than ten words to him. I know he's a high roller. But, Tom, there could easily have been more than a hundred people at that party. He probably didn't know half of them. Do we know who organized the benefit concert? That person will have the guest list for the party. Todd told me it was an invitation-only affair." Sam stood up to leave. "Your take on what happened sounds plausible. Keep me informed, won't you? Alli's folks are close friends of mine."

✳✳✳✳✳

Sam let out a long breath. "Lawrence, be reasonable. We've got to be able to get people into the apartment house without notice and we need a distraction. Tom isn't taking any chances with word leaking through his department, so he wants my team to be on the inside. The only other person at Miami Dade PD who will know about this is the chief. We can handle it, and you know Jocelyn's safety is a priority."

Sam and Lawrence had been over the same conversation several times, but Lawrence wasn't buying into the plan.

"I don't like it. That girl will be a sitting duck for those mobsters. I don't care about my safety, but nothing must happen to her." Lawrence slammed his hand down on the top of his desk to emphasize his words. "I knew you and Tom would never let me handle it my way."

"Your way would probably have you dead as soon as you handed over those notes. Our plan will work and it will give us one of her insiders. We'll have someone in custody who might slip up and give us some vital information before she can bail him out."

"I'll concede, but if my instincts tell me that something is amiss, I'll stop the whole operation. You understand that, don't you?"

"Of course I do and I wouldn't expect any less of you. Let's go over this one more time." As Sam outlined the plan, step by step, he watched Lawrence to be sure he was following along. They couldn't afford any mistakes. "As soon as the courier arrives at the door, Jocelyn will start a recorder so we get the whole thing on tape, and then she'll let the person inside. She's been given questions to ask that will give us information we need. Once the courier has the package in his hands, Claire will radio me and we'll make our move. Claire will make sure Jocelyn is not in harm's way and the three of us will enter the apartment."

"It sounds like you've got it covered. Where did you learn to think like this, Sam? I know you weren't in law enforcement."

"You forget that I'm a former Navy SEAL. This is the way I was taught to think through an operation. Once you learn it, I guess you never forget it."

"All right, but God help you if something goes wrong. You'll have me and Carter to deal with and I won't go easy on you."

Sam smiled. "Lawrence, nothing is going to go wrong! We'll have this over and done with in time for all of us to listen to the President's announcement."

*****

"Tom, we're set on our end. I've gone over the scenario with everyone and we're as ready as we're going to be. If you've got the perimeter set up then I'll see you in the freight elevator as soon as I've run the two blocks from where I'll get out of the ambulance."

The detective laughed. "Are you sure your legs can handle this, Sam? What are you doing these days to stay in shape?"

"My good man, I'll have you know I'm in training to run a marathon. Two blocks will be nothing. I'll have to pace myself because of Claire, but I think she's a runner, also. Don't worry about us. We won't even break a sweat."

"I'll see you at four forty-five at the back door of the apartment house. By the way, how did you get Lawrence to agree to this plan?"

"He saw the logic and agrees it will work. But he made it very clear my head will roll if anything happens to Jocelyn."

Chapter Twenty-six

Jocelyn

Everything seemed to be working as planned. The ambulance had just pulled away from the building, Claire had just gotten back to the apartment, and within a few minutes the rest of the team would be at their assigned stations. She glanced at the clock once more to make sure that she would be ready for the expected visitor, then opened the sliding glass door and stepped out on the balcony.

Postcard perfect—blue sky, fluffy white clouds, hot, balmy, and sandy beaches. It was the kind of day the Chamber of Commerce could use to lure thousands of tourists to Miami. Except the tourists were leery of coming near a city where drug wars and violence blocked out the beauty this kind of day offered.

Jocelyn leaned over the balcony and wondered at the paradox of Miami, the place she had called home since her birth twenty-seven years ago. Good and evil; beauty and ugliness; tranquility and travesty. It was all there and it was unnerving. She heard the traffic flow past on Biscayne Boulevard and watched in the distance as a speedboat pulled a skier across the bay. Could the beauty she looked at really mask the horrors she had been told existed? The horrors she read about every day in the news?

She closed her eyes and struggled to change her thoughts. She needed a diversion this afternoon. Her eyes were tired from working long hours on Lawrence's latest novel, and her nerves were jangled by the anticipation of a chiming doorbell. She took a breath of the salty air and tried to relax.

The trap had been set and she had agreed to be the decoy. It had seemed like a good idea at the time, but as reality hit, her bravado was fading. Any minute now the doorbell would ring and she would be face-to-face with the evil, the ugliness, the travesty. She would no longer be able to pretend it didn't exist.

She knew that Sam had her covered. She wasn't alone and she wasn't the one responsible for capturing the person who rang the bell. All she had to do was answer the door and invite a major player for one of the biggest drug cartels in this hemisphere to come inside. How hard could that be?

The ugly side of the paradox had to be stopped. Drugs were being openly shipped through the port, corrupt customs agents and police were turning a blind eye, and the rival cartels were staging unbridled warfare on the streets. Miami was a nightmare and she might be playing a small role in stopping it. All she had to do was open the door.

Lawrence had helped orchestrate the plans that she was part of and she believed with all her heart that he had made her safety a priority. If she knew who was going to be on the other side of the door, it would make it so much easier.

The sudden unwelcomed chime of the doorbell broke the quiet and, startled her in spite of all her thoughts. She took a deep breath and opened the door.

*****

"What a surprise," she gasped. "I wasn't expecting to see you." Jocelyn stood transfixed as she looked into the face of Jeff Cannon.

"Hello, Jocelyn. It's nice to see you again. I'm glad you seem to remember me. I'm Jeff Cannon. May I come in?"

"Ah, yes. Where are my manners?" She stammered. "Please, have a seat. If you're looking for Lawrence, he isn't here. Is there something I can do for you?" She was perplexed and not thinking clearly. Was this the person she was supposed to meet or was he here for some other reason? Her knees were shaking and she decided she needed to sit down.

"I'm here on behalf of a client. I was told that Mr. Fitz would have a package for me to pick up this afternoon at five o'clock. Why isn't he here?" Jeff walked around the room as though he was looking for something.

"An hour ago, he began having trouble breathing and had a pain in his chest. The paramedics just rushed him to the hospital. He asked me to wait for the person who was to pick-up the package. I can get it for you." Her hands began to shake and she wondered if he could see how nervous she was. "If you'll have a seat, I'll get it for you. It's in Lawrence's office. It's a rather large box, Mr. Cannon. There's so much information, we couldn't package it in anything smaller. It might be too heavy to carry if you have to walk very far." She was rambling, stalling for time so she could figure out what to do. "Just sit down and I'll bring it to you."

"Stay where you are, Jocelyn. I'll get it. Does that door lead to the office?" He was looking at the room where Claire was hidden.

"No, no! That's not the door." She jumped up and ran to block the door. "This is the spare bedroom. The office is over there beyond the dining room."

"Why so nervous, Jocelyn? Is there something behind that door you don't want me to see?"

"I'm sorry. I was just trying to point you in the direction where the office is located."

"Get out of my way! Who are you hiding in that room?" He grabbed her roughly and tried to move her out of the way.

"Let go of me." She shouted. "I don't know what you're talking about." As the words came out of her mouth the door opened and Claire stepped into the doorway with her gun drawn.

"Take your hands off of her!" Claire demanded.

"Who the hell are you?" Jeff's face contorted as he shouted and tightened his grip on Jocelyn. He yanked her in front of him like a shield.

"Now! Let go of her now!" Claire's voice was emphatic and threatening as she cocked the pistol and aimed it at him.

In a panic, Jeff launched forward and forcefully shoved Jocelyn into Claire. This sudden movement caught Claire off guard, causing her to fire the gun. As Jocelyn and Claire fell to the floor, he rushed to make his escape out of the apartment. As he reached for the doorknob, Sam flew through the door and struck him across the head with the butt of his gun. Jeff staggered and tried to regain his footing, but Sam grabbed him in a headlock and pulled his arms behind him. As the two men struggled, Tom kicked Jeff's feet out from under him. Sam and Jeff crashed to the floor where Jeff continued to scramble to free himself from Sam's hold.

"Don't move or I'll blow the top of your head off," shouted Todd. He ran into the room with his gun pointed directly at the heap of struggling men.

Tom moved out of Todd's line of fire and watched as Jeff realized the fight was over. He pulled Jeff up and away from Sam and quickly handcuffed him. Then, he shoved him against the wall and began reading him his rights.

Sam got to his feet and ran to where Claire was holding Jocelyn. At first he thought they were both unharmed, then he saw that Claire was trying to stop the flow of blood from Jocelyn's abdomen. "My God! Jocelyn's been shot. Get an ambulance here now. Claire, keep applying pressure!"

"It hurts, Sam." Jocelyn whispered. "It hurts so much."

"You'll be all right, Jocelyn. Just hold on. An ambulance is on the way." He grabbed a throw off the back of the couch and used it to help Claire apply pressure to the wound. "The bleeding is almost stopped. You'll be all right." He continued to apply pressure as he talked gently to Jocelyn.

Todd had already called the operator as Tom led Jeff toward the door of the apartment. "I'll be back as soon as I get this guy in the patrol car that's in the alley. My guys will take him downtown and book him." Both men were breathing hard and it looked like Jeff was limping.

"You can't book me on anything! I'm an attorney and all I was doing was visiting a friend. There isn't a charge you can find that will stick!" Jeff shouted as the detective pushed him out in the hallway.

Until they reached the elevator, everyone could hear Jeff shouting and railing against the police. "My friends will have me out of that place before your booking agent can write my name in the book. You're going to pay for this!"

Ignoring the chaos in the hallway, Todd rushed to help Sam. "How is she? She'll be all right, won't she?"

"I'm trying to keep her from going into shock. She's lost some blood, but I think I've pretty much got it stopped." He lowered his head close to her face. "How are you doing, Jocelyn? Talk to me."

"I feel funny, Sam."

"Try to keep talking to me, okay? Don't move. Just lie still until the paramedics get here. I don't think your wound is that serious even though it hurts. Just keep talking to me."

"What happened, Sam? What did I do wrong?" she whispered.

"You did everything right. Don't worry. Jeff Cannon has been arrested and you're going to be okay. That's the important thing."

Todd looked from the floor where Jocelyn was lying and noticed that Claire was as white as a ghost. "Claire, what do you need? How can I help?"

"I shot her, Todd. He pushed her into my gun hand and I shot her." Claire was visibly shaken and Todd hurried over to where she was leaning against the wall.

He touched her shoulder and tried to get her to look at him. "It was an accident. You couldn't have done anything differently. Come over here and sit down. I want the paramedics to take a look at you when they get here."

From a distance, they heard the sound of sirens and Sam prayed they would arrive in time. In all the confusion, no one remembered that the President was holding a press conference. In his press conference, he would make a landmark announcement to launch a federal war against the drug trade.

*****

Within minutes of arrival, the paramedics had lifted Jocelyn onto the gurney, had started an IV, and were working to get her blood pressure stabilized. One of the paramedics had checked on Clair and suggested she come with them to the hospital where the doctors could make sure she was not in shock.

"About an hour ago, you picked up an older man at this apartment. Do you remember which hospital you took him to?" Sam asked.

"Yeah, he's at Mercy Hospital. Unless someone has come to take him home, he's still there. It was a false alarm. He wasn't having a heart attack. The doctors think it was a panic attack." The paramedics had quickly put their equipment away and were headed out the door with Jocelyn. "We're taking her to the same hospital. Follow us."

"We'll be there in a few minutes. I have to call her parents and let them know what's happened. If Mr. Fitz is still in the ER when you get there, please tell him we're on our way."

For the first time since he had burst into the room, Sam leaned against the wall and closed his eyes. After he had taken a few deep breaths, he made the call to Carter.

"Meet us at the ER at Mercy. They're taking Jocelyn there. She's been shot, Carter. But she's going to be all right."

Chapter Twenty-seven

Carter

Carter held tightly to Sharon's hand as they sat in the waiting room at Mercy Hospital. Jocelyn had been rushed to surgery over an hour ago and all they could do was wait. He looked around the room at the worried faces—Sam and Lara, Todd, Claire, Lawrence—and wondered if it had been worth it for them to use his daughter to trap Jeff Cannon. Of all people, what could this upstanding attorney in the community possibly have to do with the drug cartel and that crazy woman?

Closing his eyes, he tried to stop all thoughts except those about his daughter: His sweet Jocelyn. He remembered the night she arrived in his life and the glow of love on his mother's face as she looked in the box that held the tiny baby. How blessed his life had been.

He had fallen in love with Jocelyn from the first moment he held her in his arms. She brought joy and laughter to their house, and she never failed to amaze him with her curiosity and intelligence.

He pictured them in the kitchen of their old house, Gracie teaching Jocelyn to bake cookies or talking to her about the everyday matters of life. And, when his mother died suddenly, it was his love for his daughter that had kept him going.

The years she had lived in the guesthouse had been some of the happiest in his life. Before she moved to her own apartment, he had looked forward to coming home from work to the two women he loved with all his heart. Yes, his daughter was a grown woman, no longer a child, but he could still feel her tugging on his hand, saying, "Daddy, tell me a story."

He was proud of the adult she had become. He loved to read her column in the Miami Herald and he smiled when he thought of the work she had done with Lawrence. His little girl was talented and kind, and yet, something unbelievable had happened to her and today she was fighting for her life.

Dear God, Please don't let me lose her now. Please don't let her die.

Sharon gently shook his arm and he opened his eyes just as the surgeon walked into the room. He tried to read the look on the doctor's face, but the man gave him no clues about what he had come to tell them. Carter jumped to his feet as he prayed for good news and the others in the room gathered around the doctor.

"Mr. McDeal, your daughter made it through the surgery and the outlook is positive for a complete recovery. Because the bullet was fired at close range, she did suffer some internal injuries that could not be repaired. I'm sad to tell you that a complete hysterectomy had to be performed in order for us to save her. I know what an impact that will have on her life. She is so young and I assume that one day she was hoping to have a child. But, we had no other option. There was other damage that we were able to repair that may prolong her recovery process. She lost a large amount of blood, but there must have been some quick thinking at the scene or her chances of survival would have been less than optimistic. I know this is too much information to take in at one time, but I thought you would want to know the full extent of what we had to do. I will be available to answer your questions whenever you're ready. Now, if you'll excuse me, I need to get back."

"When will we be able to see her?" Sharon asked.

"She'll be in the recovery room for several hours, but as soon as she is moved to a room, I will have someone come and get you."

As the doctor walked away, Carter remembered something he wanted to say. "Wait, doctor. I didn't thank you for saving my daughter's life. We're so grateful to you and the surgery team. Thank you."

The doctor turned and nodded his head at Carter before he continued down the hallway.

Everyone but Carter started talking at once and relief flooded the room like sunshine after a storm. Lawrence walked over and hugged Carter. "Thank God she'll be all right. This old man's heart couldn't have taken bad news."

Carter tried to find a response, but no words came. The tension in his body was still real as he fought off tears. Yes, his daughter would live, but when she learned she would never be a mother would they be able to console her?

He turned as Sharon opened her arms and pulled him into the warmth of her love. "It'll be okay, sweetheart. I know what you're thinking and I promise you it will be okay. We'll face tomorrow when it comes. Let it go for now and rejoice with us that our girl will have a future."

*****

He sat alone beside his daughter's bed. The others had either gone home or had headed to the cafeteria. He knew Sharon would bring him something and try to make him eat, but more time would have to pass before he would be able to swallow anything.

His mind wandered as he listened to the hum of the machines in the room and the voices of nurses talking in the hallway. The sounds of hospitals were always the same, mimicking the ebb and flow of life, promising and withdrawing and then, promising again .

Jocelyn looked pale, but peaceful, and he wished that look of peace could always be there. The drug war was exacting a terrible price from his daughter and he was angry with everyone involved, even his friends.

He wanted to strike out at Lawrence for writing his damn book and involving Jocelyn, and he wanted to hurt Sam and Claire and all the rest of them for not protecting her. He needed an outlet for those feelings before they got out of control. He grabbed the extra pillow at the end of the bed and began punching it with all his might. Every blow was propelled by his rage. He struck the pillow over and over until he finally hugged it to his chest as his body convulsed with sobs.

Chapter Twenty-eight

Sam

"I'm responsible for what happened to her and I can't get that out of my head." Sam was stretched out on the bed next to his wife. "I should never have let her be a part of this operation. She was an amateur and I expected her to act like a professional."

"You did the best you could. It was a risk, but everyone agreed it was a low risk. You couldn't have anticipated or prepared for what happened. You didn't know the man would shoot her." Lara had listened to Sam go over this for the past hour and she knew it would be hours more before he would let it go and get a few minutes of much needed sleep.

"That's just it, Lara. Jeff Cannon wasn't the one who pulled the trigger."

"What are you talking about?"

"Claire had pulled her gun on Cannon and he pushed Jocelyn into her with such force that the gun discharged. Claire pulled the trigger. That's what makes this worse."

Lara rose up on her elbow and looked at her husband. "You've got to be joking."

"I wish it was a joke, but I've got Jocelyn in the hospital, Claire is distraught, and the man we arrested is a prominent attorney who happens to be the partner of people we trusted. It's also possible that Jeff Cannon may have been the last person to see Alli alive."

"What are you talking about? Slow down and start over."

"The last thing we know is Alli went to a party at Cannon's estate. He'll be questioned about that while they have him in custody." Sam's mind raced from one incident to another faster than he could process it all. "Several times in the last month, Maddie has remarked about the wealth Eric Randall and Jeff Cannon had been enjoying, and unfortunately, we seem to have discovered the reason. If they're working with the Emperitza, there's no telling how deep their involvement goes in the drug business. You know, when Elena left Eric, I assumed it was because he might be having an affair with Maddie. But, maybe Elena knows more than we think about the activities and clients of that law firm."

"Do we know anyone who's leading a normal life? This is a tangled web if I've ever seen one." She sighed. "Is Maddie really having an affair with Eric? Somehow he doesn't seem to be her type and I'd never figure her to get involved with a married man."

"I think you're being a bit naïve. I don't know who is sleeping with whom, but I've had my suspicions about those two for quite some time. Anyway, I wouldn't be surprised if Eric wasn't called in for questioning. I'd hate to see Maddie tarnished by the company she keeps. You know I trust her, but I have some questions that she's going to have to answer, before I'm satisfied that she didn't know what was going on." He stopped talking as another thought hit him. "I just remembered something. Because of all the uproar this afternoon, we missed the President's press conference."

"This is too much to think about and we both need some sleep." Lara turned over and snuggled down in the covers. "Can we talk about this in the morning?"

"You go to sleep. I've got to see if I can find out what the President announced. I'm going to turn on the television and see what's happening. I'll come back to bed in a little while."

*****

"At a White House press conference this afternoon, President Reagan announced he has appointed Vice President George Bush to head the South Florida Task Force aimed at dismantling drug trafficking and organized crime in south Florida. The Task Force will utilize the resources of the federal government, including the FBI (Federal Bureau of Investigation), the DEA (Drug Enforcement

Administration), the IRS (Internal Revenue Service), the ATF (Bureau of Alcohol, Tobacco, and Fire- arms), Immigration and Naturalization Service, United States Marshal Services, the U.S. Customs Service, and the Coast Guard. In addition, the Department of Defense tracking and pursuit capability will be made available to assist local and state government agencies. The President said, 'This task force will allow us to mount an intensive and coordinated campaign against international and domestic drug trafficking and other organized criminal enterprises.' With the appointment of the Vice President, this operation is to be initiated immediately. Governor of Florida, Bob Graham, assured the President that the state government would cooperate with this joint effort and would assist in any way possible to stem the violence and crime that has infected his state."

*****

Sam was stunned and elated. The announcement represented real hope at last and might give Miami a fighting chance. The depth of the task force that would soon coordinate an effort to clean up the city was nothing short of a miracle. But, then again, he knew better than to underestimate the influence of Eduardo DaSilva, and he was convinced that DaSilva had played some role in bringing it to fruition. Lawrence had told him the city and state had asked for help in the past but the federal government had been slow to act until now. Surely, the timing for this announcement wasn't a coincidence. For whatever reason, Sam was glad to know that law enforcement in Miami would no longer be waging a war it didn't have the resources to win. With a smile on his face, he turned off the TV and returned to bed. There would be plenty to do in the morning.

*****

"Lawrence, when Tom told me the President was going to make an announcement, I'm sure he didn't think it would be something of this magnitude. Can you tell me now whether DaSilva had anything to do with this?" Sam knew before he asked the question that Lawrence would give him a vague answer, but he had to ask.

"Don't let your imagination get the best of you, Sam. Do you really think the man has that kind of influence?"

"We both know he does. But I understand your reluctance to give me a straight answer. This task force is so much better than we could've hoped for. The Emperitza and her henchmen have to be running scared this morning. First, her courier is arrested, and now the Feds are on their way to her door."

Lawrence smiled. "If this works as planned, the backbone of her operation will be broken. At least it will be broken in South Florida. But the Vice President has to stop the money source that is creating all the corruption. Once that's accomplished, the rest of the operation won't have a chance of surviving. The drug business needed the right players in order to build their infrastructure and they found people in all walks of life that they could buy. These people make sure nothing stands in their way. It will be interesting to watch how this unfolds and to see how many upstanding people will get caught in the web." Lawrence poured himself another cup of coffee. "Would either of you like more coffee?" He held out the coffee pot to Sam and Todd.

"No thanks. I need to run. I want to stop by the hospital before I go see Tom West. Then, I want to have a long talk with Maddie." Sam was anxious to be on his way.

"What do you think the Emperitza will do next, Sam?" Todd inquired.

"I've been wondering the same thing. My guess is she'll accelerate everything. She'll get the last drop of money out of her business and then try to get the hell out of the city. That means we've got to be ready for anything. Lawrence, the price on your head just went up and she'll want that book stopped immediately.

"Since we have a new situation, I'm going to make a switch. Claire will stay with the McDeals and I'll release Patsy from her assignment. Miami Dade has guards around the clock at the hospital with Jocelyn, so neither one of them is needed there."

"Why do you think it's necessary for Claire to be with Sharon and Carter?" Lawrence wanted to know.

"The Emperitza can't get to you through Jocelyn anymore, so who's the next in line? I've already talked to the McDeals and they know not to leave here without letting us know and without taking

Claire with them. Neither of them will be going to work for a few days and they'll be spending most of their time at the hospital." Sam drank the last of his coffee and got up to leave. "Anyway, Lawrence," Sam winked at him, "this move is for Claire's sake, she needs something to think about beside Jocelyn."

"So many innocent bystanders have gotten caught up in this mess. Carter had to call Roseanna last night to tell her about Jocelyn. That poor woman has a husband and a daughter in jeopardy because of my book. It hardly seems fair."

"Lawrence, the book was a catalyst, not a cause. All we can do is hope something good comes out of all this carnage."

*****

Sam sat in Tom West's office and listened to the latest rundown. "Once the Feds decided to make a move to help us, they haven't wasted time. I've already gotten word that agents are on their way to Miami. It feels like an old western movie where the Cavalry comes riding in to the rescue. The chief told me this morning that everyone is suspect and a full scale investigation of the police department has been ordered." Tom looked worried. "This is going to turn into a witch hunt before it's over, but it'll be worth it if we can ferret out the people who are on the take."

"For an undertaking as massive as this sounds, I hope the Feds are really sending all the help that's been promised." Sam wasn't convinced. "We don't need for that task force to take months to discuss our problem. We need action. On a more personal note, how do you think this is going to impact Lawrence?"

"Get ready for fireworks. My guess is that woman is mad as a hornet this morning and she's going to be looking for a punching bag. Your man may be one of her first targets."

*****

Sam was waiting for Maddie in a booth at the back of the deli down the street from her office. When he had called to set up a meeting with her, she told him she was rushed, but would meet him for quick lunch. As he looked at the menu, he tried to plan his approach. His questions were bound to set her on edge, and the last thing he wanted was for her to see him as the enemy and shut him out.

She slid into the booth and looked at him expectantly. "What's on your mind, my friend? I can't imagine you asked me to lunch because you enjoy my company."

"Hello to you, too. You're on the defensive and we haven't even ordered lunch."

"Sam, with everything that's happening, I know you want to ask me about my relationship with Eric. But that topic is off-limits."

"Maddie, what you're doing or not doing with Eric Randall is your business. I'm here because I don't want to see you get hurt. The cops have Jeff Cannon in custody and you know there will be questions about Eric, and Elena, too, for that matter. Somebody is going to add you into the mix sooner or later. If that law firm is in deep with the cartel, you don't want to be caught in the backlash."

Her shoulders sagged and a worried look crossed her face. "Sam, I haven't slept a wink since yesterday. I know Jeff saw me when they were taking him out of the building and he probably thinks I set him up." As Sam tried to interrupt her, she waved him off. "I know that's not rational thinking. But, Jeff doesn't know what Eric might have told me. I don't want to believe that Eric is mixed up in all of this, but too many things have happened in the last few months for it to be coincidental."

"Like what?"

"Too much money, too much drug use, and an influx of unsavory looking clients. Eric knows that I'm concerned because I've voiced it on several occasions. But, Sam, I promise you that all I have are suspicions. I don't have any hard, fast evidence."

"If you are seeing him, keep your eyes open and, for God's sake, take care of yourself. If this task force is a reality, you can bet that law firm is going to be scrutinized very carefully. And, that will include anyone who may have contact with it." He looked at the frown on her face and softened. "I'm not here to judge, Maddie. You've worked damned hard to get where you are—I just don't want to see you caught in the crossfire. If you say you don't know anything, I believe you."

*****

Later that afternoon, Sam sat in the living room of the guesthouse discussing the day's events with Todd and Lawrence. The headline of the Miami Herald screamed the question on everyone's mind, "How Many Cops Have Gone Bad?" and announced the federal task force that was headed to South Florida. The faces of Vice President George Bush and Governor Bob Graham were on the front page and interviews with them were on every newscast.

"When and where the sweep will begin is anyone's guess. But, my informant tells me it's already underway." Lawrence leaned forward as he talked. "This is the most exciting news I've had in years. This town will be swarming with agents and I'm sorry I'm not in the middle of it."

"You might not be in the action, but you could certainly be in the midst of it. Either the Emperitza will heat up her pursuit of your book or she'll be too busy to care anymore. Now that Miami's not standing alone against her, she may figure your book is old news." Sam countered.

"Do you think she'll just walk away and forget about her threats to Lawrence?" Todd didn't sound convinced.

"If she feels squeezed, I think she'll use Lawrence to make a statement. This town rolled over and let her have control and that's what she's used to. She may use Lawrence to test the power of the task force."

Suddenly, the staccato rat-a-tat-tat of automatic gunfire ripped through the air. A barrage of bullets hammered the walls of the main house and pinged against the surrounding fence.

"Get down and stay down!" Sam yelled as he ran for the door. With his gun drawn, he eased his way to the outside and began crawling across the garden to the back door of Sharon and Carter's house. As quickly as it started, it ended. Then he heard the screeching of tires as the unmarked police car that was usually parked at the end

231

of the street took off in pursuit of the shooter. Sam stood up and ran the rest of the way to the house. He had to see if the McDeals had been harmed.

He banged on the door and was relieved when Carter flung open the door and yelled for him to get inside.

"My God, what was that?" Carter was shaking with anger. "They could have killed us all. You should see the windows on the front of the house! There's glass everywhere."

"Are you and Sharon all right? That's the important thing."

"If you call shaking like a leaf and mad as a hornet 'all right', then I guess we are! Thank God Sharon was in the hallway and I was in the den when it started or we might be dead."

By the time they walked to the hallway where Sharon was sitting against the wall, the sounds of sirens filled the air and someone was banging on the front door.

"Stay here with Sharon while I go to the door. Don't leave the hallway until I tell you!" Sam shouted instructions as he cautiously approached the front door and positioned himself against the wall. "Who's there?"

"Open the door. It's Sgt. Drake with Miami Dade."

Sam stood behind the door as he eased it open and saw the familiar face of the sergeant who had been guarding the house.

"Is anyone hurt?"

When Sam indicated that everyone was okay, the man continued. "It was an old black Ford, probably vintage 1960. As far as we could tell there were two men inside; a driver and a shooter. Our man took out after them, but that car was suped-up and they had a lead on us. I called for backup but I haven't heard if we caught up with them. There are some investigators on their way over here."

Sam walked out on the sidewalk to look at the damage to the house. All the windows on the front of the house, downstairs and upstairs, had been broken and the front door and stucco were riddled with bullet holes. The people he was charged with protecting were no longer safe here.

He walked back in the house and dialed Michael Anderson. "I know this is a bad time to call and ask for favors, but I may need to get Lawrence and the McDeals out of Miami. Can I send them to your house in Eleuthera?"

It only took a few seconds to get an answer. "Thanks, Michael. I'll get back to you to make arrangements. How are you and Margo holding up?"

The conversation was short and Sam hung up the phone with relief that he had an alternative safe house he could use.

After a few more words with the sergeant, he walked back to the hallway to talk to Sharon and Carter. "You know we're going to have to move until this is over. It's not safe here for anyone. They'll be back and next time we may not be so lucky."

"I feel like I'm coming unglued. This is getting to me, Sam." Sharon's eyes had the look of a cornered animal. "I thought I was tough, but this is the last straw."

"I want you to take Lawrence and go to the Anderson's house in the islands. I don't think you can be protected here anymore."

"I can't leave, Sam! Jocelyn is still critical and there's no way I can leave her." Carter exclaimed. "I agree that Sharon and Lawrence have to go. But, I'll stay behind.' He thought for a minute. "I'll take a hotel room near the hospital, but I'm not leaving Miami."

Sharon stood up and looked at Sam. "You've got to give us some time to talk this over. Carter's right. We've got to think about Jocelyn." She started walking toward the living room and then she gasped. "Look what they've done to our house!"

"Sam, we've got to have some time to talk." Carter put his arm around Sharon's shoulder. "I know the police will be here soon to ask all their questions, but we need to get ourselves calmed down before they get here and before we can give you an answer."

"Stay in the back of the house. I don't think they'll chance coming back, but you never know." He turned to leave. "I'll check with Lawrence and be back by the time the police get here."

*****

"Lawrence, be reasonable. The main house took a heavy hit and next time those thugs may find a way to get to the guesthouse. Don't dig your heels in on this. We need to make some changes. Sharon is frightened and I can't blame her."

"Carter's not about to leave his daughter. How do you think you're going to get them to go away from her? This is my fight, Sam, but that woman has made it everyone else's. I want to meet with her—face to face—and get this settled once and for all. I can't bear feeling responsible much longer."

"Don't be ridiculous! Meeting with her will never happen." Sam couldn't believe what he was hearing. "Remember, you don't call her. She calls you." He felt like shouting, but what good would it do? "She would never believe she wasn't being lured into a trap. You're not thinking this through." He hesitated. "Wait a minute. Have you decided to let her have the book?"

"Not after all we've been through to protect it. But I'll bargain with her. We know there is no way she'll be able to continue in Miami if this task force has any muscle at all. I'll tell her I'll hold off publication until she has left the city."

"And you think that will placate her? Excuse me, Lawrence, but that won't deter her for one second. You better start packing your bags for the islands."

"I've done everything your way and look at the results. What have I got to lose?"

"Start with your life! Besides, hasn't Jocelyn lost enough to keep you safe?" Being frustrated with Lawrence wasn't helping the situation, so he decided to change tactics. "Let's say I went along with your plan, then what?"

"If she agrees to the delay in publication, then our lives go back to normal and she can leave town without any backlash from what's in the book."

"The fallacy in your reasoning, Lawrence, is an assumption the lady is planning to leave town. I agree that's a possibility, but I don't think it will happen in the near future. Even with the task force, it will be months, maybe years, before she feels pinched. She owns this town. Why would she want to go somewhere else and start over? I think we let her make the next move."

"That may prove to be a deadly mistake, Sam. But, I'll give it a few more days before I ask my informants to help me set up a meeting with her."

Sam looked at Lawrence and quietly continued. "When you came back from the meeting with DaSilva, you seemed confident that something big was in the works. After the President's announcement, I assumed that was what you'd been told would happen. Am I right? Or is there something else?"

"I can't break that confidence, but what DaSilva told me is the only reason I'm willing to wait a few more days. And, I think I made myself clear about not going to the islands."

"Fine. But I have to do something to protect Sharon and Carter. When you see what was done to their house, you'll understand."

*****

"I'd love to take my wife and run away to the islands, but like I said before, there's no way I can leave Jocelyn. I'll see if I can convince Sharon to go without me. She's beginning to show signs of stress, so she might agree." Carter was standing in the living room looking at the bullet holes and shattered glass. "I've got to get this mess cleaned up but I'm afraid to call anyone. With the way things are going for us, I don't know who I can trust."

"Let me see what I can do. I'll make a few calls. But, I've got to get you all moved because there is no way you and Sharon can stay here tonight." Sam picked up a painting that had been ruined in the gunfire. "Carter, I'm sorry we got you and Sharon involved in this.

235

I'm working on a plan to move everyone to another location since I can't convince anyone to go to Eleuthera. I'll get back to you within the hour."

"Sam, I'd like to be close to the hospital. What if Sharon and I moved to one of the hotels in that area? The only place we'll be going is to see Jocelyn, and Claire will be with us."

"I'll check into it and get back with you. Let me see what's available. In the meantime, pack some bags so you can be ready when I get back to you. And, tell Sharon not to worry. Tom West and I will have someone here to start boarding up the house before you leave. I think the police have just about finished their investigation."

"Thanks, Sam. I'll let her know. But, I'm getting anxious about my daughter. Are you sure she's protected?"

"Give me an hour, okay?" Sam frowned. "The police have Jocelyn under 24/7 protection. I know there are at least two people on duty outside her door, but there may need to be more."

*****

Sam was exhausted. He needed a good night's sleep and some time with his wife. But things were happening too fast. His level of tolerance for Lawrence's stubbornness was at a low point and he needed a break before he said something he regretted.

He called Lara and asked her to meet him for coffee in the lobby of her office building. He could only take a few minutes, but his wife had a knack for making him laugh. He remembered he hadn't stopped for lunch, so maybe food and a short visit with his wife would change his attitude.

Besides, it would take some talking to convince Lara to take Sharon McDeal to the island.

Chapter Twenty-nine

Carter

He hesitated for just a minute before he picked up the phone and called Rosanne. He had to find out how Paul was doing and he wanted to update her on Jocelyn's condition. He also wanted to ask her a favor.

A young voice answered the phone and Carter felt a smile begin. "Hello, this is Carter. Is your mother home?"

As he waited for Rosanne to come to the phone he went over the things he wanted to say and he knew that Jocelyn's mother was the right person to give him an honest answer.

"Rosanne, how are you and the kids holding up? Have you seen Paul today?" He could tell from her voice that she was pleased he had called. He listened to her questions and nodded in agreement.

"Yes, it was a close call. But I'm glad to hear that he's doing better. I haven't seen Jocelyn today, but I talked to the nurse on her floor and she assured me that she's improving. I'll keep you updated. As soon as she's feeling up to it, I'll call from the hospital so you can talk to her."

He listened for a few minutes as Rosanne told him the latest news about Paul. His condition had improved and he would probably be moved from ICU later in the week.

"That's great news." He paused. "Rosanne, what do you think of calling Mark and asking him to go to the hospital to see Jocelyn? I know they aren't together anymore, but they still have some feelings for one another. She's going to need a friend to get through all of this."

Her response warmed his heart.

"Yes, I agree they've always had a connection. Thanks for agreeing to call him and if he doesn't feel right about it, I'll understand."

He said goodbye and hung up the phone. Had he done the right thing? Perhaps he should have shared his reasons with Rosanne. But she seemed to think the visit would be a good idea so he decided that would be a conversation for another day.

Maybe he was wrong to think it, but he never doubted that Jocelyn and Mark still loved each other. The church was the obstacle between them—as first cousins, the church would never allow them to marry for fear of genetic problems for any children they might have. But, as sad as he was that his daughter's injury had resulted in a hysterectomy, that injury had removed the obstacle. There would be no genetic children and he knew Jocelyn was going to need love and support to get through the grief she was going to feel once she heard that news. He and Sharon would be there for her, but she was going to need more.

He hadn't talked to the young man in years, but he was playing a hunch on this one. If Mark had changed his feelings for her, he would tell his aunt and that would be the end of it.

For the first time in two days, Carter allowed himself to smile. He had done what he needed to do. The rest was up to Mark and Jocelyn.

*****

"I brought you a strawberry milkshake and a couple of candy bars to cheer you up." Carter entered the hospital room and tried not to show his concern. "You're looking better today, sweetheart."

"Hi, Daddy. I'm glad you're here. Would it hurt your feelings if I saved those treats? I don't think my stomach can handle them right now."

"Of course not, sweetheart. Whenever you're ready the candy bars will be in this drawer and I'll ask the nurse to put the milkshake in the refrigerator for later." He watched as she struggled to talk. "You rest and I'll just sit here and read a magazine."

"The doctor is supposed to be here in a few minutes and I have so many questions about what happened to me. I remember being shoved into Claire, but everything after that is a blur. Please, Daddy, tell me what happened."

"Jocelyn, you were shot at close range and you're lucky to be alive. Please remember that. Nothing else really matters except your life. Prayers were answered for your family." He walked over to the bed and put down the small bag he was carrying. "Hey, we have a few minutes for some father-daughter time before the doctor arrives. So, let me sit here and enjoy being with you."

"You sound serious. Is there something wrong that I don't know about?"

"Rosanne and the kids send their love. You know she'd be here if she could, but Paul is still in ICU and she can't leave. Sharon and Claire stopped to buy you some slippers and a robe. They'll be here before too long." He was doing his best to change the subject. "Are you in much pain? Or, are they giving you some good drugs?" He chuckled as he tried to make light of the situation.

"Daddy, you were never very good at changing the subject. You know that, don't you? So, just tell me and get it over with. What's going on that I need to know?"

"Honey, let's wait for the doctor. He'll be able to explain things so much better."

"Don't do this to me. Please just tell me. I'm not dying, am I?"

"Goodness, no. Do you think you'd be talking to me like this if you were dying?" He reached for her hand. "There were some complications caused by the gunshot and they had to do some surgery they hadn't counted on."

She hesitated. "What kind of surgery?"

Carter let go of her hand and began wringing his own. "Jocelyn, they had to do a hysterectomy." He said the words and felt his shoulders sag with sadness. "I'm sorry, honey. But they had no choice."

Jocelyn stared at her father in shock. Then she hid her face in the pillow. "Oh, no," she whispered.

"Sweetheart, listen to me," Carter begged. "I know it hurts, but you have options. You're alive and that means you have choices." He walked around the bed and bent down so he could look into her eyes. He gently lifted her head and wiped away her tears. "You were a gift given to me when I had lost hope of ever having a family. You are my child, no matter the circumstances of your birth. And, I promise, when the time is right, there will be a child out there waiting to be yours. And what a great mother you will be." He pushed the hair from her face and placed his hand on her shoulder. "I promise."

He didn't know where the words came from or where he found the courage to try and comfort her. He had never been her comforter—that had been Gracie's job—but as he said the words, he believed with all his heart they were true.

"I love you, Daddy."

Her whispered words resounded in his ears and he felt the tension flow out of his body. His daughter would survive even this disappointment. *God, give her comfort and please let my words be true.*

*****

Later in the afternoon, he stood in the hospital corridor talking quietly with the guards when they noticed a man approaching. As the guards moved in position to protect the entrance to Jocelyn's room, the man came close enough for Carter to recognize. It made him smile to realize that Rosanne had kept her promise. He extended his hand to Mark Sanders and nodded to the guards that the young man could enter her room.

"He's family."

He didn't follow Mark into the room, but stood within hearing range. He wasn't planning to eavesdrop, but he wanted to make sure that Jocelyn would welcome her visitor. For a few minutes there was no sound from the room. Just as he was becoming concerned, he heard what he had hoped to hear. There was no doubt in the words the young man spoke to his daughter. "Jocey, I'm here. You know I'm here for you and no matter what, we'll get through this together."

When his daughter responded, "Oh, Mark," Carter knew he had done the right thing.

Jeanne Moon Farmer

Chapter Thirty

Sam

"I've got Sharon McDeal and my wife, Lara, on a plane to the Anderson's house on Eleuthra, and Carter's at the Mayfair Hotel near Mercy Hospital with Todd Madison. Claire McGuire and I are covering Lawrence. I know you've got people at the hospital and the McDeal's house, but I need some extra patrols around the hotel. The Anderson's have their own security at the island house, so I don't think that one's an issue."

Sam and Tom West sat in a booth at a diner near police headquarters going over plans for protecting all the people caught up in Lawrence's conflict with the Emperitza.

"My informants are telling me things are humming at the Emperitza's place. She thinks the Feds are bluffing and this Task Force is a joke. But, apparently she's telling everyone to make each minute count. She may be expecting a huge delivery from Columbia by the end of the week." Tom picked over his food and seemed distracted.

"How is that going to impact operations?"

"We've been told that everything and everyone is on high alert. But, the plans are on a "need to know" basis. I understand the Coast Guard is sending additional support and the Task Force is making big changes over at Port Authority. But, the kicker is the air support. They're taking some extra measures to patrol all the small airports from coast to coast that are located between Orlando and Key West."

"Did you get any information from Jeff Cannon?"

"Not a thing. He's cagey, but he knows we're after him. We're watching the judge who set his bond. It's high enough it shouldn't cause suspicion, but it's way too low for all his charges." He sounded disgusted.

"Cannon should be released some time tonight, but there will be a raid on his office before that happens. The Feds are confiscating the firm's files. Once they've got his client list, they can move forward. His release is planned so he won't have time to cover his tracks." He continued pushing the food around on his plate. "You should hear the way Cannon has been carrying on. The guy's made it known to anyone who'll listen that his rights have been violated."

"What about the Alli Anderson investigation? Anything that might connect him to that?"

"Our guys have been all over Cannon's estate and MarGrove. So far, all we know is she was at his place for a party. But, after dealing with that shyster, I know he knows more than he's telling."

"I've known his partners for years and I can't imagine they're involved, especially Elena Martinez. Have you started talking to her?"

"Not yet. I was told to let that go until after tonight's raid. The Feds don't won't any tip-off of what's coming."

"What's included in the charges against Cannon?"

"Let's see." Tom grinned. "Starting from the top, we've got attempted murder and assault, extortion, illegal imprisonment, conspiracy, and threatening a law enforcement officer. How's that for starters? And, if that doesn't work, I'll get him for spitting on the sidewalk." His grin got bigger.

"Great list, but I don't think all those charges will stick." Sam chuckled. "No wonder the guy feels maligned. You've tarnished his good name in this community."

"Right. Just wait 'til I add to that list. The man's a sleaze and I intend to prove it. How did your friends get hooked up with him?"

"From what I know, they all went to law school together."

"I hope your friends are clean, Sam. Cannon is going down and he may take them with him." He wiped some crumbs off the table.

"Change of subject. I'll get some extra patrols assigned to the Mayfair. Is there anything else I should know?"

"Lawrence is being very closed-mouth, but I think he knows something else is in the works. If I get a clue, I'll call you."

"That old man is something else. Sure hope I'm never the subject of one of his books. Gotta' run, Sam. I'll be in touch."

*****

"Do you have everyone taken care of, Sam?" Lawrence poured himself a brandy and offered a glass to Sam.

Sam waved off the drink offer. "No thanks. I'm on duty. Remember?" He offered the author a tired smile. "Yes, everyone except you. You're my only worry right now."

"Right," Lawrence replied. He raised his glass as if toasting. "You aren't here on a social visit, are you? No matter, I've had a nice day visiting with Claire. She's had many of the same kinds of experiences I had when I was active with the FBI. We've been exchanging war stories. So you can stop worrying about me."

"Glad that's working out. How's she handling what happened yesterday?"

"She's still upset and worried about Jocelyn. But she knows it was an accident and that, most likely, she couldn't have done anything to prevent it. She's a professional, Sam. She knows the risks. By the way, I talked to Carter earlier and Jocelyn is much improved. Did you know that Mark Sanders went to visit her this afternoon?"

"I haven't had a chance to talk to Carter since early this morning. I plan to stop by the hospital later. Did he say how Mark found out about Jocelyn? Her name was withheld in the newspaper story."

"He didn't say, but I'd wager that Rosanne called him. She is his aunt, you know. Mark and Jocelyn are family."

"Of course. I just had to find a connection so I wouldn't put Mark on the wrong side of things."

"I feel so out of the loop. What's new today?"

Sam filled Lawrence in on his conversation with Tom West, and then asked, "What else should we be prepared for? I know DaSilva gave you some information that you're not sharing."

"That's true. Everything he told me fits in with what's happening. But, it goes several steps beyond and involves the Emperitza directly. That's all I can say."

"Did you get any clue from him about his connection to her?"

"It's personal and goes back to something that happened long ago. One thing's for sure. There is some kind of grudge between them that didn't begin with what happened to his grandsons. That's all I know."

Sam knew he wasn't going to get any more information, so he changed the subject. He knew how to pick his battles and he was too tired to fight those he couldn't win.

Chapter Thirty-one

Maddie

One more time she followed Eric down the dark hallway to his office. She had made up her mind that tonight was the end of their affair. She had come to make that very clear to him and to see if she could find out the extent of his involvement with the sordid mess that surrounded Jeff Cannon. As he closed the door behind them, she tried to move out of his grasp.

"Let's talk, Eric. I haven't seen you in over a week and so much has happened."

He moved closer and pushed her against the wall. "You didn't really come over here to talk." He teased. "Come on, Maddie, I need you now."

As he pressed against her, she tried to keep her mind focused on something beside his body. But, she lost her resolve. His lips on hers were so familiar and inviting, and desire overcame reason. *Just one more time. One more time and then I'll tell him it's over.* Her body responded to him as it had from the first time he touched her and she began to move in rhythm with him. The hunger was there, he was there and she didn't want to stop until her appetite for him had been sated.

Somewhere in her heart she knew she should say 'stop.' This man was so wrong for her. His body had destroyed all her moral convictions and he had used their sexual energy to make her stop thinking. Yet, all she wanted to do was feel. Her heart rate increased and she felt dizzy as he increased the pressure of his touch. His mouth, his hands, she was ready for more. As they slid down the wall to the floor, she felt him fumbling with her clothes and she moved to guide his hands. *Yes, Yes, Yes.* She gasped with pleasure just as the door crashed open and bright lights momentarily blinded her. *Oh, my God. What's happening?*

Eric quickly moved away from her and she tried to rearrange her clothes so she could get up off the floor.

"What the hell is going on?" Eric screamed as he yanked up his slacks and ran his hands through his hair. "Who are you and what are you doing in my office?"

Maddie recognized the FBI jackets and realized what was happening. She also noted that Eric had forgotten she was there. As embarrassed as she was, she tried to move behind the door so she could pull herself together before the questions began.

"FBI. We're removing all the files and office equipment from the premises."

"By what authority and under what warrant?" Eric was still screaming.

The agent moved toward Eric and shoved the warrant into his chest. "By this authority. So sit down and shut up. One move to hinder this operation and you'll be arrested. All I need from you is your name and the name of your lady friend."

"I'm Eric Randall, senior partner of this firm, and I demand to know why you are confiscating my property."

"Read the warrant! Does federal investigation mean anything to you?"

Eric stomped out of the room and grabbed the phone off the receptionist's desk. As he tried to dial, an agent rushed over and snatched the phone out of his hands. "You were told to sit down and keep quiet."

As the agents moved from office to office loading boxes with files, Maddie slipped the agent who looked in charge her business card and quietly made her escape out the front door.

Driving to her house, she went over and over the scene in the law office and realized the consequences she might have to face. Nothing good was going to come out of what just happened and she knew she was lucky the agents had not detained her. As soon as she walked in her front door, she called Sam.

"I'm in big trouble. Can you come over?"

*****

While she waited for Sam, she changed her clothes and tried to do something with the tangled mess that Eric had made of her hair. She could spend hours beating up on herself for letting her sex drive get the best of her, but what was the use? Those antics were not going to set well with her boss or the entire prosecutor's office. Not to mention her father or Lawrence. She would have to pay the price, even if it meant losing her job and having to bear the disappointment, or worse, the disgust of the two men she admired most in the world.

In less than an hour, Sam had left Lawrence with Todd and he was sitting in her living room shaking his head at her emotional tirade. She left out the sordid details as she described the scene at Eric's office, but she knew Sam could fill in the blanks.

"Maddie, slow down. It happened and you'll have to deal with it." He scratched his head and looked with some concern at the woman he usually thought had it all together. "You gave them your information. They didn't try to prevent you from leaving and you're not involved. This should be an easy fix."

"Sam, don't you get it? They burst in at a very indiscreet moment! This will be all over the *Miami Herald* in the morning and I'll be finished at the prosecutor's office." She plopped down on the couch. "Why was he invaded by the FBI, anyway?"

"The feds are trying to tie Jeff Cannon to the cartel and they've got to find out who else is involved. You've told me before that you have suspicions about Eric, so don't be surprised if they're true." Then he added, "I tried to warn you."

She groaned. "They'll think I'm involved."

"No doubt you'll be questioned. Just tell them what you know. If you don't have any hard facts, leave off your suspicions."

"You sound like a lawyer."

"Then take my advice. And maybe you should start acting like the sharp attorney you really are." He looked at the pout on her face. "You're acting like a spoiled kid. You know the drill, Maddie. You've been on law enforcement's side and you know what the prosecutor's office will be looking for in this case. And, it's not the lady who got caught—how shall I say it? Who got caught in a compromising position." He laughed at her red face.

Maddie scowled at him. "Don't say anything more. This is not my finest hour. Would you believe me if I told you I went over to his office to break it off with him?" She saw the look on his face. "No, I guess you wouldn't. But, if you knew about this raid, why didn't you tell me?"

"And, miss out on your moment of discomfort?" he teased. "How could I have known you would be at that office tonight, my friend?" He hesitated. "You've told me all you know, haven't you? If you know anything else about what goes on at that law firm we better talk about it before you have to meet with the Feds."

"I don't know anything except what I've observed."

"Eric is probably going to try to find out what you know. So be careful. If he's involved, he's worried. If he's not involved, he's baffled. The only thing that will keep him from thinking you set him up is the fact the two of you got caught. He knows you wouldn't let that happen on purpose." He leaned forward and looked her in the eyes. "Maddie, fooling around may have saved your life."

*****

Tapping on her window woke her up. She sat up in bed and listened intently before she opened the nightstand drawer and grabbed her gun. It was still dark outside and she knew there were no tree branches close enough to the window to cause the sound. Slowly, she swung her feet to the floor and cautiously moved to the side of the curtain where she could get a better view of the outside. A man was standing near the window, tapping on the glass with his knuckles. She knew that body too well not to know that it was Eric.

"What are you doing? Don't you know I could have shot you?"

"Let me in. We've got to talk."

"Do you want to come through the window or shall I open the front door for you?" she quipped.

"Cut the jokes and go open the door." Eric demanded.

As she walked through the living room, she hid the revolver in between the cushions of her chair.

"You look awful," she exclaimed as he walked in the house and sat down on the couch. "And, from the way you smell, I'd say you've had a lot to drink. Why are you here, Eric?"

"What do you know about what happened tonight?" He leaned forward and pointed his finger at her. "I know you've got your head together with Sam Baxter and law enforcement, and you know what's going on at the prosecutor's office."

"That's a question you should be asking your partner. He's in hot water right now, not me."

"You think you're so smart, don't you? What are the Feds looking for and don't give me any more BS!"

"They want to know what Jeff's doing with the cartel. And, whether you and Elena are involved. That's what they're looking for, Eric, and they won't stop until the questions are answered."

"What do you know, Maddie? What do you *think* you know?" His face was distorted with anger and he rushed toward her. "What do you think you can tell them about me?"

Maddie's hand slipped between the cushions where she could grab the gun if she needed to. Outwardly, she remained calm and unfazed. "All I can tell them about you, Eric, is how good you are in bed." The look on his face told her she needed to get him out of her house. She jumped up and startled him. "I want you out of my house! I don't want to see you again."

He swung his hand at her face but she dodged the blow and caught his arm. "I don't know what you're thinking or what you're involved in, but don't you ever try that again." Her words were slow and deliberate, but there was no mistaking her threat. "Get out before I have you arrested for assault."

"Watch your step, Maddie. If something comes down on me, you'll regret it." He shook his arm loose and pulled away from her.

"You better be more concerned about what your partner told the cops before they let him go than you are about me. You know I don't have a clue about your business." She opened the door and stood beside it so he could pass. "And, Eric, don't ever threaten me again."

She slammed the door shut with relief and turned the deadbolt. *What have I gotten myself into now?*

Chapter Thirty-two

Lawrence

"I've talked to my editor in New York and the book is scheduled for release on the first of next month. I haven't changed my mind and I'd like to go ahead with the book signing party that Jocelyn has planned for that evening. As soon as she's feeling better, I've got to visit with her to make sure I know all the details."

"She's not going to be able to make this party happen and you know it. You need to cancel it for her sake and all the other reasons. I'm not going to give in on this one. It's a no-go." Sam was emphatic.

"Ah, my friend. As much as I want to oblige you, I think a business commitment goes beyond your jurisdiction." Lawrence put his fork down and folded his hands in front of him. "I'm going to ask Maddie to take over some of the details for Jocelyn, and I'll get Claire to help her. If that won't work, I'll let my agent take over. But, that party will take place as planned."

"Our friends at police headquarters and the FBI, not to mention the DEA, might have the last word on this. I'm not going to get into a contest of wills with you, Lawrence. But, we will abide by the decision of law enforcement. That's a promise."

"I know all the concerns and I think this party can work to our advantage. The Emperitza must be angry that she didn't get my notes and references and she'll be looking for an easy way to take care of me and my book at the same time."

"You've forgotten one little detail in all of this. She's not going to wait that long. She told you not to allow the publication. That's her objective and she's going to force you to close that book down. My guess is she's going to make her move within the next few days. She wants to hear you tell New York to pull the book."

Jeanne Moon Farmer

"You've made your point, Sam, and I guess I was dreaming about how it should be. Let's see what happens."

"What aren't you telling me? You seem so confident that by the first of the month the book will be in bookstores and you'll be signing autographs. That kind of confidence is coming from something and I wish you'd let me in on it so I can stop worrying."

"We'll both have to wait and see. Now why don't you finish that gourmet breakfast I prepared for you?" He chuckled as he looked at the bowl of cereal and cup of coffee. "Claire was going to prepare something nice, but you got here too early. One bad thing about this guesthouse is the shower situation and living arrangements for more than two people. Claire's taking her shower now and as soon as I knew you were going to be here, I told Todd to go home. He can shower at his house and be back here before you have to leave."

"Quarters are tight, but I'm hoping it won't be for too much longer." Sam turned and looked out the window. "The guys who are working on the main house got here about the time I did. It'll probably take them several days to repair all the damage." He turned back to Lawrence. "I know the general contractor and we had all the guys checked out before anyone was assigned to this job. But, in this town nobody is above suspicion. I'm not leaving until Todd gets back and as long as there are workmen inside these gates, he isn't to go back to his house unless I'm here to help cover you."

"You sound like you mean that."

"I'm serious and you know it."

"I do, but I don't have to like it. Remember, I'm usually the one giving those kinds of orders."

"Lawrence, I know it's hard to sit and wait. But you haven't given op orders in a long time. Please remember, downtown is giving us our directions and we'll do what we're told even if it means doing a lot of nothing."

*****

254

"Maddie, come in and join us." Claire opened the door and greeted Lawrence's guest. "I'll set an extra plate for dinner. You will stay, won't you?"

"Thanks, Claire. Sounds great. How is he today?"

"Restless and complaining. But, he'll get over it. He wants to be in the middle of the action and Tom West is not keeping him in the loop. Your dad was probably the same way, right? Once in law enforcement, one can't separate, even after retirement." She motioned for Maddie to take a seat. "He's upstairs and Todd is in the kitchen on the phone. I'll let them know you're here."

Lawrence came down the stairs as Claire turned to call him. "Hello, my dear. You are staying for dinner, I hope." He gave her a hug and motioned for her to sit with him. "Claire, I need a few minutes with Maddie, then why don't you and Todd join us."

He made sure they were in the room alone, then he hunched toward her and began talking in a whisper. "Is anything going on in the prosecutor's office that you can tell me?"

"Can you be a bit more specific? There are hundreds of cases and I know you aren't interested in them."

"Is there any talk of an indictment for the Emperitza?"

"You know I can't tell you that. Even if I knew, I couldn't talk about it."

"Keep your eyes and ears open. That's all I can say."

"Are you expecting some big break-through? We haven't been able to pin anything directly on her since she moved to town." She was disgusted. "We've had to settle for some of her lowly henchmen, and they keep going free. Judges and jurors don't seem to be on our side."

"Hi, Maddie. Good to see you." Todd walked over and gave her a kiss on the cheek. "We need some lively conversation around here. You got anything that'll lift our spirits?"

"With that greeting, I guess you didn't hear about my narrow escape from the FBI?"

"Not a word." Todd laughed. "Sam did not tell me one word about compromising situations!"

"Oh, great! Now the whole town will know." She pulled a handful of red curls across her face like a mask.

"What in the world are you talking about? Am I the last to know everything?" Lawrence looked from one face to the other and could tell that Maddie was embarrassed about something.

"That's part of what I came to talk to you about, but it looks like Sam beat me to it."

"Sam hasn't mentioned anything about you. What's happened?"

"The FBI raided the law firm of Randall, Martinez and Cannon last night. They confiscated files and equipment."

"I figured that would happen as soon as they had Jeff Cannon in custody. But what does that have to do with you?"

She exhaled loudly. "I was there. And, let's just say I was not at my best."

"Oh, Maddie, my dear. Please don't tell me my suspicions about you and Eric are true."

"I wish I'd listened to your warning and stayed away from him. Now I'll have some explaining to do. Before you ask, I've already unloaded this on my dad and gotten a lecture. I expect you'll do the same."

"That man was after you the first minute he saw you and to my dismay, he didn't try to hide it from his lovely wife."

"They're separated now, Lawrence. Elena was smart enough to leave." She wrung her hands together. "I went to the office last night to break it off with him, but things got carried away and the next thing I knew the FBI was storming the place. Like I said, it was not my finest hour."

"Were you arrested?"

"No sir. I gave one of the agents my card and got out of there. Sam and I talked it over and they weren't interested in me. I'll be questioned, but I don't have anything but some suspicions. The feds are after the client list and the files the firm has on people that may have connections to the cartel."

"That's true. But be careful. If the cartel thinks you know anything, you won't be safe." Lawrence wanted to ask more but he didn't want to embarrass her even more in front of Todd and Claire. Later he would ask his questions, especially about Elena. "Was Eric arrested?"

"No, and that seemed strange to me. Maybe they think only Jeff is involved." Maddie had regained her composure now that the conversation wasn't focused on her.

"Todd, what do you know about this?" Lawrence asked.

"Only what she's told you. The feds timed the raid so it would happen before Jeff's release, and the last I heard he was out of jail."

When the phone rang, Claire jumped to answer it. The others made small talk until she hung up the phone.

"That was Sam with some big news. A new arrest warrant has just been issued for Jeff Cannon. It's looking more and more like he's involved in the death of Alli Anderson. They want him for questioning on a possible manslaughter charge."

There was a collective gasp in the room.

"Why?" Both Todd and Maddie responded together.

"They found something that belonged to her stuffed in a cabinet aboard his yacht, plus the remnants of a pretty wild party. Sam said they found cocaine residue everywhere. As soon as they can find the guy, there's a chance he's going back to jail."

Maddie jumped up and looked at Lawrence. "I think I know where he might have gone after his release. Claire, call Sam back!"

"How would you know that, Maddie?" Lawrence said.

"He and Eric own a fishing place in the Keys. Jeff often takes his women friends down there." She stopped. "It's not in their name. Give me a minute and I'll remember whose name it's in."

"Do you know which Key?" Todd asked.

"Yes, its somewhere on Tavernier. I've never been there, but I've heard Eric talk about it."

"Why would he go there?" Claire asked as she picked up the phone to call Sam.

"He needs time to think and he probably doesn't want to face the Emperitza. Remember, he's the guy who botched the plan to get Lawrence's notes." Maddie started walking around the room.

"I think the house is in Jeff's mother's name. She's divorced and remarried, so the name wouldn't be the same as his." She continued walking. "Wait, I think her name is Jackie Garret or Garnet. It's something similar. Tell Sam to start with that. I'll keep thinking."

Everyone was talking at once until Lawrence smacked his hands on his knees. "I knew it had to be murder. It was someone with a boat who knew where the dock at MarGrove was located. It all fits! Cannon knew how to find the estate and, chances are, he knew MarGrove had a deep-water dock. There aren't too many of those on the Bay. But, I remember Sam telling me that Margo had it dredged."

The lull in the conversation was so abrupt that Maddie stopped pacing. Lawrence was trying to get up when he saw her walk quickly to the chair where Todd sat slumped over. "Are you okay? Can I get you a glass of water or something?"

Todd's head and shoulders sagged. Then he dropped his head to his knees. "I did this to her. It was horrible to think she took an overdose, but if she was murdered, I'm to blame."

Maddie placed her arm around him. "That's not true and you can't even think it."

"I left her unprotected. I let her go to that party without me."

Lawrence's voice carried across the room. "Listen to me, young man. Even if you had gone with her to the party, you would have been asked to wait somewhere away from the invited guests. There was no way for you to police her every move. The only thing you might have heard was the boat leaving the dock. But, even then, you wouldn't have thought that she might be on it."

He stopped to see if Todd was listening to him. "You're sad about her death and you miss her company. She was a dynamic young woman and I'm sure the two of you had some wonderful times over the years. But, in no way, are you responsible for what happened to her."

Todd looked over to where Claire was talking on the phone to Sam. "Ask him if he's seen Margo and Michael." He stood up so quickly that Maddie was thrown off balance. "I've got to go talk to them. They'll blame me!"

"Sit down!" Lawrence commanded. "You will have ample time to express your sorrow to the Andersons. But now is not the time. If you go over there in the state you're in, it will only make their grief harder to bear." He turned to Maddie. "There's some brandy in that cabinet. I think Todd needs something to calm his nerves."

As Maddie poured the drink for Todd, Claire finished her conversation with Sam and sat down on the couch next to Todd. "Sam knows how upset you are and he'll be here later. Right now, he and Detective West are on their way over to tell the Andersons."

She lowered her voice and spoke only to Todd. "It's hard not to become emotionally involved with some of the people we serve. They become like family over the years, don't they? Alli's death is not your fault and someday you will come to terms with it and move on. We're here to help you if you need us. In one way or another, all of us have been through what you're going through. We know it will hurt like hell for awhile, but beating up on yourself won't make it hurt any less." She took the glass that Maddie offered and placed it in Todd's hand. "Sip this and shed your tears, my friend."

*****

In the dark of the night, Lawrence laid in bed going over all the different things that had happened since he'd been kidnapped by the Emperitza. What a story it would make when he could finally write it. All the elements were there—greed, passion, corruption, and even murder. But, this story had heart. The good guys in this story loved, hated, had compassion, and were personally invested in the outcome. They all wanted the same thing—a crime-free, drug-free Miami. They wanted to feel safe in their homes and on the streets; they wanted to be able to trust law enforcement and believe in the justice system; and they wanted to reclaim the city's reputation as a vacation paradise. Those were the reasons he couldn't give up his fight. He knew at times he sounded—and felt—like a deranged old man. He didn't want to fictionalize a happy ending for his story. He wanted to witness it happening.

Good guys and bad guys created the tension in his novels and he manipulated their every action. As the author, he resolved the issues and solved the crimes. He knew the ending of the story before he put the first word on paper and his main character, Agent Joe Fielding, was always a hero. That's the way it happened in fiction.

A worried frown crossed his face and he absent mindedly rubbed his chin. But, this wasn't fiction and real people were hurt because of him. He couldn't control the variables and it was upsetting. He still didn't know how this saga was going to end.

Knowing he wasn't going to get much sleep, he turned on the light and moved to his word processor. He would write until his eyes got heavy or until he had no more words.

*****

"Lawrence, you look tired this morning. Didn't you sleep well last night?" Claire asked across the breakfast table.

"It was a long night. Not much sleep, but I managed to finish a chapter of my next novel. Maybe I'll take a short nap after breakfast."

"I've got a bit of news this morning," interrupted Todd. "I had a call from Margo earlier and the plans have been completed for Alli's funeral. On Thursday, there will be a small private service at St. Stephen's Church in the Grove and a graveside service at Graceland Memorial Cemetery. The following week there will be a public memorial service at the Jackie Gleason Theater. Apparently, Alli's agent is making the plans for that one. It'll probably be a wing-ding media event." He rolled his eyes. "Margo and Michael want us to attend the family service."

"Of course, we'll all be there." Lawrence replied.

"We'll be there if Sam gives us clearance." Claire reminded Lawrence. "If he gives us the okay, then we'll find a way." She turned to Todd. "How did Margo sound? Do you think she's all right?"

"You know Margo. She's got on her diva face. She won't let any of us see her grief," said Todd. "I forgot to ask her about Sunni. She's the one I'm worried about."

"Death of a loved one is never easy, but when you add the possibility of murder to the emotions, it can be overwhelming." Lawrence added. "Tell Sam we're planning to be at the funeral. He'll make it happen."

Jeanne Moon Farmer

Chapter Thirty-three

Sam

The cover of darkness made it possible for the law enforcement team to make their way toward the house undetected. The place had a four-foot wall around three sides with an entrance gate in the western wall. The eastern side was open to the ocean. They would have easy access to both entry points. As they approached the wall, they could see that a car was parked out front and a single light burned inside the house.

Tom West motioned for two of the men to cover the beach side and he and Sam hoisted themselves over the wall and took their place near the front porch. Silently, they peered through the window at Jeff Cannon. He was stretched out on the couch—either fast asleep or passed out. An empty vodka bottle lay on the floor beside the couch and an automatic revolver was within the man's reach on the coffee table.

The detective waited until he knew his men had time to reach the back door and then he nodded to Sam. "I'm going to the door. Cover me from this window and whistle if he picks up the gun."

Sam moved closer to the window as Tom made his way to the front door. "Open up, police!"

"He's not moving." Sam whispered. "Call again."

"Cannon, we know you're in there. Open up or we're coming through the door!"

Again, there was no movement and Sam jumped up to help with a forced entry.

Tom tried the doorknob and then motioned to Sam for the two of them to use their shoulders to forcefully open the door.

The sound of the door breaking jarred the quiet, but when they entered the house, Cannon still hadn't moved. Sam ran to check on the man as Tom moved cautiously through the house toward the back door. When the two small bedrooms had been checked, the detective walked to the back door and opened it for the other members of the team.

"Tom, he's got a pulse, but I can't rouse him." Sam shook Canon's shoulders as he called his name. "Hey, man, wake up!"

One of the officers secured the loaded gun while the other two continued to check the rooms for anything that might be useful in the investigation.

"I can't wake him up. I think we need to get him to the mainland. Can one of you call and have an ambulance waiting for us in Florida City? He needs medical attention, but it'll take hours for help to get to this isolated place." Sam checked again for a pulse.

"Sam and I will put him in my car and head for Florida City. The two of you find a way to secure that front door and then follow us. Gather up the few things that we can use and take them to the evidence room at headquarters. There's a stash of drugs in that back bedroom and a satchel of money under the bed. I'd say our friend was planning on taking a trip."

"I found his wallet and passport in the satchel, Boss. What about his car? Do we leave it here?"

"Leave the car, but bring the keys." Tom yelled as he headed out the front door. "I'll move my car closer to the house."

Sam moved to pick up the inert body of Jeff Cannon and headed out the door.

*****

"What the….What's going on?" Jeff mumbled as he tried to sit up. "Where am I?"

"Take it easy. We're on our way to meet an ambulance in Florida City. You need to be evaluated at the hospital before we take you in for questioning," Tom explained.

264

"Who are you?" Jeff growled.

"Detective Tom West, Miami Dade PD. I think we've met."

"Am I under arrest or something?"

"For starters, you violated the terms of your bail. You were not supposed to leave Dade County, remember? And, we have a few questions about Alli Anderson that you need to answer."

"I don't know anything about Alli Anderson and I don't need to go to the hospital." His voice was stronger with every word. "I want to call my lawyer. I'm not answering any questions without my lawyer."

"Suit yourself, Mr. Cannon. I'll tell the ambulance not to bother." He picked up his radio and called in. "Cancel the ambulance in Florida City. I'm bringing Jeff Cannon straight to headquarters." He replaced the radio receiver and looked at his passenger in the rearview mirror. "You can call your lawyer when we get downtown. Maybe he'd like to explain how you got to Monroe County."

"I don't have anything to say."

"Fine with me, but the DA might have a few things to say to you. They're probably preparing the paperwork for your disbarment as we speak."

There was only silence from the backseat. They drove on for several more miles when Sam turned around and started asking questions.

"Is the Emperitza after you? I'd think her goons would like a piece of you. They're probably not too impressed that you didn't get the notes you were sent to pick-up. Did you know the DA is looking to charge you with accomplice to attempted murder in the shooting of Jocelyn McDeal?" Sam chuckled. "Man, your troubles just keep multiplying. Assisting the Emperitza is going to look like a piece of cake when they pile on all the charges that are mounting against you. They're questioning Eric Randall right now and you know he's not going to go down alone. For an attorney, you got a little careless, didn't you?"

"You've got nothing on me and you know it."

"Think again, Cannon. For what you did to Alli Anderson and Jocelyn McDeal, I hope you burn. The rest of the charges don't mean a thing to me." Tom's voice was flooded with emotion. "You're a scumbag and a disgrace to the legal profession, counselor. I'll make sure the case against you is airtight. But you're a drop in the bucket. We're not going to stop until we've got the Emperitza. You can count on that. We've got the manpower now to take her down!"

*****

A ringing phone in the middle of the night jarred Sam. He shook himself awake and reached for the receiver.

"This better be good!" He groaned and tried to focus on what he was hearing.

"I'll be there in twenty minutes."

Jumping out of bed, he headed for a quick shower. As the hot water pounded on his head, he tried to understand the implications of what Tom West had just told him. Apparently, the Emperitza had ordered the execution of a rival drug dealer and his family in South Miami. Her henchmen had murdered the man and his wife, but had spared the man's children. One of the children had copied down the tag number of the car and two of the three gunmen had been arrested as they were leaving a diner in Homestead. The third man had escaped and police were still looking for him. *This could be the break that leads us directly to the woman. But, what will it take to get one of her goons to talk?*

As he dressed and headed for the car, his mind was going in several directions at once. If they got enough information from Jeff Cannon and these two hired guns, they might have the kind of details they needed to destroy the entire drug operation in the Miami area.

Sam hadn't been so excited in a long time. Even though he tried to remain cautiously optimistic, he knew the Emperitza would already have her lawyers scrambling to get her men out of jail. Her worst enemy was anyone who had information they could use to bargain and negotiate for their own best interest.

At three o'clock in the morning, the streets of the city should have been empty. But, Miami had become a city that didn't sleep. Tawdry neon lights flickered and beckoned the late-night hangers-on and the raucous clamor of music had become the city's heartbeat. There was an eeriness about the way the streetlights cast a golden glow that caught the corners of buildings in shadows and the headlights of on-coming cars reminded Sam of the frightened look he had seen in the eyes of wild animals fleeing for their lives.

It was the perfect setting for his imagination to run wild and all of his crazy thoughts had one purpose and one outcome—the capture and conviction of the Emperitza.

*****

The interrogation room was brightly lit and Sam could see through the two-way glass that Jose Moreno was unfazed by the questions and accusations that were being hammered at him by Tom and another detective. Moreno sat back in the chair with his arms folded across his chest. His responses amounted to a slurred "nada" and "where's my lawyer?"

Sam had been watching for thirty minutes and nothing had changed. He watched Tom leave the room for a brief time and then return with a smile on his face. "Mr. Moreno, your partner has identified you as the shooter. He'll testify in court that he was only the driver and you were the killer. He's told us all about your meeting with the Emperitza and her orders to execute the entire family. Your partner says that you went against those orders and let the children live."

At that point, Tom leaned across the table and got close to Moreno's face. "He says he'd rather deal with us than have to explain why those kids are still alive. He says that you are 'dead-meat' and as soon as you are out on the street, she'll have you mowed down."

From his position on the other side of the glass, Sam saw Moreno's eyes change and hoped this new information would help Tom crack the man's armor. For the next twenty minutes, there was no let up. "Tell us what you know, Moreno! Tell us where she is and how we can get to her! Is her life worth more than yours? She's not going to let you walk away from this. Your partner says you're the one who killed that two-year old kid last year? Why'd you kill that kid and let these kids live? You know you'll fry for that one—that two-year old! When you walk in any prison, they'll all be waiting to take care of a kid-killer. Nobody tolerates a kid-killer and you know it."

Tom would walk away from Moreno and then get back in his face. His comments and questions were relentless and Sam watched him wear away at the confident demeanor of the assassin. Sooner or later, there would be a crack in the façade.

"You going to let your partner nail you for all this? He'll get two or three years, but you'll get the chair or life. Doesn't seem fair, does it, Moreno? You crash and burn, and this other guy gets off easy. Where is your boss? How do you get your orders? Are you involved in smuggling drugs into the country or are you just a fast gun? Who gave the orders for that cop in LA to be killed? I've got a witness that says you did that and will testify in court."

The detective walked out of the room and approached Sam. "Isn't this the guy with the good-looking wife that Sharon McDeal told us about?"

"Yeah. Sharon decorated their house. Why?"

"Maybe that's a way to get this goon to talk. I'll threaten his wife." Tom shrugged his shoulders. "It's worth a try." He grabbed a cup of coffee and went back in the interrogation room.

"Jose, understand you've got yourself a great house on the Bay, couple of nice cars, and one hell of a gorgeous wife. Your partner says your wife's involved in all this. Must be nice to have your wife in business with you. He says she takes her orders from you and she was with you when that little kid and his momma were killed. I'm gonna send my men over to your house to pick up the little wife. Do you think she's loyal to you? I think she'll talk rather than go to jail for you! You know what happens to pretty women in prison, don't you?"

Tom turned to the other detective. "Have Mrs. Moreno brought in for questioning."

"Leave her out of this. She ain't in on nothing and you know it!" Moreno yelled at Tom. "You leave my wife out of this or you'll be sorry, copper."

"May I remind you, Mr. Moreno, that it's not in your best interest to threaten me." He turned away from the man. His tone demanded no conversation. "Have his wife here in the next hour. I've wasted enough time on this scumbag."

"Where's my lawyer? I've got rights."

"We read you your rights, Moreno. And, your attorney is probably on his way. And, we'll read your wife her rights. No big deal. We're doing everything by the book."

"Stop that guy. I don't want anyone at my house." Moreno was still yelling. "Do you hear me? Don't send nobody to get my wife."

"That depends on you. I've been asking the same questions for hours and now you suddenly feel like talking? Even without your attorney?" Tom sat down and put his elbows on the table. "I'll hold off on bringing your wife here if you give me the information I need. That's the deal."

Sam listened, but didn't believe that Moreno was going to cooperate. More likely, he would try and string Tom along. But Sam knew Tom well enough to know that he could eventually wear the guy down.

It would be fun to watch if it ended in something they could use.

Jeanne Moon Farmer

Chapter Thirty-four

Jocelyn

Her head hurt and the pain in her stomach felt like a fire she couldn't extinguish. She had pushed the call button, but that seemed like hours ago. All she could think about was how much longer before the nurse came with a needle full of something that would help her go back to sleep.

When she tried to think, everything seemed fuzzy and the details escaped her. Had she had breakfast or lunch? Who had been in the room earlier? What had her dad told her? The little things were tough to remember, but the big things totally eluded her. She couldn't remember how she got shot or how she got to the hospital. Her brain couldn't hold on to those things. The one thing she wished she could forget was the menacing look of Jeff Cannon. His face was burned in her memory and she knew she'd never forget the fear she had seen in his eyes. She knew he had touched her and it terrified her. But every time she pushed herself to remember, the pain in her head intensified and she lost the thoughts.

"How're you doing, sweetheart?"

She tracked her father's voice and followed his words as he approached the bed.

"Hi, Daddy. I'm miserable. I feel worse than I did yesterday. Everything hurts and there are so many things I can't remember."

"That's to be expected, Jocelyn. Your body has been through a lot." Carter put a bag down on the floor beside the bed. "Sharon called earlier and wanted me to bring you some of your things. I don't know if I picked out the things you need, but I tried." He smiled.

"Thanks. I'm sure it's fine. And, if you forgot something, you can always bring it later." She couldn't imagine what he might have packed, but she was grateful that he tried.

"Have you had any visitors today?"

"I think you're the only person who has come to see me since I've been here."

"You've had quite a few people stop by to check on you—Sharon, Lara, Sam, Todd, Claire, Lawrence, Mark. And, Rosanne's called several times. I didn't know whether you'd want me to call Ben, so I didn't. But I will if you want to see him."

"Mark was here to see me? When? I don't remember seeing him."

"You've been in and out of touch. That pain medicine they're giving you must be powerful stuff."

"I called for the nurse to bring me a shot. I guess she forgot."

"I'll go find out." Carter started to leave.

"No, Daddy. Wait. I'd rather talk to you for a few minutes. Then you can go find her."

"You're sure?"

"Yes. Now tell me about Mark's visit. How did he know I was in the hospital?"

"I guess Rosanne called him."

"What did he say? Or better yet, what did I say?"

"Honey, I wasn't in here when Mark came. You'll have to ask him. Now let me find your nurse. You look like you're in a lot of pain."

*****

Drifting off to sleep, she wondered what she might have said to Mark and hoped she hadn't embarrassed herself. Part of her prayed he would come back, even if it would hurt her to see him.

*****

272

"Hey, beautiful. How do you feel?"

Mark's voice floated across her mind like a song and she knew she wanted to wake up to see if he was really there or just a figment of her dreams. The drug-induced sleep made her body feel heavy and her eyelids weren't cooperating with her efforts to wake-up.

"Jocey, wake up."

There it was again. She was sure it was Mark's voice and it was getting closer.

"You've been asleep for hours. I brought you some dinner. I know how much you like my mom's chicken soup. She made it special for you."

She managed to open her eyes for a few seconds, but she wasn't sure she could keep them open. At first it was hard to focus, then she saw him.

"Mark? Is it really you?"

"It's me, Jocey. I'm here."

"Give me a minute and I'll be awake." She smiled and held out her hand to him.

"Now that's more like it. This is the first time I've been here when your eyes were open. What can I get you?"

"Nothing." When she spoke she was afraid he would leave. "Stay here, please. I'm waking up. I promise."

He leaned over and kissed her quickly on the lips. "Do you realize we've wasted years of our lives and it hasn't changed a thing? I love you and I always will. This time I'm not leaving."

She struggled to say something in protest, but he kissed her again and she knew her words would have no meaning.

"Mark, we'll have to talk. We still have issues." She whispered against his cheek.

"There are no issues that we can't tackle if we're together. Jocelyn, I'm not living another day without you so you might as well stop fighting me. We belong together and everybody agrees with me, so you're outnumbered."

"I love you, Mark. That has never changed."

*****

The doctor had given her the same news she had heard from her father and she shed her tears. The emotional pain was added to her physical pain and she didn't know which hurt the most. She looked up at her father and saw her own sadness reflected in his eyes.

"You'll never be a grandfather. You know that, don't you?" she whispered.

"Jocelyn, I never thought I'd be a father and then a miracle happened and you came into my life. I believe in miracles, don't you?" Carter took her hand in his. "I know you're heartbroken, but this doesn't have to be the end of the story."

"Does Mark know about this?" It suddenly dawned on her that it was the reason Mark had said the things he did. "Does he, Daddy?"

"Yes, Jocelyn. He knows. But, it doesn't change how he feels. It gives him hope that the two of you have a chance for a life together."

The tears began to flow again. It was too much for her to think about.

"Just don't close the door on him again without giving it a lot of thought. You can be happy, Jocelyn, if you'll give yourself a chance."

Chapter Thirty-five

Lawrence

Pages and pages of yellow legal paper were spread out on the table and he had studied his notes until his eyes were red and tired. The more information he collected, the more muddled his thinking became. The facts hadn't changed—the Emperitza ran a multi-million dollar cocaine business.

Her source was the Medellin Cartel in Columbia and she used airplanes and boats to bring the drugs into the country. She used small planes that could land at obscure airports, she had people planted within the customs agency who looked the other way, and she had couriers who could transport the drugs undetected. He knew drugs had been carried on the local transit buses and packages had been dropped in the Everglades from airplanes. He knew there had to be courier routes and a sophisticated lookout system blanketing the state of Florida, particularly the I-95 corridor from Florida to the northeast. And, he knew she had hired guns that would carry out her vendettas.

She was clever and she was crazy. He also suspected that she was using her own product. She had escaped incarceration in New York and she had turned Miami into a shooting gallery. She wasn't the only operation in town and the rivalries had created havoc. The drug wars had escalated steadily for the past ten years and the murder rate in Miami was one of the highest in the world.

His informants had given him some insight into her operation and her bizarre lifestyle, but there had never been enough evidence to directly link her to anything. Somehow there would have to be a break—someone in her operation would have to link her to one of the incidents or there was no way for law enforcement to stop her.

He picked up one of the pages and ran his eyes over his notes once more. *What am I missing? What are we all missing? What is her vulnerable point?*

The door opening caused him to look up from what he was doing and he watched as Sam approached.

"Good to see you working hard, Lawrence," Sam joked.

"I can't figure out what we're missing."

"That's why I'm here. I've been at headquarters all day listening to Tom interrogate one of the Emperitza's main guys. There's some information you might want to hear."

"Do we finally have a break in the case?"

"Don't know yet. But, the police have a guy named Jose Moreno in custody that might give us what we need to move on the Emperitza. Last night, this guy and two others executed a drug dealer and his wife in front of the dealer's kids. One of the kids got the tag number of the car and the guys were apprehended. Two are in custody and one is on the loose. We know the guy on the run has had enough time to alert the Emperitza, but so far nothing has surfaced. However, this Moreno guy has been singing his heart out to our detective friend."

"What has he told you?"

"She wanted the dealer dead because she thought he'd double crossed her on a gigantic order that was supposed to arrive in Miami two days ago. She sent her people to kill the whole family after she decided the couple had hijacked the shipment." Sam looked over his head at Claire and Todd in the kitchen and motioned for them to join him. "You all need to hear all this, too."

"Are you kidding? We've had our ears to the door since you walked in here," Claire said. "Keep going, we're with you."

"I should've known there would be no secrets in this little house." Sam looked at Todd. "You would have gotten a kick out of the way Tom handled this goon. Once Tom threatened to drag the man's showgirl wife down to headquarters, the guy started thinking a bit differently about his situation. From what I understand, the gal is somewhat of a loose cannon and maybe he figured she'd tell all she knew. But, I digress." He nodded his head and continued. "The guy admitted that he worked for the Emperitza and he as much as said she ordered the execution. Tom also hammered him about the murder of that two-year old kid. Moreno knows something but he hasn't been willing to talk. I have no doubt that Tom will wear him down."

"Will he testify? If he won't testify, the lady will walk." Todd asked.

"Tom got a sworn statement about the execution of the drug dealer and his wife, but whether he can get Moreno on the witness stand is another question."

"Sam, what about the kids? Are they credible? Can they testify against Moreno?" Claire motioned toward Lawrence. "If the DA can work with the kids, they may not need Moreno."

"Wrong, Claire. That won't get us to the Emperitza. The kids can only testify about seeing Moreno at their house." Sam interrupted. "Yes, we want Moreno. But we need his testimony to get to his boss."

"They've got enough to bring her in for questioning." Lawrence's voice was animated. "If they can get her inside headquarters, then they might have a chance of tripping her up on some technicality."

"The odds are against us, Lawrence. The lady is the bread and butter for half of Miami. She's got more lawyers and judges in her pocket than we can count. They may be able to bring down an indictment against her, but by then she'll have moved her operation out of the state."

"You're right, Sam. But, let's see how it plays out."

*****

"Maddie, have you seen Eric again?" Lawrence wanted to make sure that she was taking care of herself.

"I told you what happened the other night. He better not show himself around my house. And, no, he hasn't called." Her smile disappeared and she looked embarrassed. "Lawrence, I made a big mistake and the worst part is that you know about it. I knew better than to get involved, but I did it anyway."

"You're human. We all do things we wish we hadn't done."

"Not you. I can't imagine that you ever let anyone compromise who you are. And, I promise it won't happen to me again."

Lawrence laughed. "My dear, at your young age that's a rather rash statement. Just learn from each mistake and move on. That's my motto."

"Has Sam given you any more information about Jeff and Eric? Are they going to question Elena?"

"They may question her, but no one thinks she's involved. You know her dad's an attorney and I'm sure he's giving her good advice. She and her son will be all right." He wrinkled his forehead and thought for a moment. "I think I'll invite her over for lunch. I want her to know that she's got my support. I've always liked her, you know."

"Will Sam let you do that?"

"Do you think he could stop me?" He looked defiant and then softened. "I hate being treated like a two-year old. Of course I'll clear it with Sam!"

"This whole thing is making you grumpy." She walked over and patted his shoulder. "We'll all be glad when it's over. I know you haven't been able to see Jocelyn, but have you talked to her?"

"I tried to call her yesterday, but Carter answered the phone and said she was sleeping. They're keeping her sedated because of the pain, but she's off the critical list. He also told me that Mark Sanders had been to see her several times. What do you make of that?"

"You know more about their relationship than I do. But my guess is he's still in love with her."

"I don't think those two ever really let go of each other."

The phone rang and Maddie jumped to answer it. But Claire got there first.

"Hello. Yes. Please repeat that. Wait, don't hang up."

Claire held the receiver away from her and looked at it quizzically. "That was strange."

"Who was it?" Lawrence asked.

"It was a woman. I could tell that much. But all she said was 'I'll see you tomorrow.' Then she hung up."

"Did she have an accent?"

"Yes, but I couldn't distinguish it. She didn't say enough."

"It was either a wrong number or the Emperitza." Lawrence said off handedly. "But, what in the world did she mean? What's happening tomorrow?"

"I think it was a wrong number, Lawrence. The lady wouldn't give us that kind of warning." Maddie looked at Claire. "Don't you agree?"

"One thing I've learned about her is she likes drama. Her methodology seems to depend on her mood. She likes everything from motorcycle drive-by killing to old-style executions to mind-manipulation that intimidates those who displease her. She likes to play games with her victims, and I agree with Sam, I think she's using drugs very heavily." Claire responded.

"I know you want to attend Alli Anderson's funeral tomorrow, but after this call, I doubt that Sam will allow it." Todd offered. "That's the only thing going on that would take you away from this house."

"Then, we won't tell Sam about this phone call." Lawrence picked up the newspaper and continued reading. He knew the others were going to begin their protest and he was ready for their objections.

"Whoa, friend. Do you expect us to keep silent about this just so you can go to the funeral?" Claire said. "Lawrence, put the paper down and let's discuss this. You can't issue a statement like that and think we'll go along with you."

"The three of you gang up on me all the time. I may be old, but I'm not going to let that woman control any more of my life than I have to." He folded the paper and placed it on the table. "First of all, I plan to attend the funeral. Second, we need to be prepared for anything. And, third, I think we'll probably get to meet the lady in person if we're there."

"Tomorrow is the family service. How do you think she's going to get inside? This thing will be more closely guarded than the queen's coronation and nobody will get in that church without an invitation," Todd argued.

"Then she must know somebody who's willing to give one to her." Lawrence nodded. "I'm telling you, the lady is planning to be at the funeral."

"If you're that sure, then we need to get Sam and Tom here to figure out a plan." Maddie looked at Todd. "I still don't think it's a good idea for Lawrence to be anywhere near that church tomorrow." Then she glared at Lawrence. "Do you have some kind of death wish? Her henchmen are sharpshooter assassins, not amateurs. I know you think you're invincible, but I never thought you'd take this kind of risk."

"Wait until we've talked to Sam before you make that kind of judgment call, Maddie."

"Fine. I'll call Sam and have him set up a meeting here tonight. Let's see what they think of your hair-brain scheme." She shrugged as she picked up the phone.

*****

The small living room of the guesthouse was crowded and everyone there had his or her opinion about the phone call and the possibility of something happening at the funeral. Lawrence was adamant about who the caller was and what the message meant, and he presented an action plan that he thought might net them the grand prize.

"Tom, have a warrant ready for her arrest. This may be our one and only chance of grabbing her."

"The DA has enough evidence to arrest her for the murders of that couple in south Miami and they're trying to find the connection to link her directly to as many as two-hundred other killings over the last few years. We can get the warrant, but I doubt if she'll surface in a public place. If she sent you a warning that means she's sending a hit-man," Tom West said.

"That doesn't make sense. She wants that book stopped first. Then, she'll send someone to finish the job." Sam countered. "I'm sure she wants Lawrence dead, but it won't happen until she knows he's killed the book."

"I think things are beginning to close in on her. In the last few days, the Task Force has made some inroads into her operation and she's losing people and money. The FBI has arrested several of her top people and the Coast Guard has stopped two big shipments from coming into the port. I also know the surveillance of the small airports has resulted in the confiscation of three or four planes.

"And, when I talked to Carter yesterday, he told me that your guys arrested five men at the bus barn who'd been using the city buses to courier drugs to some of the suburbs." Lawrence was going down the list of events that had taken place just that week. "The combined efforts are paying off and she has to be feeling the heat. I think she's starting to make some big mistakes. In the past she used her brains and she built an untouchable infrastructure. Now she's acting on emotion and she's getting careless."

"You may be right. But how am I going to identify her and protect you and the others who are attending the funeral?" asked Tom. "If she shows up at the church, she'll be disguised."

"She'll be there and she'll have an army with her. I don't know her plans, but she won't come alone. Even if she plans to kill me herself, she won't come alone. So, we have to outsmart her and I think I'll be able to identify her even in disguise."

*****

Sunshine and a cool breeze off the bay greeted the mourners who had come to pay their last respects to Alli Anderson. Outside the church, the street had been cordoned off to all traffic but the three limousines carrying the family and the hearse that carried Alli's casket.

All other cars were parked in the lot behind the church after being carefully checked. The occupants had to present the proper invitation and identification before the cars were allowed to enter the area. Then cars and handbags were checked for weapons.

Snipers were positioned on the rooftops of buildings on either side of and across from the church. Inside the church, the balcony was closed to visitors and Tom had placed four policemen along its perimeter. Lawrence had been escorted to a pew that was situated under the balcony on the right side of the sanctuary.

Lara had flown in for the service but would return to Eleuthera later in the afternoon. She entered the church with Sam and they took their seats in the pew behind Lawrence. Maddie and Claire were seated on either side of Lawrence, and Todd was seated directly in front of him.

"I feel shielded against any possible thing that could happen today." Lawrence whispered to Maddie. "It's a good thing I'm not claustrophobic. You all are smothering me."

"You insisted on coming. So this is the way it's going to be." She smiled. "Sit back and pay your respects."

Lawrence watched the center aisle as the guests began to gather. Most of the faces were unfamiliar, but he recognized members of Alli's band and Mark Sanders. Sam leaned forward to identify some of the others, including her agent and manager. Fifty or sixty people were seated when there was a lull in the procession followed by the entrance of the family. When all of them were seated, Margo, Michael and Sunni began a slow walk to the front of the church.

A hush fell and all eyes turned to watch the tall, elegant woman dressed in black. Although she had been out of the limelight for seven years, her presence was as engaging as ever. She was still the Diva, commanding attention just by being in the room.

She is still one of the most beautiful women I've ever seen, Lawrence thought as he watched her proceed down the aisle with her daughter on one side and her husband on the other. *What a shame we can no longer hear her voice.*

The priest conducted a beautiful service and several people eulogized the short life of the pop star. Then, a tall, exotic woman walked to the chancel rail and began to speak.

We are all pilgrims on a journey—we carry our dreams, our hopes and our desires with us as we travel from our past to our present in search of our future. But for some of us, the journey ends before our footprints have barely had a chance to be etched into the sand. Alli's journey ended too soon, she did not live out her future, but she did live her dreams. She left her footprints on this world with her music and her zest for life.

Her time on earth has past, but her memory will linger. As she sleeps, she will be cradled in the hearts of those who knew her as a daughter, a sister, a granddaughter, a niece, and a friend. She will be there, just beyond our reach, when we think her name or remember the melody of a lullaby.

Every mother wants to sing her daughter to sleep and as Alli begins her eternal sleep, may she be comforted by the gentle sound of her mother's voice.

Margo walked to the chancel rail where Dr. Lulu Sarsyn was standing. Lulu took her hand and stood beside her as she began to softly croon the words of the lullaby. The voice that had been silent for years rang out across the church growing stronger with every note. There was tenderness and a poignancy that poured forth from Margo's heart that transformed each word into a symphony of love and farewell.

Sleep well, my child, sleep well. The angels sang for joy at your birth. Sleep well, my child, sleep well. There is no more darkness, only light.

Sounds of sobbing were heard from all corners of the church as Lawrence passed a note discreetly over his shoulder to Sam. She's here. Not sure where exactly. She's somewhere in front of me.

*****

The ranks closed quickly around Lawrence as they stood to leave the church. Sam had signaled Tom and the eyes and ears of law enforcement were alert and scanning the crowd. As Lawrence reached the end of the pew, he stopped abruptly and stared at a woman wearing a veiled hat who was approaching him. The heavy fragrance of Chanel No. 5 was unmistakable. She was within a few feet of him. Did he make the first move or did he wait to see what she had planned? He reached behind him to grab Maddie's hand just as the imposing body of Eduardo DaSilva stepped from the shadow of the aisle and stood between him and the Emperitza.

When she saw DaSilva, she hastily pushed people out of her way and tried to disappear in the crowd. Lawrence last glimpsed her as she ran behind the chancel rail to the choir loft. Sam and Tom were behind her, trying to make their way to that area of the church without alarming those who were following Alli's casket as the pallbearers moved up the aisle toward the exit.

Without another moment's hesitation, Lawrence's protection team put the evacuation plan into action and whisked him to a windowless room off the narthex. Maddie and Claire were ordered to remain there while Todd and several police officers ran out of the church to assist in securing the perimeter of the church.

Lawrence heard the officers instructing the funeral guests to remain in the narthex and to stay calm. They were told that an uninvited guest was in the building who wished to disrupt the service. "This should be taken care of in a few minutes and then you'll be free to go on to the cemetery. We apologize for the interruption, but we don't know the intent of this person and we want you to be as safe as possible."

A knock on the door alarmed Maddie. She motioned for Claire to go to the door while she moved between Lawrence and the door.

"Who is it?" Claire asked.

"Eduardo DaSilva. I need to speak with Senhor Fitz."

Claire turned to see what reaction Maddie and Lawrence had to the request, but both of them were nodding for her to open the door.

With gun drawn, she cracked open the door just wide enough for her to see the older gentleman. "Are you alone?"

DaSilva nodded his head and quickly entered the small room. "I came to warn you that she might be somewhere near the church today and also to pay my respects to Margo. However, I didn't think the Emperitza would be bold enough to be seated in the church."

"Thank you, Eduardo. I'll admit I'm more surprised to see you than I was to see her. When I saw you in the crowd, I had just passed a note to Sam Baxter to tell him she was near."

"How did you know that, Lawrence?" Maddie inquired.

"It was the overwhelming scent of her perfume. I recognized it from the night she held me captive. She must bathe in Chanel No. 5."

"You even knew the name of the fragrance. That's impressive, my friend." Maddie looked at the others and shrugged her shoulders. "After all these years, why am I surprised at anything you do?"

"It was the only fragrance my wife would wear. There is no way I would have forgotten it." He motioned for Eduardo to take the chair next to him. "How did you know she would be here, Eduardo?"

"I have made a point of knowing where she is and what she's doing ever since the death of Paolo. My reasons and my connection to her are very personal."

"If law enforcement catches her today, they have a warrant for her arrest. The dominos have started to fall, Eduardo, just as you predicted. Her empire is crumbling and her reign of terror may soon lose its grip on Miami."

"We can only hope, my friend. We can only hope."

Jeanne Moon Farmer

Chapter Thirty-six

Sam

When the Emperitza began to run, Sam and Tom took off behind her. Tom had signaled to the men posted around the church to execute the action plan they had developed if she appeared. All entrances to the building were secured and there was a rush to protect the guests. The funeral procession had been halted and Lawrence had been moved to a safe room. The guests had been ushered to the narthex of the church and were told they would be released once the intruder had been located.

"Is she alone? Do you see anyone else?" Sam yelled to Tom as he ran up the steps to the choir loft. "She had to leave through that door."

They moved cautiously through the loft to the closed door, checking each row of seats as they made their way around the altar. Neither of them had been in the church before, but they had studied the floor plans provided by the priest the night before. They knew that once they opened the door at the top of the loft they would enter a maze of hallways that led in three directions. They hoped it was to their advantage to know that there were only two outside doors.

Tom had stationed men at each of those doors, so Sam knew the woman they were chasing would never get out those doors undetected. The problem was all the places she could be hiding inside. Three other officers joined them as they were getting ready to open the door and Tom was quickly pointing out the directions each would take. As they split up, Tom went to the left and Sam to the right.

Sam was concerned that an innocent bystander might be trapped in one of the rooms at the mercy of a woman who wouldn't think twice about killing them to protect herself. In their earlier discussions with the priest, they had been assured that no one would be in this area during or after the service. Still, he worried.

With his back against the wall and his gun drawn, he side-stepped carefully down the hall. After every step, he stopped to listen for any sound that might indicate that someone was near. On either side of the hallway were five closed doors and he knew he would have to check each room. He tried to remember the floor plan—were these classrooms, offices, or closets?

When he opened the first door and looked inside, his heart skipped a beat. The room was full of racks of choir robes and he groaned. This would be a perfect place to hide. Guardedly, he made his way down the rows, checking for feet, listening for the sound of breathing, watching for the slightest movement. As he neared the end of the first row, he heard the sound of footsteps in the hallway. The steps were slow and hesitant, each one deliberately taken. He spun around and made his way back the way he had come. Just as he approached the door, it was flung open and one of Tom's men stood in front of him.

"This way." The officer whispered and motioned for Sam to follow him back in the direction of the choir loft. Seeing the hall from this direction, Sam saw a door they had missed located slightly below the stairs that lead to the loft. As the officer opened the door, two shots rang out in their direction and Sam saw the man in front of him take a bullet and slump against the door.

He laid down, returning her gunfire as he grabbed the wounded man and pulled him out of the way. Crouching low, he crawled in the direction of the shots. Inching his way inside the small storage area, he raised his head high enough to see her shadow. She pushed a storage rack away from the wall and paint cans fell off the shelf near where Sam was crouched. He jumped back and lost his balance. She seized the advantage to shoot at him as she rushed past.

Firing blindly, he shot in her direction and heard her stumble. A stream of profanity told him that he had either hit her or she had run into an obstacle. He staggered to his feet; taking steps in her direction when he heard Tom shout for her to drop her gun and put her hands in the air.

Within seconds, the hallway was filled with police officers with drawn guns all pointed at the most notorious woman in the city. The Emperitza was shouting and threatening in English and Spanish, as several of Tom's men held her arms and put the handcuffs on her.

"You are under arrest on suspicion of murder, money laundering, drug trafficking, extortion, and kidnapping. You have the right to remain silent...." Tom continued to Mirandize her as his men walked her down the hall toward an awaiting squad car.

"Sam, are you okay?" He had returned to the area shortly after the ambulance arrived to take the wounded officer to the hospital. "Looks like he was hit in his left arm and rib cage, but it doesn't look critical." He stopped walking and turned back to where Sam was standing. "My God, you're hit. Why didn't you say something?"

Tom reached out and grabbed Sam as he began to slide toward the floor. "Stop that ambulance before it leaves. We've got another casualty."

"Lara." Sam whispered as he closed his eyes against the searing pain.

Jeanne Moon Farmer

Chapter Thirty-seven

Lawrence

"Why doesn't someone come and tell us what's going on?" Lawrence was antsy. There was too much commotion and noise coming from outside the room where he was being held. "I hear sirens, Maddie. Crack that door open and tell me what you see."

"That's not a good idea. I was told to stay here with the door closed until someone came for us. It won't be long—"

Before she could finish the sentence, the door opened and a police officer walked in the room.

"Detective West asked me to let you know what's happened. Right now, we have the Emperitza in custody and she's on her way downtown. Two men have gunshot wounds and they have been transported to Mercy Hospital. We've given the okay for the funeral procession to continue on to the cemetery and you are free to join them. A car is waiting for Mr. Fitz at the side entrance of the church." He looked over where Lawrence and Eduardo were seated. "Excuse me sir, but I don't have any information about you. If you'd give me your name, I'll find out where your car is."

"I am Eduardo DaSilva. My car is waiting for me across the street. Do you know if the parents have left for the cemetery? I had wished to speak to Margo before I left." Eduardo stood up.

"I can check on that for you, sir."

"Yes, thank you." He held out his hand to Lawrence. "I must go. My plane is waiting to take me home." He shook hands and started for the door. "Maddie, I will call you soon if there is additional information that might be helpful."

Lawrence made the attempt to engage Eduardo even though he knew it would be unlikely for them to meet again. "Eduardo, you have my thanks for everything. Once again you have come to our rescue and I am grateful. Perhaps the next time you are in this country we will be able to meet for dinner and a conversation that isn't laden with problems."

The officer reappeared at the door. "Margo is in the second limousine and she is waiting to see you. If you'll follow me, sir."

Eduardo nodded his head toward Lawrence and left the room.

"I fell in love with that man the first time I met him. It's a shame he's old enough to be my grandfather." Maddie smiled and walked over to help Lawrence from the chair. "I don't know if he's one of the good guys or not. I just know he is one fine gentleman."

"I agree, my dear." Lawrence was slowly rising out of the chair. "I'm very tired. I think it would be best if I didn't go to the cemetery. Would you mind if we went back to the house?"

"Maddie, if you and Todd want to go to the cemetery, I think it will be okay for me to take Lawrence home. If you're not sure, we can find Sam and ask him," said Claire.

"I'm surprised that we haven't seen Sam or Todd. You wait here and I'll go tell them that we're going home. I don't need to go to the cemetery, but I'm sure Todd will want to go." Maddie left the room with an assurance that she would return in a few minutes.

"Claire, why don't we start for the car? I think the young man said it had been brought to the side entrance."

Before Lawrence could walk across the room, Maddie was back and closed the door behind her. "My news isn't good." She looked shaken. "One of the two men taken to the hospital is Sam. I don't know how serious it is, but Todd left to drive Lara to the hospital. Someone will call and let us know as soon as the doctors have seen him." Her shoulders sagged. "Lara must be frantic with worry." She reached for Lawrence and hugged him. "He'll be all right. I just know it. Let's get you home and then I'll see what I can find out."

*****

Claire brought them each a cup of tea and sat beside Maddie on the couch. "This day has been unreal. My head is spinning."

"Nothing could have prepared us for the events of this past week. Our friends lost a daughter, Sam is in crisis, Jocelyn is healing physically but the emotional scars will always be there, and I am an old and stubborn man who once thought this fight was worthwhile. My heart is heavy because of what I have caused."

The room was silent for a long moment, then Maddie leaned forward and covered Lawrence's left hand with her right. "You taught me long ago that the blame game is not in anybody's best interest. Your reason for this was noble and the end result will have long-term effects. You didn't create the evil; you're not responsible for the monster. I'm as sad as you are, but I haven't given up hope." Maddie leaned back on the sofa and sipped her tea. "Claire, even on a warm Miami afternoon, this hits the spot. I've used up all my energy, too."

Lawrence gazed out the window and hoped a few minutes of silence would help him let go of the heaviness that was weighing on his shoulders. He knew the lawyers would already be working hard for the release of the Empertiza and once she was out of jail, his ordeal might escalate. However, something had changed inside him and he knew any future encounter with her would be different.

He was too tired to continue the fight. He would gladly give up his life, that seemed to be the inevitable conclusion to the woman's plans, but he couldn't let the bloodshed against his friends go on any longer. They had suffered too much.

When he had rested, he would call his agent and cancel the publication of the book. He would return the advance to the publisher and pay the fine that would be imposed for a broken contract.

The sun was going down and a rosy glow had settled upon Sharon's garden. Someday he would like to sit in this chair in peace and watch a scene just like this one. Today there was too much turmoil and confusion for a scene like this to seem real and he couldn't find any enjoyment in it.

Someone was shaking his shoulder and he realized he had dozed off. When he opened his eyes, Maddie was smiling down at him.

"Todd called and Sam is going to be all right. He's out of surgery and his injuries were not as extensive as the doctors feared. Lara is with him and Todd will be back here soon. On the other subject, the Emperitza will have to spend at least tonight in jail. For some reason, her lawyers couldn't find a judge who would hold a bond hearing in the middle of the night."

There was a lilt to her voice. "Maybe there are some law abiding judges in this town after all."

PART THREE

Wake up! Wake up! Clothe yourself with strength, Zion!
Put on your beautiful clothes ... O city....
Godless and evil people will no longer come to you.
Isaiah 52:1

Jeanne Moon Farmer

Chapter Thirty-eight

Tom West

The hallway outside of the interrogation room was filled with FBI and DEA agents, the Police Chief, the head of the Port Authority, and other members of the Drug Task Force. Everyone wanted a look at the notorious mastermind of the south Florida drug trafficking business and no one knew what to expect from her.

Tom West and a senior FBI agent had been briefed and were ready with questions they knew would not get answered. They hoped that a rapid-fire approach might unsettle her just enough to get a response. Her attorneys were already on the phone with every judge in town trying to arrange an immediate court appearance and a bond amount that would ensure that the Emperitza did not have to spend one night in the Dade County jail.

When the woman was brought into the room, Tom was surprised at her appearance. He had expected someone glamorous, expensively dressed, and well manicured. Instead he was seated across from a middle-aged housewife who had let herself go. The alleged Emperitza was average height, overweight, and dowdy. Her South American heritage was evident in her black hair, dark eyes and olive complexion. The expression on her face was dour and solemn.

Was this the woman who had ordered all the mayhem and murder? Was she really the cold-blooded killer that had orchestrated execution after execution? Did she have the presence to command assassins and frighten rival drug moguls? Was she clever enough to run a million dollar business? And, how did she get into that church with a loaded gun? Which one of his men was in her stable?

"Who were you after at the funeral?"

"Why were you targeting Lawrence Fitz?"

"How did you get in the church with a loaded gun?"

"Who's your contact in Columbia?"

"When's the next big shipment coming in to the Port of Miami?"

"How many of your people are working for me?"

"Who's going to run the show if you end up in jail for the next forty years?"

"Did you order the execution of the Ramirez family?"

"Who killed that two-year old?"

"Are your rivals going to take over Miami when they find out you're in here singing at the top of your lungs?"

Question after question, over and over, louder and louder. The lady never looked up. She kept her eyes on the ground and seemed unfazed by anything that was going on around her. The agent leaned across the table and got as close to her face as he could.

"We can stay here all night. We can hammer these questions at you all night. There'll be no sleep, no dinner, no drugs. How long do you think you can go without a hit?" He took a step back and waited.

"You can sit in this room with the two of us as long as it takes. We're not going anywhere until we get some answers and your attorneys aren't getting in until we give the signal."

When he mentioned her attorneys, she looked up for a brief second. Then she lowered her head again and the questions continued.

Tom stood up and walked over to a picture on the wall. As he looked at the picture, he unobtrusively motioned and immediately the lights in the room were turned up to a blinding glare. They shone directly on the Emperitza's face and the temperature in the room rose several degrees.

As perspiration beaded on her face, she made no effort to look at her accusers or to wipe the sweat from her lips. She had become an unfeeling statue.

Tom knew this would not be easy, but he never expected hours of silence and no reaction. The questions got more intense, more personal, and they failed to get a rise out of her.

"We've got several of your people sitting over in the jail and they are telling us things that sound impossible to imagine. The case they're making against you in order to save themselves is like reading the rap sheet of Al Capone. They're blaming you for every crime that's been committed in south Florida for the last ten years. You don't look like the type of person that would do all those horrible things. Surely, they're all lying about you. Why don't you tell us your side of the story?"

Silence.

"I understand that Lawrence Fitz's book will be on the book shelves by the end of the week. His publisher says the print run is ready for release." Tom sat down and calmly continued. "I've read a draft copy of that book and Mr. Fitz portrays you harshly, doesn't he? His picture of you isn't very flattering is it? No wonder you wanted to stop that book. Once people start reading it they're going to see right through you and the fear-factor you've worked so hard to build will collapse. Yes, that book is going to make your threats seem like blowing in the wind."

She lifted her head and looked Tom in the eyes. For a split second he felt an icy chill and the hair on the back of his neck prickled.

"Burn in hell, copper." The words flew at him like the venom of a cobra and then she dropped her head again.

Tom had faced hardened, cold blooded criminals in the past and he knew some people were not redeemable. But, he had never come face to face with the degree of evil he felt in that moment. The woman had to be stopped.

*****

At five o'clock in the morning, the inquisition was over. Tom and the agent had to relinquish and concede defeat. Their rounds of questioning had not produced any results. Her attorneys had found a judge willing to hear a petition for bond at seven o'clock and their demands for time with their client could no longer be ignored.

"We aren't finished with you. You can count on seeing us again." The FBI agent flung the words at her as he left the room and her attorney's entered.

"Get us a room that isn't bugged, officer. There's no way we can have a conversation with our client with everyone from Miami to Washington, DC, listening." The attorney glared at Tom as he made his demands.

Tom gave instructions and then walked out of headquarters. His head hurt, his back hurt, and he couldn't wait to take a shower. He felt dirtier than he had ever felt and he hoped some scalding hot water would wash all vestiges of that woman down the drain. The smell of Chanel No. 5 perfume would probably haunt him for the rest of his life.

$$*****$$

"She's a flight risk! Who set her bond?" Tom was yelling. "How are we supposed to do our job when the judges do things like this?" He had returned to headquarters later in the afternoon to hear the news that the Emperitza had walked out of the courtroom on a bond that was lower than what most judges set for misdemeanors. He was angrier than he had been in years. "Call a meeting of the task force. We just lost our chance to shut her down."

Stomping out of the office, he slammed the door behind him. "What's the use? All that work for nothing."

Chapter Thirty-nine

Lawrence

"I know you've told me Sam is all right, but I'd rest easier if I could see him. Who's at the hospital with Lara? Somebody has got to be there with her." Lawrence wasn't going to take no for an answer. "Did anyone call his son?"

Claire, Maddie and Todd finally gave in to his persistent requests and decided to take him to the hospital to see Sam and Jocelyn. They agreed with him that while the Emperitza was being detained at police headquarters, there was less possibility of an immediate threat to his safety.

"I talked with Lara earlier and Sam's son will be here in the morning. Lawrence, against my better judgment, we're going to take you to the hospital. But you've got to promise to leave when we say time is up." Maddie had been out voted by Claire and Todd, so she walked beside Lawrence as they headed for the car. "After all the excitement and emotion, I don't know where you've found the energy to go out again."

"After Eduardo left the church, the police rushed me home without giving me a chance to say a word of condolence to Margo and Michael. Now there are things I need to say to Sam and Jocelyn. Please try to understand." He tried to shake the feelings of melancholy but he knew the feelings would linger until he had resolved things with the two people who were in the hospital because of him.

Hoping the people in the car would give him some straight answers, he asked about the reactions at the funeral. "Did the funeral goers know what was going on in the church?"

"They were told that an intruder was in the building and they were held in the narthex of the church until the Empertiza was taken into custody. I don't believe anyone knew the identity of the intruder or what exactly transpired." Claire answered.

"Once they had her in the squad car, they let everyone go on to the cemetery. I told the Anderson's that you were tired and had gone on home. Their minds were occupied with other things, Lawrence, and I don't think they even suspected there was trouble." Todd explained. "They're show biz people and they've dealt with overzealous fans for years. I know they thought that was what was happening."

Todd drove the car around several blocks to make sure they weren't being followed and then he backtracked across the highway for good measure.

"The shots that were fired were muffled by the traffic noise and the police had closed up everything in the front of the church to protect the guests. People probably thought they heard a car backfire if they heard anything at all," Todd continued.

"Were you surprised to see Eduardo?" Maddie asked. "Why do you think he was there?"

"I'm learning not to be surprised by anything Eduardo DaSilva does. I don't know if he had a premonition that there would be trouble today or whether he was there to pay his respects and happened to spot the Emperitza. Either way, I owe him a debt of gratitude." Lawrence wondered if he would ever have an opportunity to repay the debt. "I know he is fond of Margo, and his family was responsible for so much of her heartache. I'm not surprised that he would come to her daughter's funeral."

Driving up to the hospital made him feel uneasy. He began looking at the faces of people walking in and out of the front doors and checking the cars parked on either side of the walkway. "Todd, go around the circle again. I don't feel comfortable." His eyes were alert to what was going on outside the car and he sensed that Maddie had reached inside her purse for her gun. "Something isn't right."

Before the words were out of his mouth, a car came speeding around the circle going the wrong way and rammed into their car. The jolt threw Claire against the dashboard and Lawrence and Maddie against the back of the front seats. Claire screamed out in pain and the car horn blared as Todd was thrown into the steering wheel. They stopped abruptly as the other vehicle backed away and sped off across the parking lot barely missing people who were crossing the street.

"My God, what was that?" Maddie looked out the back window and tried to determine the make and model of the car. "Was that intentional?"

"Claire, are you okay?" Todd asked as the doors of the car were thrown open and hospital orderlies tried to determine if anyone was injured.

"Ma'am, that's a nasty cut on your forehead. You're going to need stitches." The young man helped Claire to the wheelchair and began wheeling her toward the Emergency Room.

"Leave the car here and come inside. Can you walk? Who needs assistance? We need to see if there are any extensive injuries." Hospital personnel were asking questions and trying to move them from the car into the building. "We've called the police and they're on their way. Several of us saw what happened. That other driver must be crazy or on something! He was going the wrong way and had to be going fifty miles an hour when he hit you."

Maddie waved away any help for herself. "I'm fine, but he needs some attention. You'd better bring a gurney." She pointed at Lawrence. "I think he passed out."

*****

Claire had to have stitches to close the gash on her forehead, Todd and Maddie were fine, and after a series of tests, the doctors decided it was best to keep Lawrence overnight for observation. Three of them were told to go home and get a good night's rest, and police guards were posted outside Lawrence's room. After a lot of discussion, a squad car took Claire back to the guesthouse, Maddie went to the third floor to be with Lara, and Todd stayed with Lawrence.

"Todd, go rest. They'll take good care of me." Lawrence saw the tired look on Todd's face, but knew the young man wouldn't leave him even if an army of police guards were surrounding his room.

"There's one of those recliner chairs in your room. I'll be able to sleep there much easier than I would at home."

*****

Todd had gone out in the hall to stretch his legs when a policeman walked over and handed him a preliminary report on the accident.

"We found the car over on Dixie Highway. The guy who hit you had abandoned it, and, of course, there's no sign of him. The car was reported stolen from the mall last night. They found drugs in the car and they're checking fingerprints. Something will turn up. How's the old man doing?"

"He'll be fine. They want to run a few more tests before they release him. Let me know if you hear anything else." Todd walked back down the hall and tried to find a comfortable spot in the recliner.

*****

Sunlight streamed into the room and awakened Todd. When he opened his eyes he saw Lawrence sitting on the side of the bed.

"Where you going?" he asked sleepily.

"I'd like to go home. There's not a thing wrong with me that a night's rest in a comfortable bed won't cure." Lawrence wanted to get off the bed, but he couldn't figure out how to reach the ties on the hospital gown. "Where did they put my clothes?"

"Slow down. We can't go anywhere without the doctor's discharge papers and he hasn't been in to see you this morning. Have you even had breakfast?"

"Of course not. All they've done is take my blood and wake me up every hour or so. How in the world did you sleep through them coming in here all night long?"

"I must have been tired." Todd moved the chair to an upright position. "The police don't think the accident had anything to do with

304

you. It was some guy in a stolen car that was high on something. Just a coincidence that he hit us."

"And, you believe that?"

"No, but they don't have anything more to tell us. Stay in bed and I'll see if they have anything new."

"Then I want you to go home. Wrinkled clothes and a five o'clock shadow do not become you."

*****

"Mr. Fitz, other than a mild concussion, you are doing well. I'm going to sign your discharge papers and send you home to rest. Stay quiet for the next few days and don't use your eyes too much. I'll see you in my office in one week for a follow-up unless you develop symptoms that need my immediate attention—blurred vision, nausea." The doctor handed the nurse the clipboard and reached out to shake Lawrence's hand. "Take care of yourself. At your age, a concussion must be taken seriously."

When the doctor and nurse left the room, Lawrence scoffed, "At my age, indeed!" He threw his legs over the side of the bed and motioned for Todd to help him find his clothes.

"Will you take me to see Sam? I'd like to see him if that's possible. What was the extent of his injury? I don't think anyone has given me the details."

"He took a pretty serious hit to his kidney and spleen. He was in surgery for several hours, but the doctor told Lara he should make a full recovery. With only one kidney, the doctor doesn't want him to return to work. But you know Sam." Todd talked as he handed Lawrence his clothes. "Do you feel steady on your feet or do you want me to call the nurse?"

"I'm fine. Let me wash my face and I'll be ready to go. Will you see about getting a wheel chair? I'm not sure I want to walk any distance."

*****

"Sam, you look like you could get up and walk out of here. I guess it will take more than a bullet to hold you down." Lawrence tried to make light of Sam's condition, but had to admit to himself that his friend looked weak and in pain. "Don't try to talk. I'll only be here a few minutes and I'll do the talking." He wanted Sam to know that he was stopping the publication of the book.

"I've caused chaos with my insistence that the book be published. But, enough is enough. As soon as I'm out of here, I'm calling my editor and pulling the book. Eduardo told me they have enough evidence to indict the Emperitza and many of her people, but the book has become a personal challenge for her and whether she's in jail or not, she'll continue to find ways to make life hell for me and those I care about. Our war is over, Sam. I can't allow it to go on."

Sam tried to raise himself up on his elbow, but the pain was too much and he lowered his head back down on the pillow. "You can't give in now. Miami is too important for us to let her win. This city is finally beginning to come out from under the shadow that has hung over it for too long. We all lose if you give in now." He closed his eyes. "I'm too tired to argue. Do the right thing, Lawrence. The task force, all of law enforcement, would tell you the same thing. You've got to help finish what's been started by making sure that book is on the shelf. It's our insurance against her and her kind of evil."

Sam looked at the faces of the people in the room and knew they shared his feelings.

"Miami is worth it," Sam whispered.

Chapter Forty

Jocelyn

Today, she sat at her desk addressing invitations to her wedding—an event she had thought would never happen. It had been six months since those horrible weeks when the world went crazy. Jocelyn had recovered, and with the help of her family and Mark, she had mourned for the children she would never have and was trying to move on with her life.

With the issue of natural children out of the way, the church had granted her a dispensation to marry Mark Sanders. The fact that they were first cousins was no longer relevant and they would be married in the church next month.

She looked at the names on the envelopes and wondered once again how they had survived the ordeal with the Emperitza. Lawrence was probably not as spry as he was before it all began, but he was back in his apartment, writing, researching and planning more books to come.

The novel of controversy, *The Scorpion's Sting*, had been published three months ago and was still on the bestseller list. There were only a few people who knew the part that book played in initiating a chain reaction that brought down one of the drug world's most ruthless matriarchs. Lawrence's decision to fictionalize a story about the Emperitza and her violent reign over Miami may have been the catalyst that eroded the massive cocaine business in south Florida.

The Emperitza had fled Miami as soon as she was released from jail and was apparently in hiding. She was the number one fugitive on the FBI's Most Wanted list and murder charges were outstanding against her. When she fled she had taken with her enormous amounts of money, resources, and her connection to the cartel. But, without the infrastructure she had created, and through the efforts of the Drug Task Force, the drug trafficking operations in the city were collapsing. The violence that was her trademark was diminishing and the murder rates in the city were falling dramatically. It would take years for the stain to be erased from Miami's image, but people were cautiously optimistic that the city was safer than it had been for the years of her influence.

On the days Jocelyn went to the *Miami Herald* office, she was very aware that murder and mayhem were no longer the everyday topics of conversation in the newsroom or the headlines of the paper.

As she placed the envelope with Lawrence's name in the "ready to mail" stack, she felt a rush of love for the elderly gentleman and prayed that she would have him in her life for years to come. At his age, she knew she needed to accept the reality that his years were numbered, even though she wasn't ready to accept that he wouldn't live forever. She sighed and reached for another envelope.

She would have to look-up Sam and Lara's new address. They had taken the advice of his doctors and had moved to the islands to help speed his recovery. They had leased a house on Eleuthera, very near Margo and Michael Anderson's, and would probably stay there until Sam made a choice about returning to work. Everyone except Sam thought his career in security was over, but the twists and turns of life could never be underestimated or predicted, and he was determined not to let his injuries stop him.

Maddie Sonnett had made the decision to leave the prosecutor's office and had taken a position with the FBI. Lawrence and her father fussed about her safety and wanted something better for her. But secretly, Jocelyn knew they were proud of her choice. She had combined her background in law enforcement with her law degree and was working out of the field office in Miami. Lawrence had mentioned that she was involved with the task force, and he wouldn't be surprised if someday she was part of the team that eventually captured the Emperitza.

Todd Madison and Claire McGuire had returned to Miami Dade Police as special agents on assignment; Jeff Cannon and Eric Randall were serving time in prison, although it was doubtful that Jeff would ever be released. He had been found guilty of a multitude of charges including manslaughter in the death of Alli Anderson. She tried hard to be forgiving of Jeff Cannon and the role he had played in her injuries. But, six months was not long enough for her to forget the way it felt when he grabbed her and pushed her into Claire's gun. Her nightmares were not so frequent any more, but whenever she even thought his name she had to fight off the feelings of fear and panic.

She moved down her list to Elena Martinez, her father's attorney and friend, and was grateful the woman had not been charged with compliance in any of the crimes against her husband, Eric, or their former law partner, Jeff. She had survived the divorce from Eric and had formed a partnership with her father. They had opened a law firm downtown, and Lawrence had told her Elena was dating someone she might be serious about. She knew Elena would bring her son to the wedding but she included a note for her to bring a guest.

Her stepfather, Paul Donovan, was still on disability from his gunshot injuries, but Rosanne had assured her that he was doing well. He just wasn't ready to return to police duty. As she addressed the invitation to her extended family, she thought about the night in the hospital when she looked up and Rosanne was standing over her bed. Her birth mother had left her injured husband in the hospital in Los Angeles and had flown to be by her side.

It was her mother who had wiped the tears from her eyes and had given her permission to be happy. Rosanne, who had been so adamantly against Jocelyn and Mark's relationship, was the one who told her if she still loved him to tell him and then to do something about it. "The two of you have wasted too many years already. If you still love each other, God has finally given you a way to be together. You don't get *third* chances, Jocelyn."

She put down the envelopes and thought about the names that would not be receiving invitations. She and Mark had discussed the Anderson family at length, but decided not to include them even though Mark had toured with Margo and had been in a long-time relationship with Sunni. They both understood that Michael and Margo would not leave the island to attend and an invitation to Sunni might get complicated. They knew that Sunni had recently announced her engagement to a doctor she met in New York and would be getting married next year. She was pleased that Sunni had found someone new and had moved on from her break-up with Mark and she even thought, given different circumstances, she and Sunni could have been friends.

Whenever Jocelyn thought about Margo Anderson, she regretted that she had not been at Alli's funeral to hear Margo sing. What a beautiful tribute the mother had paid to her daughter. Especially since cancer had made it impossible for Margo to ever sing in public again and had forced her to retire. When Lawrence and Maddie could talk about something beside how to capture and arrest the Emperitza, they spoke in awe of the moment Margo began to sing the lullaby. Maddie told her she thought it was the most beautiful moment of the diva's long career—a simple lullaby crooned by a mother who never really knew her daughter.

Tears welled up in Jocelyn's eyes as she tried to forget that she might not have an opportunity to sing a lullaby to a child of her own. Her heartbreak would not stop, but at least she had more good days now than bad. She wiped the tears away before they got the best of her and continued addressing envelopes. There was too much for her to do today to get caught up in a bout of self-pity. She had invitations to finish and later in the day there was a wedding gown fitting that she had to be ready for.

She closed her eyes and tried to picture her wedding. It would be small and intimate, with only family and a few friends in attendance. Her best friend from childhood, Ruthie, was her only attendant. She smiled when she thought about Ruthie walking down the aisle in an electric blue gown. The bridesmaid would steal the show from the bride. There was no way Ruthie could hide her light under a bushel. She had always been vibrant and happy, and people were naturally drawn to her. Ruthie wouldn't set out to be the star of the show; it would just happen by the sheer magnitude of her friend's smile. But, that was what she had always loved about her.

As adults, she took comfort in knowing she could talk to Ruthie about Gracie, her very special grandmother. Ruthie had loved Gracie almost as much as Jocelyn and they could share memories and laugh about their life growing up in Allapattah. They had been so innocent and carefree as children.

Wow. I sure am doing a lot to make myself cry this morning. I need to move around and think about something else!

She reached for the phone and called her father's work number.

"Hey, Daddy. How would you like to take me to lunch today? I have some errands to run and I'll be in your neighborhood."

*****

Several hours later, she walked into a deli near the Miami Transit bus barn and looked to see if her father had already taken a booth. He was always early and lately she was always late, so she wasn't surprised when he waved for her to join him.

"You're a sight for sore eyes. I'll take a pretty girl over all those bus drivers every chance I get." Carter stood up and gave his daughter a big hug.

"Thanks for lifting my spirits out of the shadows." Standing with her father's arms around her, she realized for the first time in years that her shadows were gone and she smiled. "What looks good to eat?"

"You order the Ruben and I'll order the Cuban. Let's celebrate in true Miami style!"

Jeanne Moon Farmer

EPILOGUE

It was a day for dreams to come true. She and Mark walked into the office of Catholic Family Services with hope, excitement and a bad case of nerves. Inside this building, their daughter waited for them to take her home. Jocelyn reviewed all the details in her mind and squeezed Mark's hand a little tighter. Over her shoulder was a diaper bag with all the things they thought they would need—blanket, bottle, diapers, pacifier, teddy bear, booties, change of outfit. If this child needed something else, they would have to stop at a store before they got home.

Carter had given Jocelyn a baby blanket that her grandmother had packed away in the old cedar chest, Mark's mother had contributed the bear, Rosanne had Express mailed the diaper bag from California, and Lawrence had added the outfit and booties. Their family was as eager to meet this child as they were.

The little girl they were adopting was one month old. Her birth parents were college students who had no way to care for her and the father had decided he was too young to take on the responsibility of a wife and baby.

When Jocelyn and Mark had applied to adopt a child, they had been told there was a long waiting list and it might take years before a child would become available. They had agreed it would be worth the wait and were surprised when eight months later they were told that a match had been found for them. All week they had shopped for baby items, Mark had put a crib together, and eager grandparents had helped them paint and decorate the nursery. Jocelyn was so excited she had hardly slept.

"Mr. and Mrs. Sanders, we're ready for you. Won't you come in and have a seat? Mrs. Sanders, there's a special chair for you." The caseworker smiled and pointed to the rocker in the corner of the room. "We think it's appropriate for new mothers to greet their babies in that chair. The two of you have a few papers to sign and then I'll have someone bring in your daughter."

Mark signed quickly and then handed each paper to Jocelyn for her signature. It was hard for them to spend time on formalities when all they wanted was to hold their child. When the paperwork was completed, they had to listen to the caseworker discuss the fine points of parenthood and what they should expect to happen over the next few months. Neither of them could focus their attention on what was being said, but they tried. Finally, the woman got up from the desk and walked into another room.

"I'll be right back," she called and closed the door behind her.

"What do you think happens now?" Mark asked as he started pacing back and forth. "I thought we had taken care of the paperwork and all we'd have to do is walk in here and pick up the baby."

"Sit down, honey. You're making me even more nervous."

Their anticipation was heightened by the silence and for several minutes all they could do was look back and forth from the closed door to each other.

"What's taking so long?" Mark struggled to sit still.

Before they had a chance to say another word, the door opened and the caseworker walked over to Jocelyn and placed the tiny baby in her arms. Mark jumped up to stand beside the rocking chair so he would be able to see the baby's face.

Jocelyn gently pulled the blanket away from the face of their sleeping daughter and felt an instant connection. Loved filled her and all the pain of the past few years disappeared. Warmth surrounded her—it radiated from Mark's body as he bent over her and from the bundle she was holding close to her heart. She knew she would remember this moment for the rest of her life.

She leaned over and whispered, "Hello, beautiful Gracie. I have so much to tell you about your very special name. Our story began with her, your wonderful great grandmother, and today you make the circle complete."

About the Author

Proud to be a native Floridian, Jeanne Moon Farmer loves to set her stories in the diverse cities of her beautiful home state. Like her characters, her life has been lived against a background of sandy beaches, palm trees, and unbelievable humidity. And she sees a story behind every hibiscus.

As a wife, mother, daughter, teacher, writer, and friend, she is curious about the threads that bind us to other human beings and searches for significance in the life-dramas that teach us who we are. Her writing reflects the journey of people who have been tried and tested by their own choices—some are defeated by those choices, while others learn they can rise above the consequences of those choices through forgiveness and love.

Her debut novel, Family Shadows, published in 2013, and Diva, published in 2014, are the first books in the Family Shadows series. Although each book stands alone, the characters in the story thread their way through all of the books in the trilogy.

After years as a teacher, she left the classroom to follow her passion for writing. Her writing career includes more than twenty years of technical writing in the field of education and one published work of poetry entitled Everything Makes A Difference (co-authored with Dr. Burt Bertram). Her award winning short story, Wheels of Honor, was published in the Florida Writer's Association 2012 Anthology.

She is a member of the Florida Writer's Association and two critique groups. She holds a degree in English from Florida State University where she studied creative writing with two writers who were profoundly influential, James T. Cox (O'Henry award winner) and Michael Shaara (The Killer Angels). Over the years she has led workshops on technical/grant writing and has honed her skills by attending various conferences and symposiums led by experts in the field of writing.

Joy comes from sharing life with her family—her husband, four grown sons, two daughters-in-law—and having beach sand between her toes.

Other books by Jeanne Moon Farmer...

Book One of the Family Shadows series

Family Shadows

Jeanne Moon Farmer

Incest, rape, betrayal, kidnapping - the darkest shadows that fall upon man; shadows that break apart families and destroy lives.

The McDeal's are one of the nicest families in the neighborhood. No one would suspect they live their lives in shadows.

Carter McDeal's quiet life is shattered when he is arrested for kidnapping the teenager he has called daughter for 17 years. His mother who recently died, created the lie that has overshadowed his life since Jocelyn's birth. What will it cost him to tell the truth and who will believe him?

Jocelyn McDeal's senior year in high school was supposed to be fun. But her beloved grandmother has just passed away, the birth certificate she needs to complete her college applications can't be found, and no one can verify her identity. Who is she? Where does she belong? And, why was she lied to all these years? As the evidence mounts against her father and people begin to doubt his innocence, Jocelyn turns her back on him.

Choices made years ago entangle three families and threaten to engulf them: a man may go to prison, a marriage may be destroyed, and the future of two young lovers may be cast forever in the shadows.

Was Jocelyn kidnapped as a baby? Can Carter undo the lie? Will the one person who knows the truth emerge from the shadows?

Available now at Amazon.com!

Jeanne Moon Farmer

No one knows less about love or more about a love song than MARGO.

At eighteen, a talented and driven middle-class Miami girl climbed upon a music train that didn't slow down until her stage name was known to millions of fans worldwide. Wealth, power, and fame became her only friends, trapping her in a lonely world of self-deception and destruction.

But those who love Margo refuse to give up on her.

No one in the world sings a love song like Margo. And by the spring of 1980, it's obvious to those who love her, that she is completely and utterly lost. Her twin daughters are a mess; her ex-husband is desperate to save her and her career; and her Brazilian lover turns up dead at her Miami estate.

Dark forces are in a macabre dance that count Margo and her family as expendable

As the underworld of Miami collides head-on with Margo's world, even death, illness, and broken promises reveal that love, though dangerous, can be worth the risk.

*****

An emotional, sometimes shocking, and always riveting story, *DIVA* graphically dances along the fine line between the life and death power of love. As this strong tale of seduction, power, lost souls, revenge, and redemption unfolds, it's a wild ride from the top of the music world to the shadowy side of Miami.

Available now at Amazon.com!